THE
STERLING
INHERITANCE

THE
STERLING
INHERITANCE

Michael Siverling

THOMAS DUNNE BOOKS
ST. MARTIN'S MINOTAUR
NEW YORK

THOMAS DUNNE BOOKS.
An imprint of St. Martin's Press.

THE STERLING INHERITANCE. Copyright © 2004 by Michael Siverling. All rights
reserved. Printed in the United States of America. No part of this book may be
used or reproduced in any manner whatsoever without written permission
except in the case of brief quotations embodied in critical articles or reviews.
For information, address St. Martin's Press, 175 Fifth Avenue, New York,
N.Y. 10010.

www.minotaurbooks.com

Book design by Jonathan Bennett

Library of Congress Cataloging-in-Publication Data

Siverling, Michael.
    The Sterling inheritance / Michael Siverling.—1st ed.
        p. cm.
    ISBN 0-312-31927-4
    EAN 978-0312-31927-4
        1. Family-owned business enterprises—Fiction. 2. Parent and adult
    child—Fiction. 3. Private investigators—Fiction. 4. Mothers and sons—
    Fiction. 5. Musicians—Fiction. I. Title.
    PS3619.I95S74 2004
    813'.6—dc22

                                                            20040

First Edition: July 2004

    9 8 7 6 5 4 3 2 1

For my father

ACKNOWLEDGMENTS

I owe a debt of gratitude to those who helped my story see the light of day:

Ruth Cavin of St. Martin's Press for taking a chance on me and teaching me to write better.

Robert J. Randisi of the Private Eye Writers of America for his idea that allowed the door to open for me and for allowing the likes of me to be a member.

Robin Burcell for taking the time to have lunch with an unpublished writer.

Kathy Ratermann, Laurie Voss, and Brian Sweeney for suffering through my earlier works.

India Cooper, editor supreme, who did a lot of hard work on this project.

Denise and Nicole for everything.

And, of course, Mom.

THE
STERLING
INHERITANCE

CHAPTER ONE

I'd been waiting in the dark for hours.

The room was in one of those innumerable pay-by-the-night-cash-up-front motels that litter the outskirts of River City. Judging by the traffic I could hear around me, it was the only room in the place not being treated to frequent visits by the working boys and girls with their anonymous clientele. At least the sounds of the performances that leaked through the too-thin walls helped keep me awake.

I was telling myself for what seemed like the thousandth time that I was going to give it just fifteen minutes more before giving up and going home when I heard the door lock turning ever so quietly. My heart rate jumped. I stood up from the rickety chair and took two gliding steps to the wall. The door opened a couple of feet and my quarry slipped in, quickly closed it, and fumbled with the security latch before reaching for the light switch. I could barely see the man, but I could've located him with my eyes closed by the alcoholic aroma he exuded.

I was happy to see that he was alone. Judging from the neighborhood he chose to hide out in, he could have had his choice of any number of boys, girls, or gender-indistinct persons for company. The fact that I caught him by himself was going to make my job a lot easier.

The cheap, low-wattage lighting illuminated a man cloaked in a rain-slick black coat and hat. Before he turned completely around from the door, I said, "Mr. Sterling? I have a message for you."

That turned out to be a mistake, judging by the way he yelled, spun around, and shoved a gun at me.

Without a thought, I slid a step closer to him and my hands automatically made a scissoring motion designed to snatch the gun right out of his hands. I'd been trained for years for just such a moment as this, but no amount of preparation could brace me for my shock when the gun went off as it arced out of the man's hand. The explosion stunned and deafened me, and for a split second everything seemed to freeze, including my assailant's look of surprise. Then some kind of animal survival instinct took over and I slammed the heel of my hand into his pale, round face, bouncing the back of his head into the door and sending his hat flying. He slid down in slow motion to the floor and sprawled out on the ratty carpet.

For a moment, all I could do was stare at him. Except that he was now bleeding from the nose and his gold-framed glasses were askew, he matched the photographs I'd been given, from the wispy, sparse light-colored hair to the thirty-one-year-old pudgy frame. But the Anthony Sterling I'd been sent to find was a local investment broker with absolutely no criminal background, which didn't quite mesh with the dissolute-looking—and -smelling—man who just pulled a gun on me.

I glanced around the room and spotted the gun lying on the floor. It looked to be a full-size .45 automatic pistol. I scooped it up in my shaky hand and activated the magazine release, racked the slide, and ejected the last cartridge, just in time for Sterling to scramble up to his feet and bolt for the door. Dropping the gun onto the bed, I was on him in one fast step, slapping a neck-nerve takedown on his shoulder that sent him down on his knees. I wrapped my free arm around his neck and suddenly knew what life on the rodeo circuit must be like.

I was trying to figure out how I could keep a hold on my squirming, screaming opponent and get to my cell phone when there was a loud pounding on the flimsy door, followed by the shout, "River City PD! Open the door!"

"Can't!" I yelled back. "Come on in!"

The cops didn't need a second invitation. The door instantly seemed to explode inward, unfortunately just when Sterling's struggles rolled my head into the door's flight path, knocking me right off Sterling and flopping me onto my back. There was a confused moment of shouting and foot stomping, and someone rolled me over onto my stomach and roughly pulled my arms painfully up my back. "Wait a minute! I can explain!" I said. "Sure, pal," a voice grumbled. "Everybody's got an explanation."

I was quickly and professionally handcuffed and then yanked up to a sitting position from which I could see that the room had been invaded by a gang of plainclothes cops. In this case, plain clothes meant wardrobes that no self-respecting Hell's Angels would be seen in. I guessed that I was now in the midst of a team of River City narcotics officers, two of whom were still wrestling with Sterling, who hadn't given up the fight yet.

I caught the eye of the oldest officer present, a grizzled, unshaven veteran in an old black trench coat that was dripping rainwater. He had the kind of face that, if you could read the lines carved into it, would probably tell you a very scary story. He was about to bring a police radio up to his lips when I said to him, "Like I said, I can explain. I'm with the Midnight Investigation Agency."

The officer stopped, frowned, and said, "You're from what, now?"

"I'm a private detective," I explained.

The officer made a face as if I had just confessed a particularly unpleasant perversion. I sighed and added, "My name's Jason Wilder. My ID is in my wallet. I'd show it to you, but . . ." I shrugged and let my words trail off, indicating my inability.

"Uh-huh," the officer said as he nodded toward the bed. "And is that your gun?"

3

"No, sir. That's the gun that Anthony Sterling pulled on me tonight. He's the gentleman on the floor over there." Sterling was sporting a pair of handcuffs as well, lying facedown and sobbing uncontrollably. His hands, now that I got a good look at them, were both wrapped up in soiled bandages. The officer in charge rolled his eyes in disgust and called out, "Earl! Get Crying Boy out of here. And get those people away from my door!" I could see now that a small crowd had gathered in the hallway outside, chatting and pointing at us. In most places, all the excitement would draw a lot more people out of the woodwork, but in a place like this the clientele usually take pains to avoid the police. Not to mention that the sound of a shot was hardly a rare occurrence in this neighborhood.

One of the other officers, a younger man with long brown hair and beard, dressed in street-person chic, took charge of Sterling, pulling him up to his feet and using him as a battering ram to get past the gawkers. "Look out! Coming through!" he called out as he hustled his prisoner down the hall. As Sterling was being propelled along, I heard him bleat, "You don't understand! They're going to kill me!"

The senior policeman helped me over to the bed, fished out my wallet, and flipped it open. As the remaining officers dispersed the crowd and left for parts unknown, I became aware of the ringing in my ears from the gun blast of a few minutes ago. "Now, let's see here," the officer said, holding my ID out at arm's length to read it. "How do I know this is real?" he asked.

"You know Officer Morales?" I inquired.

"Eddie Morales?"

"No, Hector. He's a patrolman. Badge 1156. He can vouch for me, and he should be working tonight."

"Really?" the officer said dubiously. He dug out a cell phone and punched in some numbers. "Yo, dispatch? This is Detective Sergeant Wentworth. Get me a hookup with Morales, badge 1156." The officer waited, not looking at me, then said, "Morales? This is Detective Sergeant Wentworth. Listen, I got a Jason

Wilder here says you know him." Sergeant Wentworth glanced from my ID to me and said, "He's five-eleven, 190 pounds, dark hair, green eyes." The sergeant suddenly grinned. "Is he ugly, you say?"

"Tell him I'm not as ugly as his cousin Maria that he tried to set me up with," I spoke up loudly.

"He says . . . oh, you got that . . . uh, huh . . . but he's legitimate, right? Okay, thanks." Wentworth clicked off his phone. "Officer Morales says to tell you that as far as you being legitimate, he's met your mother and he's certain you're adopted. But he also said you're a real dick, whatever he meant by that."

I shook my head, then regretted it because of the lancing pain my movement caused, the result of my collision with the door. "Okay, now that we got that cleared up, would you mind terribly?"

Wentworth grinned again and said, "Turn around." A minute later I was free of the handcuffs and rubbing the circulation back into my chafed wrists. "Now, what the hell are you doing here, screwing up my nice little surveillance?" Wentworth asked.

"Working. My agency was hired by Anthony Sterling's wife to find him. All I knew was that he'd gone missing several days ago."

"And he shot at you?"

"Well, maybe not," I admitted. "When he pulled the gun I did a two-hand gun take-away. Only the gun went off in the process."

"Two-hand take-away? Where the hell did you learn to do a move like that?"

I shrugged. "I was a student of Timmy O'Toole's."

The sergeant's eyes popped wide. "Terrible Timmy? Used to be a cop?"

"The same. He works for the Midnight Agency now."

"Wait a minute," Wentworth said slowly. "Wilder? You any relation to Bill Wilder?"

"My dad."

"Well, I'll be damned," he said, grinning. "So you're Wild Bill's kid? I rode with your father back in the day." Wentworth's

5

enthusiasm suddenly faded. "And I was damned sorry when he died. He was one of the best. So how come you're a private detective? I'da thought you'd be a cop, too."

"Seemed too much like working for a living."

That got a bark of a laugh out of Wentworth, then he said, "Aw, crap. Looks like I'll have to take some paper on this one." He sighed and pawed though his clothes, coming up with a pen and a small notebook. "Okay, from the top. What happened here tonight?"

I tried to get my thoughts in order quickly, sensing I was still on dangerous ground. Sergeant Wentworth's opinion of me might have been tempered by the fact that he used to work with my father—which, if it didn't exactly make me a member of the cop family in his eyes, put me in the position of a not too distant cousin—but that wouldn't cover me on the little bit of breaking and entering I committed tonight to track down Anthony Sterling. I took a breath and launched into my story.

"Well, a couple days ago, Tony Sterling's wife came to the office and hired us to find her husband. She'd already tried to file a missing persons report with the police, and someone suggested to her that she give us a try, too."

Wentworth nodded. "Go on."

"Anyway, the background investigation we did didn't turn up anything unusual. He'd never been in any kind of trouble, never had any reason to just take off."

Worthington grunted, glancing at the pistol on the bed.

I continued. "Mrs. Sterling gave us Tony's bank and credit card information. We spotted a couple of charges on his card dated after his disappearance. One of those was for this room."

Wentworth looked up from the notes he was scribbling. "Yeah. A lot of people get lost around here. Go on."

"Well, I took up a spot in the parking lot here tonight, but it started raining. Also, it's kind of hard not to get noticed in a place like this. So I thought I'd better wait for him in his room."

Sergeant Wentworth's pen stopped in midstroke. He shook

his head and said, "Let me get this straight. You broke into his room?"

"Well," I said as innocently as I could manage, "the door wasn't locked in any kind of serious way. Did I mention it was raining outside?"

"Just what," Wentworth said ominously, "did you intend to do with Sterling when you found him?"

"Nothing. Honest. All we were hired to do was locate him. I was just going to confirm that I'd found the right man and tell him his wife wanted him to come home, and then for all I cared he could have told me where to go and what to do with myself. And I really didn't expect him to pull a gun on me." I looked down at my still-shaking hands. My eyes followed the fresh furrow the bullet made in the cheap carpet and saw the pistol lying on the bed. The big gun sported a pair of grips that looked like ivory, which didn't make the thing any less ugly from where I sat. I heard myself murmur, "Scared the hell out of me."

Wentworth made an almost sympathetic-sounding grunt as Officer Earl popped his head back in the door. "Hey, Sarge, you're gonna love this one, man."

"What?"

"That dude we took out of here? We ran a warrant check on him."

"Yeah? So?"

"Seems the guy is wanted for questioning."

"What for?"

Earl flashed a toothy grin as he announced, "One-eight-seven."

Wentworth whistled loudly at the news, and I confess my heart jumped a beat. One-eight-seven is the California Penal Code's numeric designation for murder.

■

CHAPTER TWO

I awoke all too early the next morning to the ringing of my cell phone. It was still attached to the belt on my pants, part of a short trail of clothes that led from the front door of my loft to the bedroom. I reached out and snagged a piece of pant leg to reel in the electronic pest. The phone's date and time display said Wednesday, 10:42 A.M.

"If you're not a beautiful woman, I'm hanging up," I told the phone.

"You're half right. Rise and shine, sleepy boy. Time for school." It was Paul Merlyn, the receptionist at the Midnight Agency.

"For your information, Pauly, I was out late last night."

"Your love life is no concern of mine, sweetie. Your presence is requested as of now."

I moaned. "Geez. Can't Jimmy or Timmy cover whatever it is? Those old men must be good for something."

"Your guess is as good as mine. But the boss says this job's for you, and only you, baby. So it must be something easy. Come on, get up. Or do I have to come over and help dress you?"

"I surrender," I moaned. "I'll be there as soon as I can."

"And make yourself presentable. I know that's asking a lot."

I hung up and tossed the phone away and then pried myself out of bed. On my way to the shower, I reminded myself that there was one good thing about this morning. At least I wouldn't have to try to figure out an excuse for skipping my exercise routine.

I had myself hosed down and scraped off in good time. The only residue from last night's exertions seemed to be a tender spot on the left side of my head, courtesy of the police kicking the door in, and a stiff right shoulder from when my arms got yanked around behind me prior to the handcuffing. Thankfully, the gunshot wasn't ringing in my ears any more. Remembering that Paul had warned me to dress up, I put on one of my suits, otherwise known as the company uniform. I owned four, all made out of some lightweight miracle fabric that was not only wrinkle resistant but could actually be thrown into the wash, jacket and all, and put back on right out of the dryer. Considering the hygienically challenged places I found myself in on occasion, that was a godsend. The dark navy suits had numerous concealed pockets built into them, none of which I'd ever found occasion to use. I made up for the lack of variation in my wardrobe with my collection of brightly hued T-shirts and turtlenecks. I chose a blood-red tee for my ensemble du jour and headed out the door. Normally I'd walk the two blocks to the office, but as time was of the essence I went for my car, a classic 1967 emerald Mustang Fastback my dad named the Green Hornet. I shot through the midtown traffic to the 1300 block of Galleon Street.

On the corner is a two-and-a-half story Victorian made of dark old brick, its yard bordered with a formidable black iron fence. Walking along the brick path, lightly limned in moss this time of year, and up the seven steps to the porch will bring you to a massive oak door. The heavy bronze plaque to the right displays a stylized eye, with a clock inset where the iris would be, the hands pointing straight up to midnight. The sign to the right tells visitors that they've arrived at the best little private eye shop in River City, the Midnight Investigation Agency. I've come to think of the place as my own personal Fortress of Servitude.

I parked in front, jogged up the steps, and into the reception area. Seated behind a large, neatly arranged desk was a small, neatly arranged young man: Paul Merlyn, the agency's answer to the mythological Cerberus. He made an obvious display of checking his watch. "My, my, my. Don't we look positively wretched today?"

"I'd say it's nice to see you, too, Paul, but honesty prevents me. Do I go right in? Or is the boss going to make me wait?"

Paul gave me an up-and-down once-over. "No tie?"

"I hate those things. You want me in a tie, you can dress me at my funeral."

"Goody! I'll go shopping right away." He gave a head tilt toward the inner office. "In you go, sailor."

I heard the click of the lock release that Paul activated with a series of buttons under his desk. I took a moment to compose myself, then quietly opened the door leading into the wood-paneled office we referred to as the throne room. This was the lair of Victoria Wilder, ex–River City police detective and founder of the Midnight Agency. I had a special relationship with the formidable chief of operations. I was the only one in the world who could legitimately call her Mother.

She was sitting in her massive leather-upholstered chair behind the equally impressive mahogany desk. The chief's office looks more like the sitting room of a mansion, with its array of expensive furnishings, than the nerve center of the best private investigation business in the city, and Victoria Wilder fits her domain like a steel hand in a chain mail glove. Silver haired and handsome at whatever age she is (it's the one piece of information I'm expected to die rather than reveal), she's the always fashionably attired epitome of grace and charm. Just don't try to steal her purse. On her tailored tweed jacket was the jeweled brooch she invariably wore. Like the plaque on the front door, it was in the shape of an eye with a clock in the center, and with the hands at perpetual midnight.

Sitting on the floor to her left was the most recent addition to the family, a large black-and-tan German shepherd who went by the name of Beowulf. He was a former River City police canine whose career was cut very short due to a patrol car chase that ended in a crash. Beowulf lost his left eye in the accident, which caused his early retirement along with an understandable phobia where cars were concerned. The necessary operation left him with his eye socket sewn shut, and now his expression is set into a permanent wink. The sight of Mom and Beowulf together always reminded me of a comment made by Jim Bui, another Midnight operative: "One's a dangerous beast, the other is a German shepherd."

I walked halfway across the plush carpet and stood at polite attention. Mom favored me with a warm smile as she came around the desk to meet me. "Are you all right, son?" she asked affectionately.

"Sure. Other than a little excitement last night, I'm fine. Why?"

"Good," she said. Then, quick as a striking snake, she balled up her fist and struck me in the shoulder, with an extended middle knuckle for emphasis.

"Ow!"

"That's what you get for making your poor old mother worry!"

"You bully! Besides, I happen to disagree with two out of the three statements you just made. And I occasionally have doubts about the third."

Mom gave me a wicked grin. "Oh, you're my spawn, all right, kiddo. Want me to dig out the birthing video? Now sit down and lower your voice. You're upsetting Beowulf."

The dog had stood at attention throughout my assault, probably wondering if he was going to get a piece of me, too. As Mom ensconced herself upon her throne, Beowulf yawned and settled down again, no doubt certain there'd be another time. I rubbed my injured shoulder and plopped myself onto one of the high-backed guest chairs, wishing I'd had time for a last meal at least.

"It's been a very busy morning here," Mom announced. "First, I get a frantic phone call from Mrs. Sterling. Seems she's under the impression that, since she hired us to find her husband, we had something to do with his being arrested last night. I had to assure her that I would find out exactly what transpired."

I was about to respond when Mom threw up a warning hand. "Secondly," she continued, "in an effort to discover just what the hell went on last night, I find myself calling the River City Police Department. I had to use up a favor or two, only to discover that Anthony Sterling is in custody on an assault with a deadly weapon charge. Naming you as the victim."

"Uh, I can explain that."

The look Mom fired at me let me know in no uncertain terms that she wasn't quite finished with her soliloquy yet. I had just enough sense to clap my mouth shut and wait it out.

"Which brings us to the third item; it appears that Anthony Sterling is also wanted for questioning in relation to a homicide, a fact that I just became aware of. And all this time, I keep wondering where my only son is, and why he hasn't seen fit to tell me what he's been up to."

"Sorry," I said sincerely. "But after the cops found out that Sterling was wanted for questioning, they kept me up pretty late making a formal report. Besides, I figured that our involvement with him was done after I found the guy."

Mom sighed and shook her head. "What's a mother to do?" she said almost to herself. She looked up at the gilt-framed painting of Dad set above the fireplace as if she were looking for an answer to something. I looked at his portrait, too, but at times like this, I swear it looks like he's laughing at me. Mom then trained her wolf-gray eyes on me and said, "All right, kiddo, give it up. Tell me everything that went on last night. And I do mean everything."

That last admonishment was unnecessary, as I would never dream of holding anything back from the chief. I went into a complete recitation of last night's events. Mom stayed silent throughout; her only reaction to my story was a dangerous flash in her eyes when I got to the part where Tony pulled the pistol on me.

When I concluded, the queen of detectives leaned back in her chair and steepled her hands. "So Anthony Sterling pulled a gun on you?" she asked in a deceptively calm voice.

"Yep. Although now I'm not sure if he tried to shoot me or if the damn thing went off when I slapped it out of his hand."

"Speaking of hands, you say Anthony Sterling's were bandaged? What kind of injuries did he have?"

I shrugged. "I don't know. We didn't have a lot of time for idle chitchat."

"And he said someone was going to kill him?"

"Definitely. Although he seemed a bit delusional at the time. So now what? The job's done, right?"

She shook her head. "Not quite. Mrs. Sterling said her husband telephoned her from the jail and told her that some detectives want to speak with him, and he wanted her to get him a lawyer. She asked me for a recommendation, and given that our company was responsible for her husband getting arrested in the first place, I told her I'd make the arrangements." Mom consulted her watch. "In fact, the attorney should be here soon for a briefing."

"Oh? Who'd you get?"

"Abigail Glass."

"Gah!"

Beowulf's ears perked up at my involuntary reaction, but Mom just smiled. "Thanks for the warning," I said. "If you want me, I'll be checking out the far side of the moon for the foreseeable future."

"Nonsense. You need to be here to brief Abigail before she goes to see Anthony Sterling."

"Easy for you to say; she doesn't pinch your butt when no one else is looking. Did I mention I may have a concussion or two?"

"Stay put, crybaby," Mom said with a smile. "Consider this your just deserts for not keeping me in the loop last night."

I was trying to figure out if I could have a reasonably convincing fake brain hemorrhage when Paul announced via the office intercom, "Ms. Glass to see you, Ms. Wilder."

"Show her in, Paul." Mother rose to receive our guest. I stood up, too, so I could make a break for it if I got the chance. Beowulf just yawned.

The office door erupted open as if it were making way for a hurricane, but a hurricane had nothing on the Wicked Attorney of the West. Abigail Glass, to the eye, could have been mistaken for a stereotypical librarian from back when the Dewey Decimal System was brand-new. She kept her gray hair short and invariably wore either a gray or blue jacket and a sensible-length skirt with a white blouse that went with her knee socks and comfortable-looking shoes. But her quick, dark eyes, magnified through thick glasses, never stopped moving and never missed a thing. "Hey, Vicki ol' girl. How the hell are ya?" she caroled as she entered.

"Hello, Abigail," Mother greeted her warmly. "You remember Jason, of course."

Abby shot me a wicked leer. "Oh, yeah. How's it going, stud?"

"Great. Until about two seconds ago," I replied.

Abby barked an approving "Ha!" at my response, dropped her oversized brown leather shoulder bag, and came in for a landing on a chair. "What do we have here?" she asked, rubbing her hands together in anticipation. "Something juicy, I hope."

Abby Glass had already retired a rich woman from the practice of civil law. Having made her money, she turned to criminal defense practice mainly for her own amusement, and much to the chagrin of many a public prosecutor. Truth be told, I really liked the old girl, but we enjoyed pretending otherwise in public; we'd found out early in our acquaintance that we both got a kick out of keeping people off balance just because we could.

"Jason will fill you in on what we know to date," Mom said. I took a breath and launched into yet another recitation of my recent adventures. When I reached the punch line, Abby said, "That's it? That's all you know?"

I shrugged, and Abby made a *humph* sound. "Well, Vicki," she said, "the assault charge is no big thing."

"He pulled a handgun on my son," Mother said seriously.

Abby snorted. "Hell, if I caught someone breaking into my room, I'd probably try to shoot him too. Unless he was cute, of course." Abby sharply swiveled her head and shot a look at me. "The cops didn't give you anything else on the supposed homicide?"

"Nope. Not a thing," I answered.

"Humph," Abby muttered again. "Well, hell. I guess I'll have to go over to the jail and dig it out for myself. Can you let me have the boy here?"

I silently tried to communicate to Mom the idea that I'd rather be fed to Beowulf than accompany Abigail, but all Her Majesty said was, "Are you sure there'll be no conflict of interest involved? Besides, both James and Timothy have more experience with homicide cases."

"Those two relics?" Abby said with surprise. "I'da thought you'd have put them out to pasture by now."

The "relics" Abby referred to were Jim Bui and Tim O'Toole, Uncle Timmy and Uncle Jimmy to me for most of my life. The other two field operatives of the Midnight Agency, they used to be Mom and Dad's partners back when they all worked for the River City Police Department.

Abby shook her head. "Nah, let me have the kid. I don't see

where last night's episode will matter. Besides, I need someone who can keep up with me."

"Very well," Mother agreed, ignoring my strangled cry of alarm. Abby slapped me on the arm as she said, "Let's go, stud. And don't spare the horses!"

■

CHAPTER THREE

Hold it right there," I said. "For your information, I've been up over half the night and haven't had breakfast or even coffee yet. I hereby demand that I get fed or killed outright. At the moment, I'm not particular which."

Queen Victoria and Abigail traded looks, then Mom said, "Since you still have work to do today, I recommend you get yourself to the kitchen and eat. Abigail and I will telephone the jail and make the arrangements for Mr. Sterling's interview with the detectives."

"Don't take too long," Abby cautioned. "You're not getting any younger, you know."

"A half hour should be sufficient," Mom added. "And see if Beowulf wants a snack."

I saluted. "Aye, aye. Come on, Blinky," I said to the dog. As I stood up, Mom turned to the oversized puppy and said, "Go on, Beowulf. Kitchen." I swear the dog nodded in agreement as he got up and followed me.

In the queen's throne room, there's a pair of panels behind Mom's desk. To the uninitiated, they appear to be simply a part of the wall, but pressure at a certain point opens them up. The one on the right leads to the combination kitchen-dining area; the one on the left, to a stairway to the living quarters upstairs. Abigail Glass had known the family long enough to be privy to this little secret. Otherwise I'd have taken the long way around through the front reception area.

Beowulf followed me obediently to the kitchen, where I helped myself to coffee, yogurt, and some kind of health food cereal that probably contained enough fiber to make a full-size rope. If you're looking for junk food in Mom's kitchen, good luck. You'd have a better chance of finding the Maltese Falcon at a garage sale. Beowulf was treated to a biscuit made by a local baker specializing in food for overly pampered pets. Having refueled myself, I poured a second cup of Mom's delicious cinnamon-flavored coffee and decided to see what the boys in the back room were up to.

If Lady Victoria's office affects an Old World charm, the other office looks like the inside of a military bunker, which in a way I suppose it is. This is where the real work of the agency is accomplished. There are four desks, one in each corner, along with conference tables, a fax machine, filing cabinets, and numerous other workplace furnishings. Mom always says she prefers that all the ugly necessities of the business be kept out of sight—and since my own desk is back here, I guess that includes me. My desk is the closest to the kitchen door, and therefore closest to Her Majesty's lair. The opposite side of the room is the territory of Jim Bui and Tim O'Toole. Felix was absent at the moment, but Timmy and Jimmy were in residence at their desks.

Jimmy and Timmy were known in River City police circles as "the twins." Jim Bui, tall, slender, and laconic, differed at almost every point from the short, barrel-chested, and animated Tim O'Toole. Uncle Jimmy always took pains to dress like a prosperous undertaker; Uncle Timmy seemed to go out of his way to give the impression that he got his clothes from a secondhand store that specialized in fashions for the color-blind. Jimmy still had a full head of almost raven-black hair; the only evidence that Timmy's hair was once red can be found in old photographs.

At the moment I walked in, Jimmy was typing away the computer terminal on his immaculate desk. Timmy had his feet up on his own chaotic workstation. "Well, well, well," Timmy greeted me. "Guess who I got a call from today?"

Jimmy, without looking up from his computer terminal, said, "Your Viagra shipment arrived early?"

Timmy made a sour face. "No, dumbass. I got a voice mail from Dickie Wentworth over at the PD. Seems junior here got himself in a little bind last night and Dickie's boys had to go bail him out. By the way, junior, when you do a two-hand gun take-away, you're supposed to keep ahold of the gun."

Jim Bui stopped typing in midstroke and flashed a look at me. "Someone pulled a gun on you last night?"

"Yeah, kind of," I admitted.

Bui gave me a cool, appraising look as he said, "And your own handgun was where, exactly?"

"All safe and sound, locked in my briefcase, Uncle Jim."

Bui and O'Toole traded a pair of God-help-me looks, then O'Toole burst out, "Damn it, Junior! When are you gonna learn to take better care of yourself? I swear, that goddamn mutt over there has more sense than you."

"While we're on the subject," Bui added, "when are you going to give up that museum piece of a handgun and start carrying something more modern?"

"Hey," I objected, "that museum piece, as you call it, works just fine."

"It's antiquated and obsolete," Bui insisted.

"So are you guys," I fired back. "But I don't see anyone throwing you on the trash heap. Today anyway."

I was saved from further argument by Mom's voice over the intercom announcing, "Playtime's over, boys. Jason has to go to work now." Abby Glass chimed in, "C'mon, baby. I'm all hot to go!"

O'Toole's face split into a grin. "Was that who I think it was?"

I vented a theatrical sigh. "Yep. The woman who taught Clarence Darrow everything he knew. I'm going with her over to the jail for an interview."

"Any chance they'll keep her?" Bui wondered aloud.

"Adios, muchacho," O'Toole added. "Better you than me."

A short time later I found a parking place for my Mustang in front of the River City Main Jail, a solid-looking twenty-story concrete rectangle that takes up almost the entire 300 block of Ironside Street. After letting Abby out and feeding the meter (and jotting down mileage and expenses), I opened the trunk and emptied my pockets in anticipation of passing through the jail security screening. I dumped everything into my briefcase, keeping only my ID and pen. The stuff I normally carry around with me is a reflection of my working lifestyle. Namely, it has to be able to put up with a lot of abuse. My pen is a case in point; it's a chrome Fisher Space Pen, guaranteed to be able to write upside down while completely submerged in water—which I suppose would be handy if I ever had to write someone a letter to tell them I was drowning. With my waterproof Omega watch, I could even tell how long it would take. I took my trunk key off the ring, grabbed a full-size notepad, then closed up and followed the impatiently waiting Abby into the gauntlet of the jail reception area. Two metal detectors and an identification check later, Abby and I were escorted by uniformed police staff to a sterile white room on the first floor. The only furnishings in it were a stainless steel table bolted to the floor and some green plastic chairs. We were told to make ourselves "comfortable" and informed that the prisoner would be brought down shortly.

As soon as the door was shut, Abby thumbed her nose and wagged her fingers toward the upper corner of the room where a small white plastic fire detector was placed. "Camera," she said.

"I know," I answered. I guessed it had been a long time since the River City PD had to use the rooms with the two-way glass.

I heard the sound of keys jingling and the heavy door opened, admitting Anthony Sterling, now dressed in regulation prisoner orange, accompanied by a tall, distinguished-looking gray-haired black man in a white dress shirt and dark tie. "Hi, I'm Detective Dolman," he greeted us.

"Hello, Wally," Abby responded. "Nice to see they haven't fired you yet." Abby extended her hand to Sterling. "You must be Mr. Sterling. I'm Abigail Glass, and this young man is my assistant today. Your wife wanted us to be here."

Tony Sterling looked up, and confusion seemed to reign in his muddy brown eyes, which were starting to sport a pair of shiners. Whether he got them from me when I hit him last night or they were courtesy of the police or fellow inmates, I didn't know. Somewhere along the way he had lost his glasses, and both of his hands appeared freshly bandaged.

Detective Dolman opened a file folder he was carrying and asked me, "And your name is?"

"Jason Wilder."

The sound of my voice seemed to focus Sterling, who looked over at me and squinted. Suddenly his eyes popped wide open as he said, "You! You're the guy who hit me!"

"Well, you did kind of point a gun at me, you know," I answered.

Detective Dolman clapped his file folder shut. "Would the two of you kindly step outside with me for a moment?" he said through a slightly clenched jaw.

"Sure, Wally," Abby said easily.

Detective Dolman held the door for Abby and me, then pulled it shut behind him and whispered fiercely, "Just what the hell do you think you're doing? You can't bring a victim of a crime to see a suspect!"

"Settle down, Wally," Abby said. "From where I sit, you haven't got a crime. You're just using that as an excuse to give you time to cobble together a homicide case against my client. As for the assault charge you're currently holding him on, all my client did was defend himself from what he thought was an intruder, namely the kid here."

Dolman tossed his head in my direction. "And what, exactly, is he doing here?"

"Jason Wilder works for Midnight Investigation," Abby answered reasonably. "The same firm that'll be doing the defense investigation. That is, if you've got a case worth a damn to file against Mr. Sterling. Which you haven't done so far, right?"

"No," Dolman answered tightly.

"All right, then," Abby said. "Tell you what, let's stop futzing around out here. Your little assault with a deadly weapon charge is bogus at best, so let's forget that nonsense. You want to talk to my client? Fine. Let's get on with it so you can decide if you want me to rip your case apart in the courtroom or if you're just going to concede here and now and let everybody go home. What do you say?"

For a moment, I thought Detective Dolman was going to explode. In fact, he did—with laughter. "Damn, Glass," he said, shaking his head. "When are you going to get senile and leave us alone?"

Abby batted her eyes. "Why, Wally, I am senile. You should have dealt with me back in my prime."

"God spared me from that," Wally said with apparent reverence. "Okay, everybody back in the pool. Let's do this thing."

We filed back in and found Tony Sterling huddled on a chair with his face cradled in his arms on the table. He slowly brought his head up as Detective Dolman addressed him. "Mr. Sterling? I want you to understand a few things before we begin. Ms. Glass is here to advise you, and you may speak with her at any time during our conversation. Again, I have to let you know that everything you say here today can and will be used against you in a court of law should charges be filed against you. Do you understand me?"

Tony kept his eyes on me the whole time Detective Dolman was speaking, then said to me, his pale, puffy face full of pain, "I just want you to know I'm sorry for last night. I wasn't going to shoot you. But you scared me."

"Okay," I said gently. "And if it helps at all, I'm sorry I hit you. You scared me, too."

Tony looked back down at the table, his wispy blond hair falling forward, while Abby asked him gently, "Are you sure you want to do this? You don't have to say anything to anyone, you know."

Tony gave a brief nod. Dolman began his questioning. "Okay, Mr. Sterling. First, just relax. You want some water or a soda or anything?"

Detective Dolman was smooth, I'll give him that. I would swear that he was genuinely concerned for Tony's well-being. If you hadn't known that he was about to try to get the man to admit to a homicide, you'd think he was trying to be his best friend. Tony cleared his throat and said quietly, "No, thank you."

"Okay," Dolman said. "Now, we've spoken to your sister, and she said that she saw you last Sunday night at the Castle Theater. Would you tell me why you were there?"

Tony looked to Abigail with pleading eyes, and she said, "You don't have to say, Mr. Sterling."

Tony swallowed, then nodded. "Uh, okay." He turned back to Dolman. "I'd rather not say, sir."

"But you were there," Dolman stated. When Tony nodded, he continued. "Okay. Now, I want to show you something." Detective Dolman took a color photograph from his file and slid it across the steel table to Tony. It was a blown-up picture of the .45 Tony pulled on me the night before. I could see now that there was a small gold eagle etched on the white grip. "Do you recognize this, Mr. Sterling?" Dolman asked quietly.

Tony clumsily picked up the photo with his bandaged hands and held it close to his face. "Yes," he said from behind the picture.

"Is that your gun?" Dolman asked.

Tony let the picture fall to the table. He whispered, "Yes."

Dolman nodded. "Okay, fine. I noticed you had a little trouble holding the photo, Mr. Sterling. Are your hands bothering you at all?"

The simple-sounding inquiry made Tony's jaw clench, and his round face took on a stubborn cast. "I changed my mind," Tony said. "I don't think I want to talk to you after all."

Dolman opened his mouth, but Abby beat him to the punch. "Game over, Wally. My client asserts his privilege."

Dolman's dark eyes narrowed, then he smiled, a smile that was far more predatory than friendly. "Would you excuse us again, please, Mr. Sterling? I want to have another word with your attorney."

"Can I call my father now?" Tony asked plaintively. "Please? I only got one phone call so far."

"I'll see what I can do," Dolman said reasonably as he stood and opened the door again. Abby and I trooped back out to the hallway. After he shut the door, Dolman said to Abby, "I don't think your client is going to be going home anytime in the near future."

"Oh? And why's that?" Abby asked. "Just what do you have against him? He didn't say squat."

Dolman consulted his notebook. "What I've got is not one but two eyewitnesses that place him at the scene of a homicide, one of whom can make an absolutely positive identification of him. I've also got his three-day disappearance, plus he admits to ownership of the gun."

Abby stood up on tiptoe and tried to peek into Dolman's file. "What witnesses? Who are they? Who's the victim?"

Detective Dolman smiled and clapped his file shut. "That, my dear Ms. Glass, you'll just have to read for yourself when the DA gives you a formal copy of the charges."

"Come on, Wally, quit holding out on me," Abby demanded. "What's the big deal about my client's hands?"

Dolman kept his smile as he said, "I'd say our business was concluded for now, Ms. Glass. Have a good day." He signaled to a pair of uniformed officers who promptly took up positions on either side of us and silently walked Abby and me out to the main reception area.

Throughout our eviction, Abby fumed silently—until we cleared the final door into the late October sunlight. "God damn it!" she burst out. "I'll teach that smug bastard to screw around with me!"

Abby's outcry caused a few heads to turn—people who looked like they'd either just been released from the jail or were waiting to visit their incarcerated loved ones. I decided that Abby and I would do better to discuss our business elsewhere. "Come on, girl. Let's not make a spectacle of ourselves." I fetched my keys from the trunk, opened the car door for Abby, and drove us away. "Back to the barn?" I asked.

"Only if your mama has some decent booze on hand. I need a drink after that."

"Your wish is my command." I drove Abby back to my office, and shortly afterward Mom, Abby, and I were involved in a strategy session in the throne room while Abby indulged herself with one of Mom's patented martinis. Sensing my workday was far from over, I contented myself with a Coke. Mom and Beowulf abstained entirely.

After Abby briefed Mom on our in-custody excursion, the queen said, "Let's review, then, shall we? You're certain the police will file homicide charges against Mr. Sterling?"

"Yeah," Abby grumbled. "Wally Dolman doesn't bluff, and he's pretty good, too, for a flatfoot. He thinks he's got a case, all right."

Mother nodded. "I never had a chance to work with Detective Dolman, but I know he's got a good reputation. And he was curious about the injuries to Mr. Sterling's hands, you say? Interesting. Well, until we get a full report from the police and the district attorney on their case, we should probably see what we can find out for ourselves. We know the murder was committed last Sunday night, so at least we can get the reports from what the newspapers have released."

"And maybe a bit more," I added. "I've still got a buddy who works at the *River City Clarion*."

"Ah, yes. Your friend Roland. Good," Mom said. "We also need to speak to Mrs. Sterling again. Apparently one of the eyewitnesses against Anthony Sterling is his sister. We'll need her name and where to get in contact with her." Mother looked pointedly at me.

"I'm on it," I said. "I'll go see her today."

"Well, then," Mother concluded, "I believe that's everything we have for now."

Abby tossed down the last of her drink. "Except for the fact that if that cream puff Tony Sterling is a killer, then I'm the Virgin Mary."

"Actually, we have one more piece of information, for whatever it may be worth," I announced. As Mom raised an expectant eyebrow, I continued. "When Detective Dolman showed us the blown-up photo of Tony's pistol, I was able to make out the serial number and jotted it down. It may tell us something."

Abby smiled and looked over at Mom. "Damn, Vicki. That boy of yours is not only decorative, he's almost useful."

■

CHAPTER FOUR

Mom and I bid good-bye to Abigail Glass, who promised to call us as soon as she heard anything from the DA's office. When we had the place to ourselves, Lady Victoria returned to her desk, opened the carved, ornate box that contained a wireless computer monitor, and pulled out the keyboard from the top drawer (she refuses to let anything detract from the ambience of her office). I lifted one of the guest chairs and carried it around so I could watch over her shoulder as she fired up the computer.

Putting a pair of gold-filigreed reading glasses on, she said to me, "Do you concur with Abigail's assessment of Anthony Sterling as a potential homicide suspect?"

"As a matter of fact, I do. He seemed genuinely sorry for pulling a gun on me. I figure a guy more inclined toward homicidal pursuits would have just been sorry that he didn't actually get to shoot me."

"Fair enough," Mom said. "Now, let's see what the newspapers reported. I seem to recall hearing something about this occurrence a couple of days ago."

She guided the computer to the on-line version of the *River City Clarion,* the city's main print news source. Sure enough, there was a report from last Monday's edition: "The River City police reported the discovery of a body in an alleyway off Twelfth Street on Sunday night. The body had been set on fire, making identification of the remains difficult. The *River City Clarion* urges anyone who may have information regarding this crime to contact our Crime Alert Tip Line."

After scanning that short but gruesome report, I said, "Whoa."

"No kidding, kiddo. So someone gets killed and torched on Sunday, and then promptly on Monday Mrs. Sterling comes in and says her husband's missing. When did he check into that motel you found him in?"

"Late Sunday night," I answered. "Paid for a week, which the manager thought was weird, since the majority of his clientele only pay by the hour in cash."

"And the police were interested in the condition of Mr. Sterling's hands, you say?"

"Very. Although Detective Dolman was trying to be subtle."

"Curiouser and curiouser," Mom mused. She ran a map search for the Castle Theater. The map showed a location on the corner of Ketch Street and Twelfth. A quick address check brought up a telephone number, which I dutifully copied down. Mom shut down the computer, replaced the components in their respective hiding places, and said, "Well, so much for modern telecommunications technology. Now it's time to get off our duffs and get to work. I phoned Mrs. Sterling and told her to expect us this afternoon. Let's not keep her waiting, shall we?"

I helped Lady Victoria into her expensive full-length leather coat, and Beowulf and I followed her out to the back room, where we found Jim Bui still at his desk.

"James, I'm glad you're still here," Mom said. "We need a little something that's right up your alley."

Jimmy looked up and said, "I was just finishing up on that accident reconstruction. Looks like the owner of the truck involved is going to have to pay up big time."

"Well, that's some good news for our client," Mom answered, "seeing that he got stiffed by the insurance company in the first place. Good work. Now I need you to check on something. Jason picked up the serial number for a handgun. See if you can dig anything up on it."

Jimmy frowned. "That's a lot easier for the police to do, since we don't have the kind of access they do. Legally, anyway," he added quietly.

"Well, see what you can get. Jason?" I opened my notebook and rattled off the serial number.

"What's the make and model number?" Jimmy asked.

I affected an innocent blink. "Is that important?"

Jimmy damn near threw down his pen. "Hell, yes, it's important. How the hell am I supposed to . . ." He stopped when he read my expression. "Smartass," he mumbled.

"It's a Colt .45 automatic pistol," I said, trying not to laugh. "You know? A museum piece?"

Jimmy didn't rise to the bait. "I'll check it out. May not be easy."

"Oh, and one more thing," I added. "It's got custom grips on it. Looks like ivory, with a gold eagle."

Jimmy's frown deepened. In his opinion, anyone who added cosmetic embellishments to a firearm was guilty of perversion. "I'll see what I can do," he said.

"You're the best one for the job," Mom said with certainty. He was, too. Jimmy not only taught me everything I know about firearms but turned me into a first-class combat shooter, despite my efforts to the contrary.

Mom bid Beowulf a heartfelt good-bye, and we went into the attached garage, where we keep the company vehicles. Soon we were on our way, with the queen herself behind the wheel of her black Jaguar XJR.

As she navigated smoothly through the midtown traffic, she said to me, "So. Both James and Timothy came to me this morning after you left with Abigail. Seems they're concerned that you're not taking proper precautions these days."

"In addition to being a pair of snitches, they're acting like old ladies," I answered. "And for your information, I am cautious. There didn't seem to be a need to be armed last night, that's all."

"And yet you wind up in an armed confrontation. I'll say this to you just once: Don't make your poor old mother have to worry about you or have to avenge you. It would get ugly."

I sighed. "Aye, aye, Your Majesty. Understood."

"Good. I love you, son."

"I'm moderately fond of you, too, lady."

She twitched a smile. "I don't want to have to pull this car over and give you a whupping. I just had my nails done." She laughed, and I laughed with her.

"So we're off to see Mrs. Sterling?" I said. "What's she like?"

Mother checked her rearview and then gunned the engine as she raced up the eastbound freeway on-ramp. "She appears to be genuinely concerned for her husband. When he didn't come home, she called the police right away, but they told her that she'd have to wait twenty-four hours before they'd take a missing persons report. Apparently she wasn't satisfied with that, and finally someone over at the police department suggested she call us. When I explained our fee schedule, she didn't even blink, just said that she wanted us to find him no matter what it cost."

I whistled over that piece of news. The services of the Midnight Agency don't come cheaply, my own pay scale to the contrary. "So she's rich?" I asked.

"The quick background I did when we first got the case showed that Anthony Sterling does well enough in the property brokerage and investment business, although I did notice that most of his credit cards were up near their limits. We're going to need a far more detailed analysis of his business and lifestyle if we wind up taking this case. Mrs. Sterling was rather displeased, to say the least, that her husband was arrested as a direct result of your locating him."

I shrugged. "Well, you can't say I didn't do my job." I noticed that we were leaving the sprawling cityscape behind us as we raced east toward the foothills. "Where are we going, anyway?" "Marble Hills."

I whistled again. "No wonder she can afford us."

Marble Hills is an enclave out past the Golden Lake reservoir. Over the last several years, it's become a suburban retreat for those who can afford it. Turning off the main freeway, Mom drove us through an impressive array of large homes with expansive front lawns. We finally pulled up to a white two-story pocket-size mansion with a driveway big enough to land a Harrier jet on. Lady Victoria parked her chariot in the drive, and we walked to the massive carved oaken double doors, where we were met by the lady of the house.

From having met her short and rather overweight husband, I found Katerina Sterling a bit of a surprise. She was a tall, willowy woman who appeared to be, like her husband, in her early thirties, with light-colored hair that she kept short and bangs that came almost down to her large, deep brown eyes. Her features appeared too delicate to hold all the worry that they did. She was dressed simply in a dark blue turtleneck sweater and a pair of jeans. When she greeted us, her voice surprised me as well with a subtle yet noticeable Eastern European accent. "Please come in," she said as she stood away from the door.

We were admitted to a foyer and led back to a large living room with a vaulted ceiling and expensive-looking, comfortable furniture. "Hello again, Mrs. Sterling," Mother said. "This is my son, Jason." I shook her hand, noticing how cold it felt. "Do you have more news about my husband?" She indicated seats and perched herself on the edge of a leather-covered chair, clasping her hands together. Mother and I sat down on a couch opposite. "I do have news, Mrs. Sterling," Mom said. "And it's not at all good. I'm afraid the police believe that your husband may have had something to do with a murder that occurred last Sunday night."

Katerina's eyes flew wide as she cried, "Murder! No. That cannot be true. I tell you they are mistaken. Tony would not do such a thing. No." She shook her head again.

Mother's voice was gentle as she said, "I was able to get a very good attorney to represent your husband. But for now, I need to know if you still want my agency to help you in the matter of his defense."

"But of course! Mrs. Wilder, I love my husband very much, and I tell you he could not hurt anyone. When can I see him? Can we get him out of jail?"

"I believe visiting hours at the jail start at four this afternoon," Mom answered. "As for your husband's release, I expect they'll arraign him tomorrow morning, at which time the judge may set a bail amount. Or he may not."

Katerina swallowed, then nodded. "I see. What can be done for him now?"

"You can help us understand what the situation might be," Mother said. "Did your husband have any enemies you're aware of?"

"No," Katerina said definitely. "Tony is a good man. Everybody who knows him says so."

"I see," Mom said. "Can you think of anything unusual that has happened recently? Something out of the ordinary?"

Katerina looked down and said quietly, "Tony has been . . . quiet . . . for some time now. When I ask him what is wrong, he tells me not to worry, that it is just business, and that things will get better. I tell him that if it is money he is worried about, then we can sell the house. It is too big for two people anyway. Then he would just tell me no and say again that everything would be all right. But I think now that he did not want to worry me."

"How long have you known your husband, Mrs. Sterling?"

"Over three years now. We met through a church group that was going on a mission to Russia. Where I am from. I was going as a translator, but also to see some of my family still there."

"And when did you and Mr. Sterling marry?"

"This July, it is two years," she said. "Tony has always taken very good care of me."

"Of course," Mother said warmly. "Tell me, what do you know about his business?"

She shrugged. "Tony is very . . . old-fashioned, you would say. I remember when he proposed how he said that he would always take care of me. But his business he keeps to himself. It is a business he got from his father."

"Would that be Sterling Investments?" Mom asked. Katerina nodded, and Mom continued, "Your husband's father is Malcolm Sterling, am I right?"

"Yes."

"And has he been contacted about your husband's arrest?"

Katerina shrugged helplessly. "Not by me. He does not care for me. He did not want his son to marry me."

"Why was that?"

"I think he thought I was not good enough for his son."

An uncomfortable silence fell among us, and Mom reached over and took Katerina's hand into her own. "Whatever Malcolm Sterling's personal feelings are, I can see that you are a woman who cares very deeply for her husband."

Katerina looked up, and tears filled her large brown eyes. "Thank you," she whispered. She got up suddenly and walked quickly from the room. Mom leaned back in her seat and said to me, "Make a note: Need to check on the business angle and look up Malcolm Sterling."

"Already noted," I said back. "I'm both decorative and useful, remember?"

"I knew there was a reason I spent nine hours in labor because of you."

During Katerina's absence, I looked around the room. There were a number of framed photographs, all of them of Tony and Katerina in better times. The ones on the mantel were dominated by a large, ornate silver crucifix attached to the wall. My inspection of the premises was cut short by Katerina Sterling's return. She clutched a wad of tissues in one hand and said as she reentered, "Please forgive me."

"Nothing to forgive, Mrs. Sterling," Mother said graciously. "Now, if we can trouble you with a few more questions?"

"I will do anything to help."

"Have you spoken to the police since your husband went missing last Sunday?"

"Yes. There was a telephone call from a policeman on Monday in the evening. He asked me questions about Tony. I thought the police were finally going to help me find him."

"Do you remember his name?"

"Yes. He was Detective Dolman, of the River City Police."

Ah, I thought, that sly fox managed to pump Tony's wife for info and not let on that he was looking for him in relation to a homicide. Well, Abby said he was good.

"Have you spoken with anyone else?" Mom asked.

"My uncle Georgi. When I told him Tony was missing, he was worried, too. He likes my Tony very much."

"What can you tell me about your husband's sister?"

Katerina looked surprised. "Jenny? What has she to do with this?"

"I don't know," Mom said gently, "but I believe her name may have come up. What can you tell me about her?"

"She came back to here with her little daughter, Angelina." For the first time, Katerina smiled. "She has a very beautiful little girl." The smile faded as quickly as it arrived. "Tony and I want to have children." She shook herself and continued, "She was an actress, and she came home about a year ago. She said she had to leave her husband. She and Tony went into business together. She has a theater in the city. But they had a . . . falling-out?"

"Over what?"

"I do not know. I called her the night Tony did not come home, but all she said to me was to tell Tony to not come to the theater anymore."

"Have you spoken to her since Tony was arrested?" Katerina

shook her head. "I see," Mother said. "All right, Mrs. Sterling. I promise we'll do all we can for your husband."

As we all rose, Mother said, "Jason will give you his card with his direct telephone number. Please call him or me if you think of anything else or if you need anything."

I extracted one of my expensive business cards with the gold embossed eye and clock company symbol, which Mom maintained was a lot classier than the Masonic-derived Eye That Never Sleeps that the Pinkerton Detective Agency used. I added my cell phone number to the card and handed it to Katerina. "Thank you," she said as she walked us to the door. "I will go see my husband today. My uncle Georgi said he would take me if I needed to go to the city."

"Good," Mom said. "One more thing, Mrs. Sterling. Does your husband own a gun?"

Katerina looked shocked. "No. He would never own a gun. He is a good Christian man."

"Thank you again, Mrs. Sterling," Mom said. "We'll be in touch."

I waited until Her Ladyship and I were in her car and driving before I said, "Remind me the next time I'm shopping for a girlfriend to try the former Soviet Union."

"You mean you're not shopping now? I thought Sarah dumped you."

The Sarah that Mom referred to was Sarah Wells, former girlfriend and current resident of Ohio, where she was pursuing her vocation as a news personality, having received an offer to work at a television station that she couldn't refuse. We were both smart enough to call it quits before she left, knowing that it probably wouldn't work out in the long run. I still missed her, though, especially the way she'd laugh at all my jokes. Including the ones she clearly didn't get.

I regarded Mom as she concentrated on driving us back to the city. "You know, if I were of a more suspicious mind, I'd almost wonder whether you had something to do with Sarah's job offer."

"I can't take credit for everything," Mother said serenely. "Now, let's get back to civilization. It appears we still have a client—and more work to do."

CHAPTER FIVE

The sun was settling into a burnished red nest of dark clouds as Lady Victoria wove through the traffic on the freeway. "So what now?" I asked her.

"Considering the fact that Anthony Sterling will almost certainly be arraigned tomorrow morning, I suspect we can best serve our client by finding out as much as possible beforehand. In other words, the day ain't done yet, kiddo."

Mom's sudden transformations from lady of the manor to tough-talkin' ex–street cop and back again left me unfazed. I came to the conclusion long ago that if she's schizophrenic, then it works for her. I checked my watch and saw that the straight working day wasn't quite over yet, either. I flipped out my cell phone and hit a preprogrammed number.

"*River City Clarion,* Gibson speaking," came a well-known voice in response.

"Hello? Is this where I report a problem with my paperboy?"

"No, jerkwad. This is where you get your ass kicked, bothering hardworking members of the press."

"Hardly working is more likely," I said. "Hey, I need something."

Roland Gibson, longtime friend and staff writer for the *River City Clarion,* moaned theatrically. I pictured him at his desk: slight and sandy haired with spectacles, he looked like the kind of guy you'd hope your daughter would bring home—at least until you got a few drinks into him and got him to launch into his bottomless repertoire of dirty jokes. "When don't you need something?" Roland complained. "What about me? What about my needs? Huh?"

"What you need, I can't get in this country. Listen, there was a blurb in Monday's edition about a body found off Twelfth Street. Can you get any more information for me?"

"Stand by," Roland said. While I waited, I could hear the cacophony of the newsroom in the background. How he got any work done in that chaos was beyond me. "Okay, I got it," he said. "Let's see . . . River City police reported . . . yadda, yadda . . . hello! Ooo. This looks good. What have you got to trade?"

"That's a fine way to behave with a fellow member of the Epic Hero Society," I chastised him. "What ever happened to all that talk of brotherhood in the face of adversity?"

"It faded in the face of sobriety," he shot back. In fact, Roland Gibson was the guy who came up with the title of our tight little circle of friends, noting the way that all our first names happened to belong to heroic figures out of myth. Hector Morales, my patrolman friend from the River City PD, was another member. So was Robin Faye, someone else I was going to have to hit up for a favor on this case.

"Look, I'll be glad to dig around for you and see what I can get," Roland said, "but if you've got anything that looks fairly juicy, then give it up. If I don't run in something good soon, I'm doomed to the flower show circuit again."

I stole a glance at Mom, who nodded. "Okay, Wordsworth-less, here it is: Smart money says that the River City PD thinks they've got a suspect, and he's probably going to be arraigned tomorrow morning. His name is Anthony Sterling, of Sterling Investments. You want me to spell 'arraignment' for you?"

"Oh, man! I take back all those awful truths I've spread about you. Okay, I'll muck around and see if anyone's got anything more or if we're holding something back. You want to meet up at Marilyn's later?"

"Yeah. In fact, you give Hector a call. I've got to go see Robin today myself."

"Robin? You think she can help? Officially?"

"Well, I've got a case and a client. I think I'm entitled."

"Better you than me, hero. That place she works in gives me the creeps. See you tonight."

As I closed my cell phone, Mother said, "That was a good trade, I'd say. There's no way we could keep this out of the news in the first place, and if we can get some mileage out of the press in return, then well and good. Good call, son."

"Thanks. Praise from Caesar, indeed. Or would that be Cleopatra in your case?"

Mom grinned and shot past another vehicle that was in her way as the freeway looped around the man-made mountains of central River City. She dove down an exit, and we were cruising among the concrete and steel canyons as we headed for home. "How about some dinner?" Her Majesty inquired.

I checked my watch again. "Love to, but I might have enough time to squeeze in one more potentially useful interview."

Mom made a smooth turn onto Galleon Street, then asked, "With whom? Mr. Sterling's sister? Or perhaps his father?"

"Neither. I'm off to see a woman who talks to dead people."

Mom nodded sagely. "Well, then, I guess it's dinner with Beowulf and an evening walk for me. Shall I drop you at your car?"

"Thanks."

Her Majesty's cell phone suddenly chimed in (to the tune of "Für Elise"), and she deftly flipped it open one-handed. Holding it up at arm's length, she read the text message display. "Ah. Paul says we have a visitor. Malcolm Sterling has come to call."

"Really? Want me to tag along?"

"Surely. Or am I expected to do all the work around here myself?"

"So that's why I was born? Cheap labor?" I asked in mock indignation.

"Seems a fair exchange for the ten hours of labor I put in dragging you out into the world."

"Despite the fact that my grand first appearance into the world gets longer every time you mention it, I have it on good authority that I was born premature. I'm fairly certain I was trying to make a break for it."

"Brat," she laughed as she turned the corner to Galleon Street. Per standard operating procedure, we cruised the front of the office, spotting a large white late-model Cadillac in the front guest parking space. I made a note of the license number. Mom guided the Jag back to the alley, and soon we were parked back in the garage. I followed her in through the back room, where she had an all too brief reunion with Beowulf, and I noticed all the boys had departed. As soon as she settled herself on her throne, she intercommed the reception area. "Paul, please have Mr. Sterling join us."

The door opened to admit an expensively yet conservatively dressed older gentleman. He walked in stiffly, leaning on an old brown wooden cane as he addressed me. "Mr. Wilder? I'm Malcolm Sterling. I've come about my son."

I sensed Mom's mild amusement at the way Malcolm automatically assumed that I was in charge. She rose and announced, "Mr. Sterling, I'm Victoria Wilder, chief of operations. This is my son, Jason."

Malcolm and I were already engaged in a handshake as Mom's words took effect. He had a strong, calloused grip, probably the result of having to use the cane. There was a brief look of puzzlement in Malcolm Sterling's eyes, then a downward twitch of his mouth as he said, "Oh. I see."

Mother extended a welcoming hand. "Please be seated, Mr. Sterling, and tell us how we may be of service to you."

"Thank you," he said as he lowered himself carefully into the high-backed leather chair. I took a moment to size him up. He looked to be about as tall as his son, which is to say not tall at all, but Tony was soft and doughy, while Malcolm Sterling looked trim and fit for a man his age. His head was bald, with a neatly trimmed gray fringe around the ears, and his brown eyes, set behind a pair of glasses like his son's, were alert and sharp. He held himself upright even while seated, as if to maximize his height by will alone.

While I was checking him out, he was silently perusing the office, his frown deepening. He shrugged slightly, then said to Her Highness in his soft voice, "I've just come from the police department. They tell me that you're representing my son."

"Mr. Sterling," Mother began, "the Midnight Investigation Agency was first retained by your daughter-in-law, Katerina, to locate your son, who had been missing since Sunday. This afternoon, Mrs. Sterling again requested our services to aid your son in the event he is arraigned on criminal charges. As for legal counsel, your son is currently represented by Abigail Glass, an excellent criminal defense lawyer."

"I know," Malcolm said, making it sound like a sigh. "Tony told me so today. When I saw him in jail. What I want to know is, just what kind of trouble is my son in?"

"We'll know far more about that if the district attorney prefers charges against him tomorrow," Mom answered. "For now, it appears that the police think that your son is somehow involved in a homicide."

Malcolm's knuckles turned white as he gripped his cane. "Murder? Tony? Impossible! You can't expect me to believe—"

"It's irrelevant what you believe, Mr. Sterling," Mother said, cutting him off. "What's important is what the authorities believe. Or believe they can prove."

Malcolm Sterling's features took on a sad cast, a look they seemed accustomed to. "I still say it's ridiculous. Have you met my son?" he asked, almost plaintively.

"I have," I volunteered.

Malcolm shot a look at me. "And do you think my son could do such a thing?"

Other than when he almost shot me? I thought. I wisely elected to say instead, "I agree it seems unlikely. But as"—I almost said "Her Highness"—"my mother mentioned, it's not our opinion that counts here. You say you spoke with Tony today? What did he tell you?"

Malcolm sagged a bit. "By the time I found the jail, I was told I couldn't see him until four o'clock. Then I was referred to a detective, who managed to arrange for me to see Tony. But when I finally got to see him, he said that he couldn't talk to me there and pointed to a sign that said all visits may be recorded. He just asked me to get him out of there somehow and said he'd explain everything to me then."

"The detective," I asked, "was his name Walter Dolman, by any chance? Tall, good-looking guy?"

Malcolm looked blank for a moment. "He was black," he answered vaguely.

"That's probably him," I said. "He's the guy who's working on the homicide. Did he ask you any questions?"

"Yes, he did," Malcolm responded. "Said he wanted to know what my son would be doing around Twelfth Street last Sunday night. I told him that I certainly didn't know, but if there was trouble, then I was certain that Tony's sister was involved."

"Jenny?" I asked.

"Yes," Malcolm said heavily. "She's the one you should be looking at, not my son. I told the detective as much."

"Why do you say that, Mr. Sterling?" Mother asked.

"Because all her life she's always been in trouble. She is nothing but trouble. And I'm afraid she may have managed to get Tony mixed up in something. She came back from God alone knows where last year and talked Tony into letting her sign a contract to manage some property. By the time I found out about it, it was too late. I foolishly thought that Tony could be trusted and turned over all the business affairs to him when I retired. If I had thought there was a chance of anything like this happening . . ." His voice trailed off.

"Would that property be the Castle Theater?" I asked.

Malcolm's eyes came up from staring at the carpet and fixed on me. "Yes." He thought for a moment, then said, "Mr. Wilder, I'm certain that my son is innocent of any wrongdoing and therefore will not need your services any longer. Now, I'll be happy to pay you for any trouble you've taken so far, but—"

"Mr. Sterling," Mother interrupted gently but firmly, "as I've mentioned before, we've been retained by your daughter-in-law. She's the only one who could release us from our contract at this date."

Malcolm Sterling blinked, as if surprised to be told he couldn't do something. "Oh, of course," he said.

"Besides," Mother added, "we won't know until tomorrow what the actual situation will be. Not to raise a false hope, but in fact there may be no arraignment tomorrow, although all the indications we've seen so far tell us that there will be, and you should be prepared for that."

Malcolm sighed, looking defeated. "Very well. Would you be so kind as to tell me how I might get my son released from jail? I understand there's a procedure for bail and such."

"If your son is arraigned tomorrow, then the judge may set a bail amount," Mother explained. "Or he may be held over if deemed to be a flight risk. It's really up to the judge."

Just at that moment, the concealed panel from the kitchen flew open and admitted Beowulf, followed closely on his four heels by Felix McQuade, who announced, "Hey, isn't anyone gonna take Fur Boy for a walk? He's been buggin' . . . whoops!"

Felix was suddenly aware he was the focus of the room. Not that our technologically inclined wonder boy is shy, mind you. He's happy to talk at great length about how he's the "smartest biped on the planet," to use his words. Tall and painfully thin, with a wealth of wavy black hair that surrounds an angular face set with eyes perpetually hidden behind dark-blue-lensed glasses, he was dressed in his never varying black. Mother picked him up less than a year ago, after he'd gotten arrested for hacking into the wrong government computer center. Since gainful employment was part and parcel of his terms of court-ordered probation, a mutually beneficial deal was struck: Felix got to work for us, and Mom didn't send him packing back to jail.

I was trying hard not to laugh at the comical expression on Felix's face as it dawned on him that he'd committed a faux pas deluxe when I caught sight of Malcolm Sterling. I almost didn't recognize him; he was smiling, his eyes fixed upon Beowulf. "What a beautiful animal," he said. Looking over to me, he asked, "May I?"

I shot a look over to Her Highness, who gave an almost imperceptible nod. "Sure. He hasn't eaten anyone today."

Malcolm nodded his thanks, then eased himself off the chair onto one knee with the aid of his cane. He held out his hand. "Here, boy. Come here, please."

Beowulf swiveled his head to get his one eye focused on Mom, who said, "Go ahead, Beowulf."

The dog took a couple of steps toward Malcolm, who stretched his hand out and started scratching behind his ear. "Good boy," he cooed. "What happened to you, huh? What happened to your eye?"

"Line of duty," I answered. "He's officially retired."

Malcolm kept his attention on Beowulf as he said, "Aw. That's too bad, fella. Good boy." Beowulf gave a small approving wag of his tail as Malcolm sighed and heaved himself upright with his walking stick. Waving off my move to assist him, he said, "I used to work with a shepherd. I've always thought they were God's best creatures." He sighed again, and the sad-looking Malcolm Sterling we met when he first arrived returned. "Well, then, if there's nothing more I can do for my son?"

"We won't know until tomorrow," Mom said as Beowulf took up his accustomed position beside her desk.

Malcolm nodded. "Very well, then. If you hear anything, please call me. I left my telephone numbers with your man out front."

I escorted Malcolm Sterling to the door, and after I saw him out, I turned to see Felix, Beowulf, and Mom all looking in my direction. "Who's the gimp?" Felix asked.

"That, dear boys, was a walking, talking atavism," Mother announced. "Reminds me why I burned my bra in the first place."

"Were you wearing it at the time?" I inquired innocently. Before she could find something to throw at me, I checked my watch. "Gotta run. If we're still working on this case, then I may just have time to catch a friend of mine who could help."

"I gotta run, too," Felix added. "I, uh, got some important stuff to do. And stuff."

As Her Highness waved me off, I heard her say to Felix, "Not until we have had a long discussion concerning etiquette and the proper manner in which to enter a room."

And as I bailed out the front door, I heard Felix moan, "Aw, geez. Can't you just shoot me and get it over with?"

CHAPTER SIX

The sun was low on a cloudy horizon, cutting between the taller buildings of the city, by the time I arrived at the white two-story structure at the upper end of Buccaneer Street that houses the remodeled combination crime lab and coroner's office. I was afraid I'd be too late to catch my friend Robin Faye before she got off her shift. I found a parking place right next to the one ominously marked RESERVED FOR MORTICIAN USE ONLY, grabbed my notebook, and jogged up to the double glass doors and into the rotunda reception area. The crime lab section was housed in the right wing; I turned left toward the security-glass-encased portal that guards the morgue. I pressed the buzzer, and a nasal, feminine voice responded through the speaker, "May I help you?"

"I'm here to see Robin Faye."

A pause, then I heard, "I'll see if she's still here. Hey, Frank! Tell Robbie she's got a live one up front."

Less than two minutes later, there was a click and a side door opened up. "Wild Boy! What brings you here?"

I turned to see Robin Faye, all six-foot-two with womanly dimensions to match, leaning out of the door. She wore a smile that lit up her café-au-lait complexion, and her tightly braided hair, midnight dark tinged with gold, was bound up into a crown. I'd never venture a guess at what my Amazonian friend weighed in at—you'd have to take into account the massive amount of gold jewelry she invariably wore—but if anyone could make a plain hospital green work smock look stylish, she was the woman to do it. "Hello, my princess," I greeted her. "Room for one more?"

Her smile twisted into a grimace at the old *Twilight Zone* line. "I told you once: You ever wind up coming here as a customer, I'll kill you. How's your mom?"

"Still ruling her kingdom and abusing the peasants. Namely me."

"Well, I'm sure you deserve it," she said airily. "Now, what brings you here? Besides the fact that you can't live without me, etcetera, etcetera."

"First and foremost, we're having a society meeting at Marilyn's tonight. Can you make it?"

"Oh, yeah? Count me in. I've been missing you boys."

"Great. See you tonight." I turned as if to leave, then did a dramatic pause, slapping my forehead. "Oh, yeah. Almost forgot in my joy of seeing you again. You wouldn't happen to have an incinerated body lying around here since, say, last Sunday night, would you?"

Robin lowered her head and gave me her best suspicious stare. "And if I did?" she asked with slow caution.

"Well, I was sorta kinda hoping that you'd have a little information you could share. Not for myself, of course, but on behalf of my client."

Robin tilted her head, narrowing her large golden-brown eyes. "Is this legit?"

"I'm almost positive it is."

"Does your mystery body come with a name?"

"That's what I was hoping to learn from you."

"Sunday, eh? Ah, yes. I believe I'm acquainted with the gentleman to whom you refer." Robin held the door wide open for me. "Well, your timing's good. Most of the day shift went home already, making up for the weekend rush. So come into my parlor, good sir, and meet my guests."

As the door closed behind me, I found myself in a white

hallway with a tile floor. I followed Robin through a pair of steel-plated swinging double doors and into a cavernous, hospital-smelling amphitheater with rows of metal-covered overhead lamps that cast harsh light down through the room. The far wall held a large number of square stainless steel hatches, and I was happy to note that none of the metal operating tables, with their curiously unsettling grooves built in, were currently occupied. I tried to cover up the sudden chill that had little to do with the lowered temperature in here. "We have a visitor," Robin announced loudly as we entered.

"Robin? Not to be disrespectful or anything, but I don't think your guests can hear you."

"Hey, just because you're a member of the living-impaired doesn't mean people shouldn't be nice to you. So you're here to see Nicholas?" Robin asked over her shoulder.

"Is that the guy from Sunday night? Found off Twelfth street?"

Robin walked over to a corner desk, slid into a wheeled chair, and started tapping the computer keyboard. A moment later she said, "Yeah, that's him. Severe burns and all." Robin looked up and gave me a beautiful smile. "You want to meet him?" she asked invitingly.

"God, no!"

My friend looked bemused. "So why are you here?"

"I wanted some info. Stuff that hadn't made the paper yet. I've got a client who's going to be arraigned tomorrow, and I was hoping to get some information early."

Robin sighed. "That's one of the sad things about being deceased. No one wants to see you anymore. Okay, Braveheart, I've got his chart up. What do you want to know?"

"Well, for one, who is he? You said his name was Nicholas?"

Robin smiled. "Now, he's one of our special cases. You see, we don't know what his real name is, and he's been very shy about telling us. So in the meantime, I give them names. You know, so I can address them properly during the various procedures."

I had a brief bad moment when my mind suddenly wondered about some of the "procedures" that occurred in this place. I clamped my imagination down and asked, "So what do you know about him?"

Robin spun in her chair and consulted the computer monitor. "Let's see. His face was no help because of the fire damage. You want to see the photographs?"

"I repeat: God, no!"

"Baby," Robin half whispered. Louder, she said, "Let's see. Caucasian male, 228.4 pounds—he was a big boy. Age twenty-five to thirty-five. No identification in clothes. No wallet. Gold necklace with no identifying jeweler's marks and an imitation Rolex, made in Korea. It was pretty melted." Robin swung around to me. "You'd think he'd gone out of his way to give me a puzzle to play with. Seems our friend here had nothing in his pockets." She swung back to the screen. "Okay . . . ah, 0.29 blood alcohol." She looked over toward the lockers. "That was rather naughty of you," she said in the direction of where I assumed Nicholas was currently residing.

"You said there was nothing in his pockets? What about his clothes?"

"Let's see." Robin clicked through a couple of screens, then said, "Common store-bought stuff. Nothing expensive, no custom-made items. Nothing looked new."

"Damn. Isn't this weird?"

"Not as weird as a lot of people who've come to visit me here," Robin said easily. "For instance, there's my good friend Marie."

"Who?"

"Marie," Robin said again. "She came to us just over three years ago. Someone put her into a Dumpster and set her on fire. Kind of like our friend here. Anyway, Marie's been very shy about telling us who she is, too, but that's all right. We'll figure out her true name someday."

I shook my head, trying to rid it of the sad thought of being gone with no one to remember you. "What was the cause of death on our guy? Was it the fire?"

"No. He arrived with a knife wound and a gunshot wound. Someone set him on fire after he was dead."

"Say what? He was stabbed and shot?"

Robin nodded sadly. "Yep. Penetrating puncture wound through the right renal gland, that's kidney for those of you who skipped biology, at a forty-five degree ascending angle, which means he was stabbed with an upward motion, causing massive hemorrhage. Death would have been almost instantaneous. The blade used was single edged, with a wide back. Rather unusual, almost triangular."

"Bleah. I almost hate to ask, what about the gunshot wound?"

Robin scrolled down on her screen, then said, "Close-quarter gunshot wound to the upper abdomen, just under the xiphoid process; that's his sternum to you. Avulsion of tissue in the area, along with parts of his clothes that were forced into the wound channel, shows that the gunshot was fired almost point-blank. A single .45-caliber, full-metal-jacket bullet was recovered from the subject's fifth thoracic vertebra." Robin read silently for a moment, then murmured, "Interesting."

"What, dare I ask?"

She turned to me. "The bullet was fired into Nicholas at a forty-five-degree angle as well. It appears that he was shot while lying down."

"Okay. So he was stabbed in the back, then shot in the chest while lying down, then set on fire?"

"Yep. No doubt about it, he had a really bad day," she said sympathetically.

"Anything you want to add to that little understatement?"

"Not unless someone comes forward to claim him. Or we can get a match on the dental work. His hands were mostly gone from the fire, so no fingerprints, naturally."

"Right. Naturally. How was he set afire?" I held up a hand as I saw Robin draw in a deep breath. "In plain, simple terms, please."

She smiled. "Well, to put it into a term that a plain, simple man can understand, turpentine."

"Turpentine?"

"Yes. Sometime after Nicholas's body was insulted by stabbing and shooting, someone poured turpentine over the body and lit it."

I snapped my notebook shut; this was enough for one day for me. "Okay, my princess. Remind me I owe you a drink tonight at Marilyn's."

Robin rose from her chair. "I hope this was helpful to your client. By the way, you could come visit me more often, too, you know. As much as I love my people here, it is nice to have a two-sided conversation for a change."

I laughed. "Okay, Just so long as you don't invite me for an indoor picnic."

On our way to the lobby, I turned and asked her, "By the way, why do you call him Nicholas?"

"Well, I have to call him something, don't I? Besides, we pride ourselves on treating our guests like royalty around here. Marie, for instance, was named in honor of Marie Antoinette. I named him Nicholas after the last czar of the Russias, mainly because of the dental work he had while a member of the living. It looks like he may have spent his formative years somewhere in Eastern Europe."

A thought hit me. "Or maybe Russia?"

"Sure," Robin said. "It's a possibility."

That made Robin's guest my second Russian for the day. "Okay, princess, I'll see you tonight at the club," I said as I walked to my car.

Night had fallen while I was in Robin's domain, and my appetite seemed to have fled along with the sun. I was feeling pretty worn out, too, a hangover from last night's fun and games, and I was now sorry that I'd promised to meet my friends later at Marilyn's. But I owed the gang a drink at the very least, and my friends were far more dear to me than sleep.

I found myself starting to drive aimlessly through the neon-lit streets and thought that, as long as I was killing time while waiting for my appetite to resuscitate, I might as well accomplish something useful. I decided to do a little reconnaissance of the Castle Theater and get the local geography in order, as I was fairly certain I'd be visiting there on the morrow. I steered the Green Hornet in the direction of Ketch Street and joined the slow-motion parade of cars that is laughingly referred to as the rush hour. Eventually I was able to make my way over to the block of Twelfth Street between Ketch and Jib. Parking was now plentiful, as the weekday's mass urban exodus was in progress. I found a space across the street from the alley in question. I shut off the engine and took a good long look across the way.

One thing was certain: It was a god-awful place to die. The alley was dark and about as inviting as the maw of a shark. I shrugged and thought I might as well check things out while I was here. According to Detective Dolman, there were two eyewitnesses to Sunday night's events. I've found out that occasionally it's useful in this business to put yourself in the place of a witness, to see for yourself what can and can't be seen.

I got out of my car and looked up and down the street. There were fewer than half a dozen people about, and they all seemed to be concentrating on getting off the street as soon as possible. The businesses on Twelfth were all closed up now, with skeletal metal shutters locked against the night, and I heard a low rumble of thunder roll across the sounds of the traffic in the distance.

I went to the trunk of the car, unlocked it, and opened the briefcase that was inside. It held a compact collection of equipment that's useful in my line: camera, voice recorder, binoculars, and other assorted items. I retrieved the palm-size camera and my small Surefire Executive tactical flashlight and checked them both to make sure they were operational. Recalling my recent series of lectures on safety and survival, I unlatched the upper compartment of the armored case where I kept my handgun. It was a stainless steel .357 Ruger Speed Six, with a 2.75-inch barrel and bobbed hammer. The gun was made back in the 1970s, and it had a couple of custom modifications to enhance accuracy and safety. The revolver, like my Mustang, used to belong to my father, and even though Uncle Jim Bui tried like hell to make me trade in the museum piece, as he called it, for something more modern, I was used to the old gun and always managed to qualify with it on the combat shooting courses.

I undid my belt and slid the Galco Speed Master holster on, then checked the revolver's cylinder to make sure it was loaded. Although the gun was chambered for magnum loads, I opted for heavy-grain subsonic .38 rounds, having never been in fear of encountering rogue elephants in the city. I slipped the gun into its holster, shrugged into my black raincoat, closed up the briefcase and car, and took a slow walk across the street to the alley.

The building on the left was a closed hotel, surrounded by a tall metal fence topped with razor wire; the structure to the right of the alley was plain gray stone a few stories high. Pale amber streetlights wanly illuminated the first few feet of the alley, and I fired up my flashlight and played it around the opening. The wall to the right was covered in a collage of graffiti, and the concrete floor was strewn with inner-city flotsam and jetsam; broken bits of glass glittered here and there. The smell that wafted out was worse than the looks of the place.

I walked forward, sweeping the ground with my light, until I came to an oblong scorched patch a couple of feet away from a pair of closed metal doors that were camouflaged with layers of years-old street artists' paintings. As I crouched down to get a better look, I was speared by the beam of another flashlight, coming out of the depths of the alley as a harsh voice called out: "Freeze, you bastard. Stay right where you are!"

CHAPTER SEVEN

I launched myself up and back, away from the glare, while swiveling my own light toward the voice and sending my camera flying in the same direction before I swept my coat back and got a grip on my gun. My camera clattered as it skipped across the ground, and I got a glimpse of my alleyway neighbor through the glare. "I said hold it!" the voice shouted again.

"You, too," I called back. We seemed locked in a duel, battling with our flashlights. I could see that my opponent had his free arm up shielding his face. I used mine to keep my revolver ready in case I needed it. "What the hell are you doing back here?" the gravelly voice inquired.

There are times when the simple truth works as well as anything. "Taking pictures," I said. "I'm a private investigator."

There was a surprised grunt in response. "You from the insurance company?"

Then again, there are times when a simple lie works pretty well, too. "Yeah," I answered.

The owner of the guttural voice lowered his flashlight, shining it on the ground near my feet. "Oh," he said. "You probably want to see Jenny."

I lowered the beam of my own light. As my overcharged vision started to clear a bit, I could make out the guy I shared the alley with. His apparent size was not reassuring to me. "Right, Jenny," I said.

"Follow me," the man said as he walked toward me. I saw him

stoop down and pick something up, then as he came up to me he extended his hand, which held my little camera. "Here, you dropped this."

I reluctantly let go my grip on my gun as I took the camera from him, noting that he was about half a head taller than I was. Without another word, he continued up the alley toward Twelfth Street. Pocketing my camera, I followed, finally getting a good look at him as he reached the sidewalk. My first impression was that I had just made the acquaintance of a leather-jacketed troll, straight out of mythology and tromping around in a big pair of biker boots. His shaven head and heavy features looked like a large lump of dark clay that someone once tried to make a sculpture out of, only to give up in the first few minutes.

My companion turned left and started trudging toward Ketch Street with a stride that I had to half jog to keep up with. His long arms swung in rhythm, one hand holding the large flashlight, the other what appeared to be a tire iron. At least the impromptu exercise had given my adrenaline-fueled heart rate a chance to do something other than make my arms and legs shaky. "Having a little trouble around here?" I innocently asked my new acquaintance.

He didn't answer at once, then grunted and said, "You believe in ghosts?"

"Me? No, not really."

"Neither do I," he rumbled back. I followed him around the corner and saw the Castle Theater. I stopped and craned my neck back to try and get perspective. The front of the structure resembled a rough-built flagstone castle, straight out of the story-books. The edge of the roof was lined with series of evenly spaced rows, like flat missing teeth, representing the balustrades where archers would fire their arrows at an invading army. The broad entrance was a stone archway, with a heavy black metal chain on either side anchored to a semicircular wooden walkway designed to resemble an open drawbridge. In the center of the opening was a small turret, looking like a giant-size rook chess piece, that was the ticket booth, and standing silent guard, one on either side of the gate, were a pair of life-size stone knights carved onto the wall, identical except that the one on the right had lost his head sometime in the past.

The marquee above the entryway—unlit, but clearly visible in the lights from Ketch Street—read: MASQUERADE BALL AT THE HAUNTED CASTLE THIS FRI! PRIZES FOR BEST COSTUME! MIDNIGHT MOVIE MADNESS! This contrasted with the handwritten sign taped to the glass lobby doors: CLOSED UNTIL FURTHER NOTICE. Throughout my life in the city, I must have been by this place hundreds of times, but it had never been open for business in all my memory.

My large escort stopped just short of the doors, finally noticing that I had quit following him, and stood there glaring at me. I smiled and hurried to catch up to him as he pulled a large, jangling collection of keys from his belt. He unlocked the door, and as I stepped into the faded-red-carpeted foyer, the aroma of popcorn heavily laced with butter washed over me and reactivated my appetite. Across the lobby in the dim indirect lighting I could see a pair of tattered leather-covered double doors that led into the theater proper and a darkened concession stand to my left. My guardian troll started stomping up the right side of a set of curving stairs. I followed, and we were soon at the balcony entrance. My friend walked past the first set of doors and knocked on a plain dark wooden door marked MANAGER. He pounded a couple of times, then a husky feminine voice called from within, "Enter if you dare."

My escort opened the door and led me into a small office with brick walls painted off-white. There was one old desk covered with papers, a set of three green metal filing cabinets, and a pair of unsteady-looking chairs. The only decorations were a series of childlike crayon and watercolor pictures taped to the brick. The occupant was on the telephone as we entered, holding up a hand for silence as she resumed her conversation. "Sorry, Rex . . . Look, as far as I'm concerned, it's still full speed ahead . . . Yeah,

I know. But I'm going to get that covered . . . You're sure you can't get me a loan? Yes, I'm sure you want to get me alone, I get it, funny boy. Ha, ha. Trust me, we'll have a show if I have to get up onstage and shoot myself out of a cannon . . . Okay, great. You're a doll. Thanks!"

During my eavesdropping, I studied the woman. From the little I'd heard from her father and brother, I had built up a rather unflattering expectation. The woman before me appeared to be in her late twenties, maybe thirty at most, with lustrous dark, almost black hair pulled back from her face by a blue bandana that failed to match the deep blue of her eyes. The other Sterlings I had met both came equipped with smallish facial features; she had strong ones, the geometry of her face adding up to a balance of beauty. The oversized gray sweatshirt she wore didn't conceal the athletic body it clad, either.

She hung up the phone, then closed her eyes and raised her hands to her temples, gently rubbing them, as she said, "If you're here with more bad news, better give it to me now."

The troll said, "Found this guy out back, Jenny. Says he's from the insurance company."

Jenny opened her eyes and gave me a rueful smile. "Did you bring a check with you?"

"Uh, no," I answered.

Her smile took on an ironic twist. "Didn't think so," she said. "That would be way too convenient. Look, what else can I tell you? I already explained that I didn't have anything to do with that new contract. And if my brother says different, then he's wrong."

I was getting in deep and sinking fast with my little lie about being from the insurance company, and as intriguing as the free information I was getting was, the bottom line remained that this woman was a potential witness against my client, her brother, and I had best do what I could to get on her good side.

"Ms. Sterling? May we speak privately for a moment?"

"Chance," Jenny said automatically. "Not Sterling. As for privacy, Bruce knows everything that goes on around here."

I silently shook off my surprise at the leather-clad thug's name. "It has to do with your family, Ms. Chance," I said.

Her lovely blue eyes narrowed in speculation. "And you are?" she asked.

I produced my ID. "Jason Wilder. I'm a private investigator."

Jenny took my identification and studied it, reading aloud, "Midnight Investigation Agency?" She looked up at me and said, "You represent the insurance company?"

"Actually, I was being a little less than truthful," I confessed.

I felt Bruce's presence a step closer to me. Jenny leaned back in her chair. It creaked ominously. "And why should you be any different from all the other men in my life?" she wondered aloud. "What's all this about, exactly?"

"As I said, this concerns your family. Specifically, your brother, Tony."

Jenny's eyes took on a speculative cast. Finally she said, "Bruce, would you mind?"

I heard a low growl that could have come from Beowulf, then Bruce said from behind me, "I'll be right outside." He stomped heavily over to the door and let himself out, closing it quietly behind him.

Jenny Chance rested her elbows on the desk, locking me in with her bright blue eyes. "What's this really all about? And why did you lie and tell Bruce you were from the insurance company?"

"Well, I was out in the alley behind here when I met your friend Bruce. I was afraid he was going to kill and eat me."

"The alley? What were you doing back there?"

"Taking pictures."

"Pictures? Where that man was killed?"

"Yes."

"Wait a minute," she said sharply. "I've already spoken to the police about that. You said this has to do with my brother."

"I know. I'm afraid the police think your brother was the man responsible for the homicide. Or didn't they tell you that yet?"

Jenny took in an audible breath. "Tony? They think Tony did that?"

"I'm afraid so."

She shook her head. "That's . . . just ridiculous. There's no way."

"The police have listed you as one of the witnesses they intend to use against him," I cut in.

She leaned back in her chair again; this time it squeaked mournfully. As she stared at me, I said, "Tony's in jail right now because the police think he did it. The reason I'm here is because Katerina Sterling has hired my agency to investigate the matter. So if you think Tony's not responsible, it would help him best if you told me everything you've told the police so far."

She gave me a look that told me she was evaluating that idea, then said, "The cops have got it all wrong, I can tell you that much right now. Tony couldn't kill anyone, and he especially couldn't set anyone on fire like that. Did the police ever figure out who that poor guy was?"

"Not yet," I answered.

She shook her head. "I'm sorry, I can't talk about this right now. I've got a circus to run," she said ruefully. "I'm still trying to figure out a way to get this theater up and running before Friday night. Look, I do want to help my brother, and I'll be glad to talk to you, maybe tomorrow?"

I was reluctant to walk away without getting Jenny's story; in my business, you don't want to miss any opportunities—or give people time to improve whatever story they plan to give you. "What's the problem?" I asked.

She frowned. "The problem is I've got a ghost that occasionally drops by to wreck the place. The last time it happened, my movie projector got trashed, and I just found out how much it costs to repair those monsters, let alone replace them. That, and the insurance company wants to stiff me because they say Tony and I changed the policy, only I didn't. My damn brother must have done it on his own. In the meantime, I'm stuck trying to figure out a way to get back into business. So, unless you know something about fixing an ancient movie projector, I don't think there's a lot we can discuss tonight."

I had a flash of inspiration. "Can you show me?"

She shrugged. "Follow me." I did, noting her graceful walk. Jenny led me past Bruce, who was on guard duty in the hall, to a door marked EMPLOYEES ONLY, took out a key, and opened it. She turned on the lights, and I saw we were in the projection booth, white-painted brick like her office. In the middle of the floor was what appeared to be a Star Wars laser cannon, aiming out through a space in the wall. Attached to the back of the thing was something that might have been a pair of stereo turntables. On the side wall was a skeletal metal floor-to-ceiling rack holding large octagonal metal boxes. The projector had a side panel open, and it looked like something had clawed its way out, leaving a trail of broken electrical wires in its wake.

I turned to Jenny. "When did this happen? Did you have the doors locked at the time?"

She crossed her arms and said, "Sometime late Saturday night, after we closed up at about 2:30 A.M. I wasn't here at the time, but I got a call from one of the kids at about eleven on Sunday morning. And yes, I was told that they locked up for the night. Whoever did this broke the projector's lens, too. Luckily, we had a spare."

I saw that the door leading in here seemed unforced. I also saw the black smudges of the remains of fingerprint powder. "I see the cops tried to get some prints."

"Yeah," Jenny said. "They covered the place. Made everyone here give them a set of fingerprints, too."

"That's so they can eliminate your prints from the possible suspects'. Standard procedure. Tell you what, if I can get someone over here who can fix this thing, will you talk to me about your brother now?"

"Fix the projector? How much money are we talking here? If I had the cash on hand, I'd have had someone working on it already."

"No charge," I assured her. "Or rather, let's just say that I'm renting your time. What do you say?"

She looked at her watch. "Well, I've got an eight o'clock curfew. I'm not about to let my daughter go to bed without a goodnight kiss from her mommy. But if you can get someone over here now, then sure. You've got a deal."

I checked my own watch and saw we had almost two hours before eight. "Fair enough." I took out my cell phone and dialed Felix. "Dude, you're cuttin' into my *Cowboy Bebop*," he complained when he picked up.

When speaking with Felix, you occasionally have to let your brain slide into neutral. While all of his words are in English, they often don't seem to be in any particular order. Whatever it was he was currently doing, it involved music; I could hear a driving jazz sound track in the background. "Duty calls, my friend. I need your technical wizardry."

I heard him sigh. "Now?"

"Now," I affirmed. "Get yourself over to the Castle Theater, Twelfth and Ketch streets. And bring your bag of tricks, or I'll tell Her Royal Highness just what you've been using her high-speed Internet access for."

"I'm there, dude," he said with alacrity.

Jenny regarded me quizzically. "Who was that?"

"That was my part of the bargain," I answered. "Now, is there a place we can talk?"

CHAPTER EIGHT

Jenny, with Bruce following way too close behind, led me
back to her office. At the door, I turned to Jenny's pet monster
and said, "There'll be a young man riding up here who answers
to the name of Felix. Could you wait for him downstairs and let
him in when he arrives?"

Bruce swiveled his massive head to Jenny, who nodded. He
grunted and trudged off to the stairway. Getting a better look at
him in the light, I tried to make a guess at his age, but it was a
toss-up whether the lines and craters in his moonlike face were
the result of long years or high mileage—or both. "If I didn't
know better," I said, "I'd almost think he didn't like me."

"Bruce doesn't care much for people. Except me and Angelina," she said as she opened her office door.

"That's your daughter, right?"

Jenny smiled, overpowering the light in the room. "My angel," she said warmly. As I sat down, she handed me a large picture from the desk. The woman in the professional portrait was
Jenny, smiling radiantly with her head held close to a blond blue-
eyed girl who could have been left on earth by the fairies. "Wow,"
I said inadequately.

"She's my world," Jenny said with pride.

I thought of Malcolm Sterling saying that Jenny had always
been trouble and ventured what I hoped was an innocent-
sounding remark. "That must make your father a proud grandpa."

Jenny's smile disappeared like a candle being blown out. "Father," she said with more than a hint of scorn, "has never seen her. Do you know the old man?"

"I met him today. And I was wondering what he might have meant when he said you were trouble."

Jenny sat down behind her desk. "Trouble, eh? That's putting it mildly, for him. I usually get accused of being in league with the Antichrist. What else did he say?"

"That whatever trouble Tony may be in, he was certain you'd be the cause of it."

"That's the old man, all right. But what does this have to do with helping my brother?"

"Well, the one thing everyone seems to agrees on—you, Katerina, and Malcolm—is that Tony couldn't kill anyone. It might be helpful if I knew the whys and wherefores, just in case we have to convince a jury of the same thing."

Jenny looked thoughtful for a moment, then said, "Okay. If you think dragging out my whole sordid family history will help."

"It may."

"Fine," she sighed. "Tony's always been kind of, well, backward and shy. I always blamed that on the fact that he never seemed to be able to come up to the old man's expectations."

"Expectations of what?"

"Everything," she said. "Athletic, academic; you name it, Tony failed at it. And the harder old Malcolm pushed, the worse Tony got. Me, I had it easy. Except for seeing to my straight-and-narrow upbringing, the old man mostly ignored me."

"Oh?"

"Yeah. I always figured it was a firstborn-son kind of thing. After a while, I gave up trying to please the old man myself. Besides, I had my hands full raising Tony."

"Raising Tony? Isn't he older? What about your mother?"

"In a way," she said softly, "I was Tony's mother. Ours apparently had the good sense to run off shortly after I was born."

"Oh. Sorry."

She waved a hand, warding off sympathy. "It's okay. I really used to hate her for that, you know? Back when I was younger. But as I got older, I started to realize that maybe she just couldn't take it, being married to the old man. I guess I can't blame her for being weak." Jenny seemed to shake herself out of her reverie. "Anyway, like I said, I was kind of the mother figure for Tony. The old man would punish him whenever he caught Tony crying. I was the only one who would hold him afterward. Then came the time when I couldn't take it anymore."

"What happened?"

Jenny cradled her chin and looked up somewhere; into the past, I assumed. "It was my seventeenth birthday. Some friends and I took off to celebrate at Kennedy Park. Unfortunately, the cops caught up with us, and the next thing I know, I'm being dragged home in the back of a patrol car. So there I am, standing in the doorway with Malcolm, who hadn't even noticed I was gone, and right in front of the cop he looks at me and calls me a whore."

"Ouch."

"Yeah," she said with a bitter smile. Then she looked at me. "You know, he could have just beaten me; that would have been fine. He could have yelled at me and called me a screwup; that'd be okay, too. But for him to call me that was just . . . wrong. So that was it for me."

"What happened?"

"That night, I packed some clothes and filled up a backpack with everything I thought could be valuable. By this time, Tony was out of the house and away at college. I left Malcolm a note, telling him not to bother to look for me, that I had helped myself to my inheritance and that I was gone for good. And I got myself to the bus station and took the first one heading to Los Angeles."

"Did your father ever try to find you?"

"Hell, no. If he thought anything at all, I'm sure it was 'good riddance'. I made my way to Hollywood. I was going to be a star, you know. Only it didn't quite work out that way."

I felt that I could have written the rest of her story myself. I've worked a lot of missing persons cases—too many—and I've lost track of all the ones that start with an unhappy teenager running away to that sinkhole full of drugs and predatory monsters called Hollywood and end when the kid gets swallowed up completely. Jenny Chance seemed to have survived all that, and now I had to know how. "So what happened then?"

"Well," she said, "I did what I could, worked at any job I could find with all those other would-be movie stars. I was hungry a lot, and I slept in some god-awful places. Then one day I met a man who told me that a girl like me could make some money in the movies, if she was willing. So I did," she said, with defiance in her voice.

I was trying to figure out what I could say to that when she went on, "I became a stuntwoman."

I shook my head in surprise. "A what?"

"A stuntwoman," she repeated. Then she batted her gorgeous eyes and fanned herself with one hand as she said in a flawless southern accent, "Why, Mr. Wilder? Whatever did you think I meant?"

I laughed. I couldn't help it. She laughed, too, a lovely sound. "You got me on that one," I said with admiration.

She gave me a wry smile. "Not that there was a lack of offers coming from the so-called adult entertainment industry, but I turned those down, I'm proud to say. Anyway, I stared getting steady work, not that you'd recognize me, mind you. All the speaking parts went to size zero bleached blonds with cocaine habits. But I did all right for myself. A lot of it was a blast, learning how to jump from buildings, shoot guns, do martial arts fight scenes, take a spill on a motorcycle, that sort of thing. I even got pretty good working the special effects side, setting up explosions and stuff. Then I met Angelina's father, married him, and had to quit doing gags for a living."

"Gags?"

"Stunts," she explained. "A little hard to do when you're pregnant."

"Was Angelina's father a stuntman?"

"Troy?" she asked with surprise. "Hell, no. Troy Chance was always going to be the star of the family. He had the looks, all right, but he needed his own stuntman to open a car door. Only problem was, I found out too late what he did for money when he wasn't working, which was most of the time."

"What was that?"

"Well, remember those cocaine-addicted actresses I mentioned?"

"Yeah."

"He was the supplier."

"Oh."

"Yeah, 'Oh,' that's what I thought, too. I decided that Angelina needed a better chance in this world than having a drug dealer for a father, so I took half of all the money he thought he so cleverly hid from me and got the hell out of there. I came home to River City."

"What did you do then?"

"Well, first I tried to introduce Angelina to her grandfather, only Malcolm seemed disappointed that I hadn't actually fallen off the face of the earth and refused to see us. Which was pretty screwed up, even for him. Tony, on the other hand, was great. I'd kept in touch with him while I was away. And I was happy to see that he married well. Katerina is a sweetie. She's told me that Father doesn't think much of her, either."

"What happened between you and Tony? Katerina told me that you two had a falling-out."

"Yeah," Jenny sighed. "Over the theater. When I got back to River City, I told Tony that I was looking to stay and raise my daughter. By this time, Malcolm had turned over all the family property investment business to Tony. I convinced Tony to let me reopen the Castle and run it. This theater has been in the family forever, only Dad never did anything with it. I sank most of the money I managed to get from Troy into the deal, and Tony had the papers drawn up." Jenny smiled then. "When old Malcolm found out, he damn near blew his stack."

"Why?"

"Probably because he'd rather see me starve. Anyway, for the first time in Tony's life, my brother stood up to the old man, telling him that it was too late and that he'd see this was going to be a good thing. By then all the contracts were done and we were in business."

"When did you have this falling-out?"

"Just a week ago," she said. "Out of the blue, Tony comes to me and says we've got to sell the place. I told him that we were actually starting to turn things around and make a profit and that I was making headway getting the theater ready to host some real shows. I wanted to start producing plays and turn the Castle into a place where some of the high schools could get a decent theater arts program going." Jenny's eyes and voice had begun to take on a glow, but it faded as she said, "I guess it's in the blood. One of the few things I was able to find out about our mother was that at one time she was an actress. I always kind of thought that after my mother left the old man, he kept this theater for sentimental reasons. But he hasn't got a sentimental bone in his head," she sighed. "I figured that Malcolm finally got to Tony and that he was putting pressure on me because of the old man. I accused him of that, but all Tony said was that he needed the money and this was the only way. So I told him to get the hell out and take me to court if he had to, but I wasn't going to let him out of the contract."

"What happened last Sunday night?"

Jenny shook her head. "That was strange, to say the least. My day started when I got the call that the movie projector had been busted up. I came over here and chased everyone out of the projection booth. I didn't want anyone to see me cry. I called the cops. Then I spent the day calling everyone I knew in the business around town, trying to see if I could get it fixed or replaced. I finally gave up and locked the place up to go home."

"Was anyone else here?"

"Just Bruce. He always insists on walking me to my car. I was halfway down the street when I remembered that I needed to get the insurance paperwork out of the office so I could call them first thing in the morning. I turned around and let myself back in, and got the paperwork, and as soon as I got back outside I heard the shot."

"You were in front of the theater?"

"Right."

"How do you know it was a gunshot?"

"Hey, I did a lot of direct-to-video action films. I know what a gunshot sounds like. Anyway, at first I wasn't sure what to do. Then I heard a scream. It sounded like it came from up Twelfth Street, and my car was parked on the corner. I peeked around the building, and I saw the light from the flames coming from the alley. I thought the theater might have been on fire, so I ran like hell up the street to see. That's when I saw . . . what was out back. I called 911 on my cell phone right away, and then I saw Tony's car driving up Twelfth."

"You're sure it was Tony's car?"

"Oh, yeah. No doubt. He's got a big white Land Rover, and I saw him behind the wheel. It was kind of surreal; I had no idea what he'd be doing there at that hour, unless he was looking for me, but he drove right past going like a bat out of hell, so I figured he saw something that spooked him. The police asked me if there were any other witnesses, so I told them my brother might have seen something." She shook her head. "I never dreamed they would think he'd do something like that."

There was a knock at her door. "Jenny?" Bruce said. "There's some kid here."

I said, "Ah. Must be the repairman I ordered for you."

I followed Jenny to the door, where Bruce and Felix were

waiting. "Never fear, the genius is here," Felix announced. "So what's the gig?"

I was happy to note that Felix was wearing his large black backpack over his equally dark trench coat. "This way, genius. I'll show you." I took Felix over to the projection room, opened the door, and stepped aside. "Here you go. Make it work."

Felix's dark glasses slipped down his nose as he ducked his head to get a look. "Make it work? This thing is older than you are, dude. What the hell am I supposed to do with that?"

"Hmm," I mused. "Guess I'll just have to tell Her Highness that we need to call the probation department and have them send over a replacement for you. Someone with less ego and more competence."

Jenny looked at Felix and said, "Tell me, what's your favorite movie?"

Felix swiveled his head, giving Jenny an all too obvious appreciative examination. "My favorite movie? Why?"

"Just tell me."

"Well," he said, "I kinda dig real old movies. You know? Made back in the eighties and stuff? Like *Brazil* or *Blade Runner* or *Buckaroo Banzai*."

"Tell you what, Felix," Jenny said warmly. "You get this thing up and running, and I'll get a copy of *Buckaroo Banzai*. You can have a private showing, if you like."

Felix's eyes grew wide. "Really? For true? *All* right!" He shrugged out of his backpack. "Now we're talking. Stand aside, genius at work here."

Jenny checked her watch. "Bruce? Could you stay with Felix and let him out when he's done? I want to get home to Angie before she has a chance to tie the babysitter up again."

Bruce nodded his massive head. "Walk you out," he rumbled.

"If you don't mind, I've got a few more questions for Jenny. I'd be happy to walk her out myself."

The look Bruce flashed me said silently that what he wouldn't mind would be breaking me into bite-size pieces. Jenny said, "Okay. I'll get my coat. Call me if there's any problem."

As Felix was pulling tools out of his bag of tricks, I followed Jenny to her office. She retrieved a plain blue windbreaker and an old brown leather purse, quickly kissed her fingertips and placed them on her daughter's photograph, then turned to me. "I have to go check the doors one last time. Come on, I'll give you the two-dollar tour."

■

CHAPTER NINE

On the stairs back down to the lobby, we heard a clanging noise coming from the projection booth, followed by Felix shouting, "Ah! Got you! Thought you could hide from me, did you? C'mere!"

Jenny cast a worried look over her shoulder. "Are you sure your friend knows what he's doing?"

"Felix? Sure," I said with a certainty I certainly didn't feel. "We only hire the best at Midnight."

My remark was punctuated by another Felix outburst. "Bastard! Don't you try to hide from me!"

"Felix has a rather special relationship with machinery," I explained. "He doesn't fix things as much as he beats them into submission. But he hasn't failed yet, to my knowledge."

"If you say so," Jenny said skeptically.

To get her mind off Felix's noisy efforts, I said to her, "Where did you pick up Bruce? Did he come with the furnishings here?"

Jenny started walking again. "Almost," she laughed. "He showed up here a little over a year ago. I was in the process of putting together some vignettes from Shakespeare. I had an open casting call and put the word out to the local colleges. Bruce Roberts showed up the first night and asked me if there was anything he could do, so I put him to work as a stagehand. He showed up for every rehearsal, doing just about everything backstage from painting scenery to running tech." She must have caught my quizzical look. "That's operating the lights and sound. Anyway, opening night arrives, and one of the guys for the scene from *Hamlet* is a no-show. I'm all set to drop the scene from the show when Bruce comes up and tells me he can do it."

I shook my head at the mental picture of the leather-clad monster dressed in a pair of tights. "You're kidding," I said flatly.

"Nope," Jenny said with a smile. "He goes on and does a flawless performance as the ghost of Hamlet's father. He must have learned all the lines by watching the rehearsals. After the show, he just kind of hung around and appointed himself as my assistant manager. I don't have any idea what he does for a living. I sure as hell can't afford to pay him. Although at his age, which I have to guess at since he never talks about himself, he could be a retired millionaire for all I know. Personally, I think it was my little angel that won him over."

"Your daughter?"

"Yeah. You should see the two of them together when she's here 'helping Momma,' as she calls it. She spends almost the entire time perched on his shoulders. I must have saved a fortune on pony rides because of Bruce."

We had paused in front of the double lobby doors. She smiled and tossed her head. "This way," she said as she pushed the swinging door open.

The theater was huge. Blue light glowed from a series of what looked to be cast-iron torches affixed to the walls on either side; soft white light shone from the "candles" in the round chandeliers suspended from chains. The walls were painted with stylized frescoes depicting knights, ladies, and creatures out of myths, faded now and dim in the low light.

Jenny noticed that I had stopped in my tracks as I took the scene in. "It's beautiful," I said sincerely.

"Oh, yeah," Jenny agreed softly. "The one thing Malcolm ever did right; he never let this grand old girl get torn down. And she's a real theater. Built originally to host plays and concerts or show movies." She took my arm. "Come on, I want to finish up here and get home to my daughter before she goes to bed." I followed her down the sloping aisle, carpeted in faded red like the lobby, and watched as she disappeared through the curtained side exit. I heard a door rattle, then she reappeared. As I followed her toward the stage, I asked, "Who do you think would want to put you out of business by breaking your movie projector? I hate to say it, but it kind of sounds like an inside job."

She stopped, then said, "Yeah. I thought of that, too."

"Any disgruntled employees around here?"

"No way," she said, resuming her steps. "Everyone who works here is either from the River City Junior College drama department or a volunteer like Bruce."

"Who has keys to the place?"

She stepped up some stairs that led around a full-size orchestra pit up to the stage, which was cloaked with a faded curtain that put me in mind of the Bayeux Tapestry. She slipped behind the curtain and held it for me. "There are three sets that I know of. Mine, Bruce's, and Tony's."

"Oh."

"Yeah," she said. I turned in a circle to look around, then up at the catwalks and the grid hung with lights above the stage. Jenny continued, "I considered the possibility that Tony may have been responsible. But it doesn't make sense."

"Why? You said yourself that he wanted you to agree to sell the place. Wouldn't putting you out of business kind of push you in that direction?"

"Tony knows me well enough to know that I don't quit once I've got my mind set on something."

I waited while Jenny checked three doors along the back of the stage. The two on either side were single metal doors. In the middle was a wide set of doubles; it was outside them I found the ugly scorch mark on the concrete alley floor. We left the stage by the opposite set of stairs and walked uphill to the last side exit, where I waited for Jenny to check that door. When she returned to the aisle, I handed her my business card. "Here. I put my cell phone number on it, in case you think of anything else that could help Tony. May I have your number? In case I have any more questions?"

Jenny cocked her head to one side. The bluish light from the walls made her large, lovely eyes appear to be lit from within. "Sure," she said. "Just answer this one first: Who's 'Her Highness'? I heard you mention her to Felix."

"Ah. That would be the boss, the woman who runs the Midnight Agency. Variously known as Her Royal Majesty, She-Who-Must-Be-Obeyed-Or-Else, and on occasion Mrs. Wilder."

"Your wife?" Jenny asked quickly.

"No. She Who Spawned Me, as she herself puts it. Her names are pretty much legion, come to think of it."

Jenny laughed, a low, throaty sound. "Sounds like my kind of woman," she said.

Suddenly a bright beam of light lanced out from the upper wall, accompanied by Felix's war cry, "Woo-hoo! Who's da man!"

Jenny looked up, whispered, "Damn" reverently, then ran full-tilt up the aisle. I chased after her, trying to keep up, but the girl ran like a gazelle, and I found watching her preferable anyway— a fact that damn near caused me to slip on the stairs to the upper galley. I arrived to find Jenny clutching Felix in a firm hug, his jack-o'-lantern grin almost as bright as the light beam from the projector. "You did it!" Jenny cried.

Felix, with obvious reluctance, pulled away from Jenny. "Well, sure. Did I mention I'm a genius and stuff?"

Bruce was over in a corner taking in the scene; I noted with interest how his deep-set, almost black eyes fixed on Felix with a baleful glare. I walked to the humming machine and looked inside the panel. Patches of black electrician's tape were set here and there. "How'd you get it to work?" I asked.

Felix grinned. "Ah, nothing to it, for a guy of my superior intellect. Besides, it was an amateur demolition job."

"Amateur?" I queried.

"Definitely," Felix answered. "Only a goddamn cheapass vandal would try to bust up this thing by cutting wires and stuff. If you really wanted to mess it up, all you'd have to do would be to put some Super Glue in the gears. I just patched things up a bit, and ta-da!"

"Well, I don't care how you did it, you're my hero," Jenny said warmly, causing a flush to rise over Felix's pale features. She looked at me and added, "You, too. For bringing Felix here."

"Hey," Felix said, "all in a day's work for us hero types."

Bruce cut in. "I think you'd better get going, Jenny."

"Yeah, you're right," she said. "I've got a date with my angel—hopefully before she manages to stuff another babysitter down the toilet."

Felix packed up his tools, and the four of us trooped down the stairs. After shutting off the lights, Jenny ushered us out and locked the front doors. I reminded her that I wanted her phone numbers, which Bruce seemed not to like at all. As Felix and I watched Jenny and Bruce cross Ketch Street—she sent a last radiant smile over her shoulder toward us—and walk to the parking garage across the way, Felix said in a whisper, "Whoa. Beauty and the Beast."

"That's not fair, Felix," I chided. "She's not that bad looking."

Felix grinned. "Yeah. Right. Like you weren't checking her action out. I saw how you looked at her."

"Isn't it getting past your bedtime?"

"No way. Nighttime is my time. Check you later, dude," he said as he unlocked his helmet from his Nighthawk motorcycle. I took myself in the opposite direction, walking back along Twelfth Street to my car. I was suddenly feeling washed out after too little sleep, too little food, and way too many adrenaline rushes for the day, all of which my time with Jenny Chance had made me forget for a while. I had an uncomfortable flush of feeling as I thought of her—thoughts I knew I had no business entertaining in my business. On the way to my car, I reminded myself that people are often not what they seem. As attractive as Jenny Chance was, her own father thought she was trouble. Jenny, on the other hand, painted a pretty grim picture of the soft-spoken and dog-loving Malcolm Sterling. Yet they agreed in their opinion of Tony Sterling: Both were certain he couldn't kill anyone.

As I came up to the alley, I sighed, remembering that all I intended to do originally was stop by quickly to get the layout of the area and take some pictures. Ah, well, I thought, I'll just snap a few photos and go directly to Marilyn's to meet the gang and get some dinner. I pulled out my little camera, hoping I hadn't screwed it up by throwing it at Bruce earlier this evening; any damage would certainly come out of my paycheck. I was clicking on the power to the internal flash when I heard two things at once: the tiny whine as the camera charged up, and the sound of groaning metal emanating from the alley.

I put my back to the wall and took a quick peek up the alley, seeing nothing but darkness at first, then a small glimmer of light over at the near wall, the wall that connected to the backstage of the theater. I leaned my head against the cold stone, wondering what to do next. Another creaking metallic protest decided my course of action. Time to try to catch someone in the act. Act of what, I wasn't certain.

I got out my flashlight left-handed and positioned my thumb on the activator while I held the camera in my right. On a silent count of three, I leaned in, aiming the camera down the alley. "Hey! Smile!" I called out.

The flash from my camera was almost simultaneous with a startled "Son of bitch!" and the ringing sound of a metal bar bouncing on the pavement. I thumbed my flashlight and shot the beam down the alley, just in time to see a pair of figures running away from me. "Hold it!" I yelled.

Running after them probably wasn't the smartest thing I could do, but off I went, my light sweeping the ground ahead of me as I ran. The rapidly departing duo suddenly disappeared, dodging left into an adjoining alleyway. I slid to a stop at the corner, shoving my camera into my coat pocket and coming up with the revolver before I darted my head out for a look. My quarry was running full-out ahead of me, a flashlight of their own leading the way. I brought my gun up and sighted, realizing at that moment that I wasn't about to shoot anyone in the back, especially as I didn't know who the hell they were or what they were doing. As the running pair reached Jib Street, I saw them diving into a large dark-colored SUV that gunned its engine and took off before the rear door could be closed, half dragging a pair of legs as it went.

My head felt light as I leaned against the brick wall, catching my breath. That, I told myself firmly, was enough for one day. I reversed my steps through the alley, spotting a large crowbar on the ground by the theater's double back doors. The bar was lying squarely in the middle of the scorch mark, and my light reflected back from the bright gouges cut into the doors near the handles. I swept the alley once again with my light to make certain I was alone, then got my camera back out and finished the job I started a short eternity ago, taking extra care to photograph the door with its brand-new damage. When I was through, I carefully picked up the crowbar, wondering if there would be any fingerprints on it, and carried it back to my car.

As I laid my find in my trunk, I took another long look around, noting how empty the streets were in this area at this time of night. My phone was ringing. I let myself into the Mustang and answered it.

"Hey, J. W.," came Roland Gibson's voice. "Where the hell are you? We were trying to decide if we wanted to send out a search party or just order another drink."

"Order one for me, too, Rollo old boy. And tell the waiter to cook up a Wilder Special, *avec fromage.*"

"What kind of drink, O Demanding One?"

"Make it a Ragnarok on the rocks," I said. As I heard Roland's appreciative reaction, I added, "It's been that kind of day."

CHAPTER TEN

Marilyn's Nightclub is River City's own Art Deco homage to a time when men and women dressed for their evening's entertainment. The Castle Theater was an actual landmark of times gone by, but Marilyn's was an artful fraud. Back in the eighties, the owner made a point of salvaging the furnishings from numerous clubs and restaurants around town that had gone out of business. Everything from the full-size turn-of-the-century bar to the blue mirrored tiles in the ceiling to the giant gilt-framed painting of the club's patron deity, Marilyn Monroe, had been saved from the trash heaps of progress.

I was sharing a curtained-off private booth in the dining area with three of my closest friends, a privilege we had become accustomed to after the Midnight Agency extricated the owner's son from a bad situation. While we never accepted anything on the house (a standard Mother strictly adhered to), the family and I were offered certain other perks on occasion. The cheeseburger I had just consumed was one example, an item you'll never see on their expensive menu, and the drink I had was another. The Ragnarok was Roland Gibson's own design, a concoction of Bacardi 151 and Jolt Cola. The bartender kept the Jolt just for our private use.

I was taking my first sip, having felt the need to cushion my stomach with the burger first, when Roland announced, "That's the screwiest story I've ever heard."

I had brought my friends up-to-date on my escapades between

79

bites. Throughout my storytelling, handsome, mustachioed, morose Hector Morales glared at me as he drank his soft drink. He would soon leave to report for uniformed duty on the River City PD graveyard shift. Robin Faye smiled, dark eyes dancing in the light from the candle on the table. Roland predictably took notes, looking for something he could use at the newspaper.

At Roland's pronouncement, Robin said, "You hush! I think it's romantic."

I almost swallowed my sip of liquid fire the wrong way in reaction. "Romantic?" I asked. "Since when are shot, stabbed, and barbecued corpses romantic?"

"Not that, silly boy," she chided. "The whole idea of restoring that lovely theater! A castle? With a beautiful maiden inside?"

"Um, actually she's a mother," I said.

Roland checked his notes. "I thought the stiff was stabbed, shot, and then set on fire. Didn't I get that right?"

While Robin gave Roland a reproachful look, Hector said, "Forget the stiff. What about those guys you caught trying to break in, man? What are you going to do about them?"

I took another sip. "I guess I should give Jenny a call, but I kind of doubt they'd come back tonight. Hey, Hector, are you patrolling anywhere around the Castle these days?"

"Nah," he replied. "I got the South City beat. But I can pass the word to some of my buds after roll call to keep an eye out. You think they're Russian?"

"Well," I mused, "I've got one possibly Russian stiff"—I caught Robin's look—"er, living-impaired individual found behind the theater, plus my client is married to a Russian woman. That, and the brief impression I got of my failed burglars tonight was that they were Caucasian and had a funny way of cursing. Hopefully, I got a decent photograph of the crime in progress."

"Well, take my word," Hector cautioned. "You got Russians here in town, and then you got Ukrainians. Don't ever screw up and call one the other, or the fight's on, man."

"Got it," I said. "You get anything else at the *Clarion,* Rollo?"

Roland pretended to look back through his notebook. "Let's see . . . yep, I got a lot of nothing right here."

"Nothing?" I echoed. "What the hell good are you?"

"I'm good for another drink, that's for sure," he said with a grin on his bespectacled features.

"What now, Jason?" Robin asked.

I had finished my drink, and it seemed to have finished me as well. "I quit for the day," I announced. "Hopefully, tomorrow Anthony Sterling will either be let go, in which case my job is over, or he'll get arraigned, in which case the court will set a date for the preliminary hearing, and that'll give us more time to work on it. Either way, tomorrow looks to be a better day."

"So we're going to have time to get back to a workout schedule?" Hector asked. He was my primary shooting and hand-to-hand sparring partner, and I passed on to him all the lessons that Jim Bui and Tim O'Toole had so painstakingly taught me over the years. I had once offered to teach both Robin and Roland the finer points of combat, but Robin is totally nonviolent, whereas Roland is strictly noneffort.

"You owe me big time," Hector continued. "Man, I'm trying to get onto the narcotics squad, and here I got one of their sergeants calling me up and asking about you. For a minute, man, I was all set to deny you."

"Narcotics?" I said. "What, you're tired of having a home life? You can get into some real ugly stuff there. Trust me, I know."

"Battle not with monsters," Roland intoned, "lest ye become a monster." He clapped his mouth shut as Hector looked down at his cola and Robin reached over and placed her hand gently on mine, her large eyes twin wells of sympathy.

"I forgot about your father, man. Sorry," Hector said quietly.

"It's all right," I said. "I just don't want to go through anything like that again. You know?"

"I got to do something to get out of patrol." Hector said, "I want to get my gold shield."

"You will," I said. "Besides, you could always come and work for my mom."

Hector silently made the sign of the cross. "She's worse than my old academy PE instructor," he said with reverence.

I stood up. "Okay, kids, I'm off."

Robin frowned. "You're not going to call that Jenny and tell her what happened at the theater after she left?"

I glanced at my watch. "Yeah, I guess I should," I said reluctantly. "Not that she needs any more worries at the moment."

"What she needs," Robin said with certainty, "is an epic hero. But I guess you'll just have to do in the meantime."

We bumped fists in our ritual of greeting and departure, and I made my way to the bar to pay the bill. As Roland slipped his coat on he said, "For God's sake, try to do something interesting for a change. I'm tired of rewriting your obituary."

I waved as Robin corralled him and propelled him toward the door, much to the amusement of the other patrons in the bar. I paid up and went out through the lightly falling rain to my Mustang. I made a point of driving carefully, not trusting my sleep-deprived and alcohol-fueled senses, and managed to make it back to my loft without incident.

I'd been trained to notice other people's living spaces, to look for subtle and not so subtle clues to a person's personality. My own living space would probably confuse anyone who tried that with me. All my furnishings were what Mom called "relic hand-me-downs" from my maternal grandparents, from the Oriental rugs to the carved wooden tables and credenzas to the sloping sleigh-bed headboards I owned. I had no idea what these things were worth, but I could appreciate the subtle beauty they all possessed. As I shrugged off my raincoat, I recalled something my ex-girlfriend Sarah once said to me. She suddenly insisted that I ask Mom for a raise, and when I asked her why she thought I should, she held her arms out to encompass my rooms and said, "See? You can't even afford new furniture!"

In addition to the Old World charm, my apartment was

home to all the twenty-first-century amenities. The large credenza against the wall supported my big-screen televison and stereo, while the glass-fronted bookshelf held my video and music collection. The dining room table, with its carved dark wood legs, was the home of my laptop computer with its keyboard and peripherals. Roland Gibson once dubbed the style of my apartment "When Worlds Collide."

I changed into my bathrobe, got out my notebook, and fired up my computer. I spent the better part of an hour putting together my preliminary report for Her Highness, as she would doubtless not only be interested in the new developments but would also like to know what I'd been doing to justify my expenses. Then I retrieved my camera from the briefcase and docked it to my laptop, uploading the pictures I had taken in the alley. The first one was a disappointment; I only caught one of the perpetrators looking up. He had a pale face with a deer-in-the-headlights look and dark hair that blended in with his dark clothes. I didn't have the software to do any enhancement, so I attached the photos to my report and e-mailed the whole thing to the office. Jimmy Bui, or better yet Felix, could probably do something with them, I thought.

I looked over to my mantel clock. It was close to eleven, and I wondered if it was too late to telephone Jenny Chance. Not that I wouldn't mind speaking with her again, but considering the news I had, I doubted she'd get any pleasure out of talking to me. I retrieved my wallet, found her number, then sat on my leather chair next to my antique end table with my brass lamp and my black plastic modern telephone. At the office or at home, no one who works for Midnight ever uses a cordless phone. There are commercially available devices that can receive the transmissions from the cordless models. I know; I've used one myself from time to time.

I punched in Jenny's number. She answered on the fourth ring.

"Hello?"

"Hi, Ms. Chance? This is Jason Wilder."

"Hey, hi," she said in her rich, husky voice. "I'm glad you called. Listen, I was wondering when Tony was supposed be in court tomorrow. Do you think I should be there? And by the way, it's Jenny. 'Ms. Chance' always sounds too close to 'mistake.'"

I laughed. "Okay, and please call me Jason. As for Tony, I'm not sure when he's due in court. If he's going to be arraigned, then it should be sometime in the morning. But I don't know which department his appearance will be in yet. I could call you and let you know tomorrow, if you'd like."

"I would," she said. "Thanks. You know, the more I think about it, the stranger it all seems. Connecting Tony with that poor dead man has just got to be some kind of mistake."

"I hope so," I answered. "Listen, the reason I called is, there was a little trouble after you and Bruce left the theater tonight."

"Trouble? What kind of trouble?" she asked sharply.

"I caught a couple of guys hanging around in the alley. Looked like they were trying to break in."

"God—" she stopped herself—"darn it. Sorry, I just got Angelina to sleep. Did they get in?"

"No. I was able to chase them off. I doubt they'll be back tonight."

"Did you get a good look at them? What did they look like?"

"Well, I managed to get a photo of one, at least. It may help the police, I hope."

She sighed, then said, "Look, I really appreciate all you've done. Especially what you're doing for Tony. But I want to give Bruce a call and see if he can go over to the Castle and check it out. I'd hate to see all of your friend Felix's work go to waste right now."

"I understand. Sorry to be the bearer of bad news."

"Hey, not your fault. Let me give Bruce a call, and I'll call you right back, okay?"

"Uh, sure." I gave her my home number, half wondering why I did that, then hung up. She called back in less than five minutes.

After we exchanged hellos, she asked, "So what's your favorite movie?"

"My what?"

"Favorite movie," she repeated. "Since I offered to get your friend Felix a showing of *Buckaroo Banzai*, I figured the least I could do is make you the same deal. So what do you like? Cops and robbers stuff? Film noir?"

"At the moment," I confessed, "I'd probably have to say any film with you in it. You got me intrigued with your talk of being a stuntwoman."

"Oh, really?" she said, a hint of pleasure in her voice. "Well, I've got my old resumé on video. I seriously doubt you'd want to sit through a complete showing of *Blood Bowl III*, or its even better sequel, *Blood Bowl IV*, although *Future Cop VII* might be right up your alley."

"Hmm. I seem to have missed those particular epic-sounding major motion pictures."

"Well, in the meantime, why don't you come down to the Castle tomorrow night? I'll get you in free. We're showing Fritz Lang's *Metropolis* with the Giorgio Moroder sound track. Better yet, come to my party on Friday."

"Party?"

"Yeah. I'm putting on a masquerade ball at the Castle. I've got music lined up, and thanks to you and Felix, there'll be some classic horror films. I'll have a free ticket for you at the box office. Have you got a costume you could wear?"

"Costume? Other than when I dress up and impersonate an adult, no."

"What, no trench coat and fedora? What kind of private detective are you, anyway?"

"Funny, my mother and co-workers ask me the same question frequently. And as to the free ticket, thanks, but I'll have to pay my own way. We at Midnight are forbidden to indulge in graft and corruption."

"Really? I can't even give you a bag of popcorn?"

"Sold. Just don't tell my boss."

She laughed, then I heard a small, plaintive "Momma?" from the background. "Uh-oh. Now we've done it; we've awakened the angel."

"Okay, I'll let you go," I said.

"Yeah. I'm still expecting Bruce to call, hopefully to say nothing's wrong. Sorry I ran off at the mouth there; I'm just kind of nervous. Just a minute, sweetie," she called to her daughter.

"Okay," I said. "Good night. Call me if you think of something or need anything."

"Careful," she said, "I just may do that. Good night."

I sat there holding the phone away from my face and frowning at it. I suppose I could have pleaded the fact that I was tired, or blamed it on the Bacardi, but all in all, I didn't have an excuse for coming on to Jenny Chance the way I did, seeing how she was a potential witness in my case.

Ah, well, I thought as I hung up the phone, tomorrow should be a lot less hectic. I promised myself I'd sleep in a bit to make up for the overtime I'd put into this case already, then treat myself to a heroic-size breakfast.

Naturally, it all went to hell from the start.

CHAPTER ELEVEN

I awoke to the melodious and irritating call of my cell phone, resting in its charger on my dresser. As I hauled myself from beneath my covers, I ruefully thought that I should have had the good sense to turn it off. When I caught a glimpse of the number of the calling party, I knew my instinct was correct.

"Hi, Mom," I said.

"Good morning, son," Her Royal Highness answered perkily. I saw that it was just shy of 8:30 A.M. By this time, Mom had already walked the dog, checked on her rose garden, and gone though her tai chi routine before having her breakfast. I swear the woman never actually sleeps.

"I received a call from Abigail Glass," she continued. "Anthony Sterling is on calendar for arraignment this morning in Department Four. She wants you to be there."

I made a face at the phone. "And before you start making faces," Mom said, "I want you to tell me, are you feeling all right?"

It's times like these that I believe Mom is either psychic or has my apartment bugged. Probably both. "Sure," I responded. "Why?"

"Because I reviewed your so-called report that you e-mailed last night. I came to the conclusion that I either have to have your head examined or go back to all those schools I sent you to and ask for a refund. Or maybe you're under the influence of drugs?" she asked brightly. "You can tell me, I'm your mother."

"That bad, eh?"

"I've read better reports from rookie police officers with high school equivalency diplomas. And who taught you how to take photographs?"

"Well, the subjects in the picture weren't exactly willing participants," I answered. "But you did at least get the gist of the report?"

"Barely," she acknowledged. "And I confess, the parts I could figure out intrigue me. Now, how soon can you get over to the courtroom?"

"If I left right away, I'd be arrested for indecent exposure."

I heard Mom sigh. "I see. Okay, get your lazy butt into gear and get over there as soon as you can, within the limits of decency, of course. I'll go and cover for you in the event they call Mr. Sterling's case before you arrive."

"Thanks."

"You owe me." She hung up.

I was about to run for the shower when I remembered a promise I made the night before. I got my wallet and found Jenny Chance's phone number.

"Hello?" she said.

"It's Jason. Listen, I just found out that Tony is going to be in Department Four this morning."

"Department Four," she repeated. "Where's that?"

"It's on the first floor of the main jail, 315 Ironside Street."

"Okay. Thanks. I just dropped off my daughter at preschool. Are you going to be there?"

By royal command, I thought. "Yes. I'm going to be with Tony's attorney."

"Good. I'll be there, too. Good-bye. And thank you again."

"Sure. Anytime," I said, and then sighed as I closed the phone and headed for the shower.

An all too short time later found me dressed in one of my dark blue suits with a matching turtleneck and driving through the gray, rainy streets on my way to the jail. I figured there wouldn't be a chance of finding street parking, so I immediately drove to the public garage one block up. There, I stripped down to my ID, pen, trunk key, and notepad, grabbed my folding umbrella, and hiked through the rain down Ironside Street to the familiar and ever uninviting main jail. I'd almost reached the front entrance when I ran into Roland Gibson coming out. "Hey, Rollo," I called.

"Hey, J. W. For once, you gave me a good tip," he said.

"How's that?"

Roland consulted his notebook. "Anthony Sterling. Just got himself arraigned for homicide upon a person unknown," he read.

I sighed. "Great. Looks like I'm still working for a living. Did they set bail?"

Roland stuffed his notebook into his coat. "Yeah. The DA guy wanted to hold him no-bail, but Sterling's attorney argued them out of it. Down to a mere million bucks."

"Ouch." That translated into a $100,000 surety bond, providing Tony could find a bail bondsman willing to take the chance on him.

"Gotta go," Roland said. "Hey, I need you to get me a list of all the players here. Especially the babe."

"What babe?"

Roland grinned. "The one that your mom is keeping company with. Black hair, blue eyes, and a big pair of—"

"Yeah, right," I said, cutting him off. "I think I know to whom you refer."

"You do? Is that the Jenny Chance you mentioned last night? More important, does she have a sister?"

"Actually, she's got a friend who's just your type. His name's Bruce."

Roland shot me a look over his glasses. "You're cold, brother. Anyway, get me a list. I was trying to get an angle myself, but your mom threw me out. Said it was nice to see me again, then asked which hospital I preferred to be sent to in the event I attempted to interview her clients."

"She's always been soft on you. She usually asks people who's their next of kin."

Roland waved and hurried down the street. "Catch you later. Over the many drinks I'm certain you owe me."

"Later," I responded. I folded up my umbrella and forged ahead into the jail's reception area. After clearing security, I wove through the people crowding the courtroom hallway until I spotted Her Majesty Victoria holding court with Abigail Glass, Jenny Chance, and Katerina Sterling. Malcolm Sterling was there as well, standing a little apart from the women. Mother must have been feeling particularly feral today, judging by the tan tiger-striped suit she wore beneath her expensive overcoat with matching wide-brimmed hat. Abby still looked the part of the librarian from hell, while Jenny was clad in her blue windbreaker with a colorful sweater and (nicely fitting, I couldn't help but notice) jeans. Her dark hair glistened in the overhead lighting. Jenny had her arms around Katerina, whose long beige coat was wrapped tightly around her. Her pale features seemed almost white now, counterbalanced by the dark circles beneath her eyes. Malcolm, dressed like an expensive attorney, looked quiet and thoughtful.

Mom spotted me through the crowd. "Ah, here he is at last."

Jenny turned and gave me a smile that seemed to warm me up considerably. " 'Bout time, too," Abby complained. "You missed the first round of excitement."

"So I heard. Now what?" I asked.

Malcolm Sterling spoke up. "Could someone tell me how I go about getting my son released on bail? I've never had to do this sort of thing before."

"I'll give ya a quick and dirty rundown," Abby said. "Then I've got to get myself over to the DA's office and see what they really got."

We were interrupted by the ringing of a cell phone, which turned out to belong to Malcolm Sterling. "Excuse me," he said politely as he stepped away and answered. I noticed that the absence of his cane made him move slowly and stiffly.

I maneuvered over toward Jenny, who caught my eye and nodded in the direction of her father. "I'm surprised to see him here," she whispered.

"Why?"

Jenny's eyes narrowed. "If you'd heard Malcolm give poor Tony the 'You've got to stand up for yourself and be a man' speech, you'd be surprised, too. Maybe the old bastard's mellowing with age." Katerina silently frowned, as if she didn't approve of Jenny's comment.

I was facing in Malcolm's direction, so I caught the sudden shocked expression that crossed his face. He started speaking rapidly, then shut off his phone and stood there staring at it like a man who just noticed he was holding a scorpion. It didn't surprise me that my ever vigilant mom had noticed, too. She said to him, "Mr. Sterling?"

Malcolm looked up and blinked. "That was Heidi, the secretary at my . . . at my son's office. The police are there with a search warrant."

"Oh, are they now?" Mom said with interest.

Abby piped in, "Aha! They must be really scrambling if they're tossing his office at this point in the game."

"Is there any way we can stop them?" Malcolm asked.

"I'm afraid not," Mom said with authority. "The best we can do is get someone over there and see what, if anything, they turn up."

That was my cue to sigh, as I realized that my breakfast was moving off into the distant future. "I guess that makes me someone," I said.

"You're not the only one, kiddo," Mom said to me with a smile. She addressed Katerina. "Mrs. Sterling? If the police are searching your husband's office, you can bet there's another team over at your residence even as we speak. I recommend we get you home as soon as possible."

"My home?" Katerina whispered with shock. "Why would they do that?"

"Looking for evidence," Mom explained. "I should have expected this. Now, I suggest we move, people!"

Mom's command galvanized everyone into motion, with the exception of Malcolm Sterling, who stood there looking confused. Leaving him behind, Mom led us through the crowd and out the doors into the rain. As we cleared the building, a short, round older man in a black overcoat and hat hurried up to us. "Katerina?" he greeted her in a soft but definite accent.

Katerina detached herself from Jenny and ran into the man's arms. Whatever restraint she had broke down as she latched on to him and started crying. The man patted her back gently and said over her shoulder, "I am her uncle Georgi. What has happened to Tony?"

Uncle Georgi had a pale, slablike face adorned with bushy salt-and-pepper eyebrows above sympathetic brown eyes.

Before anyone could answer, Abby opened an umbrella and announced, "I'm off to go raise some hell with the DA. You kids have fun harassing the flatfoots." She hurried down the street, lugging her shoulder bag.

I deployed my own umbrella, offering it to Jenny to share. She nodded, and I stepped in next to her, catching a faint but noticeable aroma of jasmine.

Mother approached Katerina and her uncle. "My name's Victoria Wilder, Mr . . .?"

"I am Katerina's uncle Georgi," he said. "I take it Tony is not coming home today?"

"No, I'm sorry to say," Mother said sympathetically. "And for right now, we have to get Mrs. Sterling back home. The police are probably there with a search warrant."

Uncle Georgi's eyes made a flashing reaction to Mom's statement. "Police? At the house?"

"Yes," Mom affirmed.

Georgi nodded. "You are the detective helping Tony, am I right?"

"I've been retained by your niece," Mother said.

"Ah. And you will stay with her while the police search, right?"

"Correct."

He nodded again. "Ah." He gently disengaged from Katerina until he held her at arm's length. "Little one? You must listen, please. This woman will help you now, and then I want you to call me and tell me all about it, yes? You must call and tell me what I can do. For you and for Tony."

Katerina, nodded twice, then said something in rapid Russian, nodding again. "Good girl," Georgi said encouragingly. He looked up at Mom. "I leave her to you to take her back home for me?"

Mother nodded. Georgi actually tipped his hat, revealing a full head of steely gray hair, before turning and walking away in the rain. Mom said, "I'm parked across the street."

"I'm around the block on Hurricane," Jenny said.

Mom took Katerina in charge. "This way, Mrs. Sterling. Jason? Keep in touch."

"Your wish is my command, etcetera," I answered her.

As Jenny and I walked through the rain, she said, "So that was your queen mum, huh? She gave me a bit of a shock when Katerina introduced us this morning. She shook my hand and gave me a funny smile. Said she had recently read some nice things about me. What did she mean by that?"

I tried desperately to recall any editorial commentary regarding Jenny Chance that I might have slipped into my report from last night. "I, uh, sent in a report of our interview yesterday," I said.

"Oh, really? And you said nice things about me? Like what?"

"I think I'm expected to swallow cyanide or something before I reveal anything from a confidential report."

Jenny laughed softly. "Um-hmm. I think I'll have a little chat with your mother. Girl to girl." She turned serious. "I'm still a little surprised that old Malcolm is actually coming through for Tony. I'm glad to see that."

We stopped at the corner, and Jenny nodded in the direction of Seventh Street. "I'm parked up there."

"Oh. Okay. Here, take the umbrella."

"What? No, it's okay. I'm not going to melt in the rain or anything."

"Please," I insisted.

She smiled, all the way up to her beautiful blue eyes. "Are you sure you're not going to rust? I'd hate to see you get your knight-in-shining-armor suit all tarnished. Tell you what, I'll take you up on your offer, and you take me up on mine. Come to the movies tonight. Or catch the matinee, if you can. We have the best hot dogs in town," she said invitingly.

"Please, don't mention food, I'm running on empty this morning. All right, you win. I'll come by as soon as I get through with this little chore Mom palmed off on me. Besides, I have a notorious weakness for tubular food."

"Good. See you then?"

"It's a date," I said as I quickly walked across the street to the parking garage. I reluctantly took my eyes from her, just in time to keep from tripping over the next curb. I ran the rest of the way to my car, where I got out my case notes and looked up Tony's work address, part of the information Katerina supplied us with when she hired Midnight Investigation to find him in the first place. I saw that Tony had his office over on Lighthouse Street just about midtown. I started up the Mustang and headed out to join the parade of traffic, wondering how much trouble I could get into before lunch.

CHAPTER TWELVE

The address on Lighthouse Street belonged to an office building shaped like an elongated Aztec pyramid, plated in gold-colored glass. After circling the block, I elected to take advantage of the underground parking (despite the exorbitant rates), found a berth for my Mustang, and took the elevator to the thirteenth floor, which was disguised as the fourteenth floor according to superstitious architectural practices.

The central elevator let me out at an inner rotunda, with corridors leading off like the spokes of a wheel. The door to Sterling Investment Services was guarded by a River City policeman in black raid gear. "Hey, how you doing?" I said to him, trying to sound casual.

He shook his head at me. "Sorry. Can't let you in. Police business."

I smiled and produced my identification. "Sorry. Got to. Working for a living," I said in imitation of his professionally discouraging staccato style. The officer was young, probably close to my own age, and I figured he must have been recently promoted to the detective squad to get a bum assignment like door guard when everyone else would be having a lot more fun inside. Holding my ID, he opened the door and leaned in. "Hey, Detective? This guy says he has to come in."

"Who?" I heard from within. Detective Walter Dolman opened the door the rest of the way. He gave me an unwelcoming frown as he said, "What are you doing here?"

"Missing breakfast," I answered. "But besides that, I was told to come here and watch real live police types doing what they do best. I figured that doughnuts would be involved."

Dolman did smile then. "That part was at the briefing. I take it you still represent Tony Sterling?"

"Yeah. Why wouldn't we?"

Dolman's smile became secretive. "Oh, no reason," he said airily. "Well, if you're going to observe, come on in and find yourself a corner to stay in. You didn't bring Ms. Glass with you, did you?" he asked suddenly.

"No. She's over at the district attorney's office, giving them a hard time instead."

He nodded. "Good enough. Come on in."

I stepped past the detective into the office reception area. There were two other officers in here, an older man and a serious-looking woman, both dressed in black jumpsuits like Dolman's with RCPD emblazoned in bright gold letters. This was obviously one of the high-rent office suites, evidenced by the fact that the right side wall was floor-to-ceiling smoked glass, providing a great view of the city and its buildings, old, new, and in between. Arrayed on the other walls was a collection of silver-framed photographs, many of which showed River City as it was in years past. "Find anything interesting?" I asked casually as I surveyed the room.

"Not yet," Dolman answered. "Harold there just cloned the secretary's computer."

Harold, apparently the older policeman, was over by a neat desk with a brass nameplate that read HEIDI MULLIGAN. He was in the process of packing up a heavy-looking metal briefcase stuffed with electronic gear. "And where is the secretary?" I asked.

"Got the day off," Dolman replied. "We let her call Mr. Sterling after we got here, and he told her to go ahead and leave."

No doubt about it, the man was a good poker player. "But not before you interviewed her, right?"

Dolman just smiled, and I took a stab in the dark. "She happen to mention anything about, say, persons of Russian descent?"

Dolman's smile didn't waver, but I saw his eyes tighten around the corners a bit. "Russian descent, you say?"

"Yeah."

Dolman seemed to weigh his options, then said, "You tell me something first. What do you know about Anthony Sterling's sister?"

"Jenny? Not a lot, really. Seems nice," I said, wondering what the hell Dolman was getting at.

"You know she was at the theater the night of the homicide, don't you?"

"Yeah. She works there. So was Tony Sterling. What's your point?"

"Just curious. We may have to talk to her again, that's all."

"I see," I said, not liking the way the detective said it. In my brief acquaintance with Walter Dolman, I had learned that he tended to couch the most important issues in a very casual way. "So," I said conversationally, "about those Russians?"

We were interrupted by the arrival of yet another officer, this one a muscular African-American man, who announced, "Got it, Detective." He held up a heavy, tubular piece of metal with a pair of handgrips.

"Okay, Derrick, go to it," Dolman said, waving at the inner office door with the nameplate ANTHONY STERLING affixed to it.

"What are you doing?" I asked.

"Entry procedure," Dolman said pleasantly. "The secretary said she didn't have a key for the office door. We called building maintenance, but their keys didn't work, either."

"So you're just going to bust it down?"

Dolman shrugged and Derrick grinned, getting a grip on the door-basher and hefting it up.

"Hold it," I said. "I may be of assistance here."

Dolman looked at me curiously; Derrick, Harold, and the female officer looked annoyed, as if I were interrupting some expected fun. "How about you let me try to get that door open without busting it off the hinges?" I offered.

"You got a key?" Dolman inquired.

"Not exactly, but I've opened a locked door or two in my time."

"This I've got to see. Okay, young man, have at it."

I heard a muffled "Oh, man!" from Derrick as he stepped back, holding the battering ram. I laid my notebook down on the secretary's desk and took out my wallet. Among its contents was a black-and-gold plastic case designed to look like a credit card. I ran my thumbnail along the edge and opened it up, revealing a flat five-piece lock pick set. I selected a hook pick and the torsion bar, knelt down, and went to work on the lock. The officers crowded around behind me to see what I was up to.

"You usually carry burglar tools around?" Dolman inquired pleasantly.

"Yeah," I said as I inserted the ends of the pick and torsion bar. "I'm immensely popular with my friends when they lock themselves out of their homes."

"You know they're illegal to carry, right?" he said.

"I've got a locksmith's license. Right in my wallet next to my CCW," I said.

Dolman made a suspicious sound at my use of the shorthand for "California Concealed Weapon Permit." "You got a gun on you now?" he demanded.

"Me? Nah. What would I want a gun for? Here I am, surrounded by River City's finest. I've never felt so safe."

I was running my mouth without really engaging my brain, concentrating on feeling out the pins in the lock. I encountered some unexpected resistance, removed the pick, and peered in. I fetched my key ring flashlight, shined it inside, and saw a small, shiny piece of what looked like metal that was stuck inside the lock. "What's wrong?" Dolman asked from behind me.

"There's something jammed in here. Give me a minute." I

selected a rake pick and slipped it into the lock, fishing around to get a grip on the obstruction. I was able to pop it out after a few tries. Dolman bent down and grabbed the piece off the carpet. "What's this?" he asked as he held it up to me.

"Looks like someone broke a piece of a paper clip off inside."

Dolman frowned. "Why would anyone want to do that?"

"It could have happened if someone was trying to pick the lock without the proper tools," I said.

"Can you do that?"

"Sure. Lock picks are great, but they're not really necessary, if you know what you're doing. I could pick a lock with a safety pin, if I had to. As a matter of fact, I could open a pair of handcuffs with just a paper clip."

Dolman smiled. "Hmm. I think I'd like to see you try that, too. So somebody tried to break in here, eh? Looks like we're getting warm."

I went back to work on the lock. "So what's all this about Russians?" I asked conversationally.

"So what's with your question about Russians?" Dolman retorted.

"Just curious," I said, "seeing as how our murder victim may have been one."

Dolman knelt down, quite close to me, and asked in a quiet yet dangerous voice, "How in the hell did you know that?"

My fingers slipped, and I felt some of the pins slide back into place as I realized I might have overplayed my hand. I couldn't afford to get my friend Robin Faye into trouble. "Oh, you know, brilliant detective work and stuff," I answered offhandedly. "I do get paid for this, you know."

"Yeah," Dolman said flatly. "I know. I did some checking up on you and your company the other day. Your mother used to be on the police force, right?"

I took out my pick, trading the hook for the rake and inserting it. "Yeah."

"Why did she quit?"

"Ask her," I recommended. "If you're not lucky, she may tell you."

Dolman let it go. "What do you know about, shall we say, persons of Russian descent?"

"Well, let's see. First, there was this thing they called the Revolution, and then—"

"Skip ahead a bit, will you?" Dolman asked.

"All right. From what I can see, there are at least three different angles. One, the homicide victim may be Russian. Two, Tony Sterling's married to a Russian lady. Three, I ran into a pair of gentlemen as they tried to break into the Castle Theater last night, right about the spot where our nameless victim met his fate. I could be mistaken, but I thought they sounded foreign. One had a funny way of swearing, anyway."

"Really?" Dolman mused. "Hey, are you sure you can get that door open? I've got things to do today."

"You find any angles I didn't?" I asked.

Dolman hesitated, then said, "The secretary said that there were a couple of guys who showed here both Monday and Tuesday, looking for Tony Sterling. She knew they weren't clients of his. And she did mention their accents."

"Ah. Interesting indeed."

"So how about it?' Dolman asked. "You going to give up and let Derrick have a crack at the door now?"

I stood up, stretched my cramped fingers out, and turned to my audience. "Oh, I got the door unlocked," I said. "I just didn't tell you before now because we were having such a good conversation."

Harold and Derrick both stifled a laugh, but the silent female detective gave me an unmistakable glare. Dolman himself smiled and said, "Well, I'll be . . . Damn, you're a shifty one."

I tried not to look too smug as I replaced my picks in their flat case. I made a gracious "after you" wave of my hand to Detective Dolman, who gave a small bow and opened the office door.

And then flew back as a thunderous exploding bolt of fire stuck him full in the chest.

Everything seemed to happen at once. All the other cops started yelling, whipping out guns as they stormed the inner office, and the young officer by the door burst in, waving his own gun around. The bright jet of flame quickly evaporated into a thick, black cloud of smoke that stung my eyes and closed my throat. Dolman, flat on his back, started twitching as a cluster of flaming, popping incendiary jets bloomed from his chest. A blaring, ear-splitting siren went off, and water sprayed from the ceiling. The female detective dived down next to Dolman, and I found myself on his other side. Instinctively I slapped my hand on the flames, burning myself in the process.

"Get it off him! Get it off him!" she shrieked. She was cutting away Dolman's jumpsuit with a knife. Pulling open my own knife, I grabbed hold of Dolman's jumpsuit near the shoulder, stabbing in and sawing down the side of the tough material, getting a shower of minuscule meteors on my knuckles and hoping I wasn't cutting the twitching detective too much. The woman and I ripped a smoking flap of cloth away from his chest and saw that the sputtering fires were embedded in his bulletproof vest. I dropped my tool and ripped off the Velcro straps. For a split second, the woman and I had a tug-of-war, then I yanked on my side and threw the burning vest back over my shoulder. Harold immediately smothered the smoking, burning mess with an up-turned wastebasket.

Then it was over. Dolman coughed and groaned, his arms and legs moving randomly. "What the hell was that?" he croaked.

Nobody had the answer. I sat there, panting, water soaking me and the expensive carpet, the blaring siren and stink of burning hell all around, and all I could think of were Dolman's words: *We're getting warm.*

CHAPTER THIRTEEN

I hate hospitals.

It's the smell that gets to me, the aromatic alchemy that always reminds me of when I was told that my father was dead. I was pretty much able to ignore it when I visited Robin at the city morgue, but waiting at River City General to be treated for my burns left me with way too much time on my recently damaged hands. The only good news I got was that, although he suffered significant blunt trauma from the shotgunlike blast, some nasty burns, and smoke inhalation, it looked like Detective Dolman was going to be all right.

The bad news was that the bitter-faced female detective, who introduced herself as Lori Banks, was now in charge of the Sterling case, and she made it clear that she didn't like me one bit. Her dark, suspicious eyes regarded me with unconcealed contempt as she said, "I don't know what kind of arrangement you had with Walter, but I don't play those games. What do you know about the Russians?"

Banks seemed to have come through the ordeal a bit wet but unscathed. I had just said good-bye to the doctor and was easing my sodden turtleneck back on, trying not to use my bandaged left hand. "Other than what I told Detective Dolman earlier today, I know *nyet*."

"Don't be funny," Banks shot back.

"He can't help it, dear," came my mother's voice from the

emergency room doorway. "Then again, looks shouldn't count for everything."

Banks's head swiveled like a gun turret as Her Majesty made a studiously casual entrance. I knew better; I noticed how she quickly scanned me from head to toe, making certain all my parts were accounted for. "Are you all right, kiddo?" she asked me.

"Yeah. No worse than the times you caught me playing with matches."

"Who are you?" Banks demanded.

"Victoria Wilder. I've come to collect my son. And you are?" Mother inquired coolly.

"Banks. Homicide. And I'm not through with your son yet."

Mother smiled that pleasant smile of hers, the kind a female tiger probably smiles when she spots a water buffalo with a leg cramp. "I'm sorry, officer, but if you want to speak with a member of my staff, call the office and arrange for an interview. Come, Jason."

I manfully resisted the urge to stick my tongue out at Detective Banks as I collected my wet suit coat. Banks crossed her arms and announced, "I said, I'm not through with him yet."

Mother took a few steps closer to the detective and said in a low, venomous voice, "Don't try to act tough with me, kid. I was busting heads and taking names while you were trying to figure out how to chew gum and walk at the same time. Now be a good little detective and back off."

Detective Banks opened her mouth, but nothing came out. Mom spun on her expensive high heels and made a graceful exit. I wagged my still-working fingers at Banks in farewell and followed suit. As I caught up with Mom in the hospital hallway, she said quietly, "That's the caliber of detectives they're putting out these days? It makes me despair; it truly does."

"Well, what can you expect from a woman who thinks beige is a good hair color?"

Mom gave me a quick grin and then sobered. "You really okay?" she asked, looking at me sideways.

"Yeah. Poor Detective Dolman caught a chestful of something nasty, but his vest stopped it. I just got a little toasted trying to get the stuff off him."

Mom took a quick glance at my bandaged left hand. "What happened?"

I shrugged. "I got a look in Tony's office while we were waiting for the medics to show up. It was a bunch of what looked like plumbing clamped to the front of his desk, and fishing line running from it along the floor. When the door opened, it fired off the thing. Whatever it was, it shot out something that burned like a son of a bitch."

In the hospital parking lot, I was sightly cheered to see that it had stopped raining, but the chill breeze that came in its place shot refrigerated air through my damp clothes. "So now what?" I asked.

"Now I take you home and put you to bed. Congratulations, you just earned a vacation."

"What? What do you mean?"

"You're on the injured list, kiddo."

"For this?" I said, holding up my hand. "I'm okay, really."

Mom shot me a suspicious look. "Since when have you ever argued with me over time off? Except to badger me for some? Are you certain you didn't hit your head on something?"

"Well, this Sterling thing is kind of my case."

"Was your case," Mom corrected me. "I'm exerting my prerogative and taking it over."

Mom always took on the most difficult cases that came to our door. I was always assigned the easiest ones. This time, that thought really bothered me. I knew better than to say so, though.

"What's going on now?" I asked as she steered her Jaguar out of the parking lot. "Just out of curiosity."

Mom checked the traffic and darted out onto Hurricane Street, heading back toward midtown.

"It's been a busy day all around," she said. "I had just reached Katerina's home when I got the call from the office. Paul thought I should know that my only son had telephoned to ask for our hospital insurance information 'just because.'"

"Yeah, well, I would have called you directly, but I knew you were busy. The cops insisted that I go to the hospital, too. What happened after Pauly snitched me off?"

"I called Timothy to come and relieve me at Mrs. Sterling's house. He arrived just after the search warrant team got there. I'm expecting him to call with his report as soon as they're done."

I looked at my watch and saw that it was now just coming up on 1:30, about three hours after I arrived at the hospital. "Okay. Then what?"

"Then I flew to River City General, where I was informed by the staff that my son was cooked medium rare, and I got you checked out of there. Your turn."

I cranked the heater up a bit to try to thaw out, then said, "I found Dolman and his crew in Tony's office. They couldn't open the inner door, so I volunteered. That's when poor Dolman got it in the chest." A shiver that had nothing to do with the temperature ran though my body as I realized that if I had opened the door from where I knelt after picking the lock, I would have been shot with flaming death right in the face.

"I see," Mom said seriously. "So the question remains, who set the trap? And why? And who was the target? Anthony Sterling is the logical choice!"

"He was pretty adamant that someone was going to try to kill him. At least that's what he claimed when the police dragged him off the other night, and now it looks like he knew what he was talking about."

Mom glanced at her Lady Rolex. "Well, if people are out to get him, then maybe getting out of jail isn't such a good thing for him. He might be safer in custody."

I watched as Mom angled onto Twenty-sixth Street. "Where are you going?"

"As I told you, I'm taking you home."

"My car is still at Tony's office."

"We'll have it picked up later."

I had enough. "Stop the car," I said.

"I beg your pardon?"

"I mean it. Stop the car. I'm sick and tired of being treated like a kid. Now stop this car and I'll make my own way home, thank you very much."

Queen Victoria was silent for a moment, then said, "I see. Perhaps you're right. Very well, then, where shall I drop you?"

"Over at Tony's office, the 2100 block of Lighthouse."

"Then what do you intend to do?"

"That depends. Am I still off the case?"

"Certainly."

"Okay. In that case, I think I'll take in a movie."

"I see," Mom said again. "I take it you'll be at the Castle Theater?"

"Maybe," I said offhandedly.

Mom chuckled. "For what it's worth, I was impressed by Ms. Chance."

"You were?"

"Definitely. And I had no trouble at all spotting her this morning outside of court. In the future, you might do well to remember to be a little less lyrical in your descriptions of individuals in your reports."

No doubt about it, I was never going to write another report under the influence of Bacardi 151. "Okay," I said meekly.

"Be that as it may," Mom continued, "this morning your Ms. Chance went directly over to poor Katerina and did her best to comfort her. You could damn near feel the temperature drop when she saw her father there, though."

"Yeah, she's got a few family issues. Speaking of Malcolm Sterling, did he get Tony out on bail?"

"I believe that was his intention, although I lost track of him after we all left the jail in a hurry. How's your hand?"

It still hurt like hell, I didn't say, on my palm and a couple of places on the back near my knuckles. "Fine. I wonder what was in that blast?"

"Sounds almost like white phosphorus," Mom replied. "Although if it had been, it would have chewed straight through anything it landed on. What a particularly nasty trap," she mused.

We drove silently through the canyons of the city for a while. I was feeling cold, hollow, and shaky, and I really wasn't looking forward to driving myself home, but after I stood on my hind legs the way I did, I didn't leave myself a graceful out. I was shaken out of my self-pity by the sound of Mom's phone.

"Hello?" she answered. "Hello, Abigail . . . No, he's all right; pigheaded, but I believe that to be a gender trait . . . I see . . . Interesting . . . Okay, dear, keep me informed."

As she clicked off her phone, I asked, "What was that about?"

"Work," she said simply. "Something you're excused from for a while."

"Give it up," I demanded. "Or do I let myself out right here?"

"For that tone of voice, I should let you," she shot back. "Very well. Abigail said that Anthony Sterling wants to talk to the police. She thinks he's looking to make a deal."

I whistled. "Whoa. So maybe I've been wrong about him all along? I wonder what made him want to talk all of a sudden?"

"We'll know more as it occurs," Mom said. "And if you're good, I'll tell you all about it."

We arrived at the gold-toned monolith that housed Tony's office, and I got a flashback to the waking nightmare I had experienced there just a short time before. As quickly as everything had happened, the worst part was waiting for the ambulance in the indoor rain with the Klaxons wailing, and Dolman groaning on the sodden floor and the whole place smelling like a broken sewer pipe in hell's front office. "So what are your plans?" Mom asked.

"As long as I'm unemployed, I think I will go to that movie," I said.

Mom gave me a thin smile. "Well, if you're insisting upon calling on a lady, might I recommend you go home and take a shower first? You positively reek, my love."

"Yeah? And here everyone tells me what a glamorous profession I've got."

As I started to get out of her car, she reached over and laid a hand on my arm. "I'm sorry if I was short with you today. I worry about you. It gave me a bad turn when I heard you were in the hospital."

I sighed. "Me, too. Sorry, that is. Keep me up-to-date on the Sterling case?"

She nodded, "All right. But you'll have to forgive me if it seems strange to see you take such an interest. Or is it one of the participants you've taken an interest in?" she added with a raised eyebrow.

I stepped out and said before shutting the door, "You're a detective. You figure it out." She gave a quick, appreciative laugh as she gunned the engine and darted back out into the traffic. I shook my head, and went in search of the public entrance to Sterling's building, passing one of the River City Crime Lab vans sitting in a no-parking zone. For a moment, I was tempted to go back up to Tony's office to see what was going on, but then I decided to take Mom's advice. Besides, I thought to myself, if Tony wound up making a deal with the police and DA, we were out of the case for good. And as much as I was looking forward to seeing Jenny Chance again, I dreaded telling her that it looked as though her brother was about to confess.

I got my car out of hock and joined the afternoon parade of traffic. I had the heater cranked on full and was driving cautiously one-handed when my cell phone vibrated for attention. I waited to answer until I could pull over. Roland Gibson's excited voice greeted me. "Brother, you're never going to believe what happened."

"Let me guess. There was some excitement over at Tony Sterling's office today?"

"Yeah, how did you . . .?" His voice trailed off.

"I was there, Rollo."

"You bastard! You've been holding out on me! After all this time I've pretended to be your friend."

"Tell you what, you tell me what the official line is, and I'll tell you the facts, okay?"

"Deal," he said quickly. "What we have thus far is that a policeman was shot while executing a search warrant, but they're not releasing the officer's name or anything about a suspect in the shooting yet. So what's the scoop?"

"Well, the shooter won't be answering any questions, on account of the fact that it was a booby trap set up in Tony's office and designed to blow away the first idiot that walked in there. And by the way, yours truly was damn near the aforementioned idiot."

"Jesus," Roland breathed. "You okay? Where are you?"

"Just out of the hospital," I said. "I'm all right, but whatever was in that blast had a nasty incendiary along with it that almost cooked the detective who caught it in the chest. His bulletproof vest stopped it, fortunately."

"Oh, my God," Roland said. "This just gets better and better! Who was the cop that got it?"

"You don't need that. And I don't want to get anyone's family upset."

"You know, except for this disturbing tendency toward morality you display every so often, you're not half bad. Okay, I can go with this, right?"

I thought for a moment. "Yeah. Don't see why not."

"Okay, my turn," Roland said. "You're never going to believe the stuff I dug up on your client's family."

"What do you mean?"

"What would you say to the fact that Anthony Sterling's own mother was once wanted for grand theft?"

■

CHAPTER FOURTEEN

What are you talking about, Rollo?"

"I've been puttering around in the morgue files," Roland said, "and your Malcolm Sterling was prominently mentioned in a few articles dating back to the 1970s."

"Such as?"

"Like Odysseus of old, Malcolm Sterling went off to war. Only in this case, when he got back home, there was no faithful Penelope waiting for him."

"Could you run that past me again? Without the mythological subtext?"

"You are such a literary ignoramus," Roland sighed. "Okay. Dateline, the turbulent 1970s, when disco was king and—"

"This is where I hit the fast forward," I interrupted.

"Okay. Malcolm Sterling comes back home from defending our country abroad. When he gets back, he finds out that his former business partner, one Anthony Worthington by name, has skipped out, after draining all the firm's bank accounts."

"Ouch."

"Oh, it gets better. Not only does this Worthington guy leave for parts unknown with all the money, but Sterling's wife goes with him."

"Double ouch."

"I said it got better, didn't I? How's that for a 'welcome home, soldier'?"

Leaving Malcolm behind with two children to raise. "What was the wife's name?"

"Let's see . . . Ah, here it is. Angelique Sterling. Looks like she used to manage the Castle Theater, which I thought was interesting."

"So what happened? To the Worthington guy and the wife?"

"Doesn't say," Roland answered. "The last news story talks about how arrest warrants for embezzlement and grand theft were issued naming Anthony Worthington and Angelique Sterling, also know as Angelique Raven. Her maiden name, I guess. In the pictures I got with the story, they make a handsome couple, for a pair of thieves, anyway. But that was over twenty-five years ago."

Damn. I wondered how much of this story Jenny knew. "Okay, Roland. Thanks for the info. Would you fax me a copy of that story to the office?"

"Sure. Anything for a so-called friend. Remember, you owe me." Roland hung up.

I sat there in my Mustang with the engine idling, wondering what to do next. Finally, the need for food and warmth compelled me to drive the rest of the way home. I wolfed down one of those energy bars made out of some jawbreaking foodlike substance, washed it down with Gatorade, and stripped off and hit the shower. I spent a long time under the water, even though I had to shower with my left hand wrapped in a plastic bag to keep my bandages dry. I finally got out and toweled off, wondering what to do with myself. I knew I wanted to see Jenny again, but any news I could offer would be unwelcome at best, and it was always a bad idea to mix personal feelings with professional actions. Then again, according to Her Imperial Highness, I was off this case anyway. Besides, a hot dog sounded really good to me right then.

I put on some jeans and a dark sweater and grabbed my old reliable leather jacket, eyeing my pile of abused business suits in the process and making a silent promise to use some of my downtime for catching up with my laundry. The Green Hornet and I played dodge-car with the traffic and arrived at the parking garage across from the Castle at a little after four; I found a spot on the fifth level. I walked to the Ketch Street side to look at the theater. In the gray light of day, the old place looked a little forlorn, an old building left behind when all of its neighboring structures had been transformed into far more modern, if far less interesting, edifices.

I took the elevator down, crossed the street in the company of numerous other city dwellers, and walked to the drawbridge opening of the Castle, where I found a young Asian woman with rainbow-colored hair inside the turret-shaped ticket booth. "May I help you?" she politely inquired.

"I think so. Jenny Chance said I could come by. My name's Jason Wilder."

She smiled broadly. "Oh, so you're the one?" I shrugged, and she said, "Just a moment, please." I watched as she picked up an old black telephone handset and spoke into it, smiling conspiratorially up at me. She hung up. "Go right in, sir."

"Thank you," I replied, wondering if I had reached that advanced age when all the girls would start calling me "sir." I was headed for the front doors when I caught sight of Bruce lurking in the doorway. Like the girl in the booth, he was wearing black slacks, a white dress shirt and black bow tie, and a gold-and-black vest embroidered with a collage of knights and castles. Even dressed as he was, he looked the part of the troll at the gate. I smiled and said pleasantly, "Hello again. I guess I'm supposed to come on in?"

He nodded his boulderlike head and stepped aside. As I entered the portal, the familiar smell of popcorn washed over me and I could hear the sound of a movie in progress coming from behind the leather doors. Over by the concession counter were two young men, both dressed in the Castle uniform; one had long dreadlocks, and the other's hair was a spiky, upthrust patch of orange over a face that was adorned with an interesting collection of metal piercings.

"Hey, you!" I heard a warm, welcoming voice from above. "Up here!" Jenny was looking down at me with a full-out killer smile. She was dressed in the black-and-gold outfit, too.

"Hey, there," I called back. "Is this the part where you let down your hair so I can climb up?"

She flipped a handful of her dark tresses over her shoulder. "Wrong damsel. You're thinking of Rapunzel. You're stuck taking the stairs."

The closer I got, the more her smile seemed to fade. "What happened to your hand?" she asked when I met her on the landing.

"Um, long boring story at best. I'm sure it looks worse than it is."

"So what's the news about Tony? Did the police find anything at his house?"

I was saved from having to answer her by a small voice piping out from her office, "Mommy!"

"Whoops," Jenny said, "we've just received a royal summons. Coming, angel! Follow me."

I did, and saw a blond, blue-eyed, and beautiful little girl, dressed in a miniature version of Jenny's theater uniform, kneeling in the chair at Jenny's desk, busily scribbling away with a crayon. "All done," she said without looking up.

"You do fast work, baby," Jenny said as she slid in from behind and picked the girl up. "Angelina? This is our friend Jason. Say hello."

Angelina took a look at me, smiled, then buried her head into her mother's shoulder. "We're a little shy," Jenny explained, "and I've taught her to be careful with strangers. It's okay, honey. Mommy knows this man. He's nice."

I ducked my head, trying to catch Angelina's eyes, which caused her to giggle and put one little hand over them. "Pleased to meet you," I said softly. I picked up the picture Angelina had been working on and crouched down next to the desk. "Ah. An artiste."

"Oh, she is that," Jenny agreed. "You should see some of the murals she's done on the walls of the apartment. I'm going to hate having to explain them to the manager."

"Tell him that he's got an Angelina original. Surely worth money someday."

Jenny laughed and took the picture from me. "What's this one of, honey?"

Angelina poked her head up. "You. And Bear."

There was a stuffed bear sitting on Jenny's desk. I stood up and came around for a look over Jenny's shoulder. "Ah. Of course. And you gave Mommy green hair. That's very pretty."

Angelina nodded seriously. "Uh-huh."

"Okay, you," Jenny said as she nibbled kisses on Angelina's ear. The girl squeaked and laughed. "You go and see Uncle Brucie. Jason and I have to have a talk."

Angelina's laughter subsided, and she gave a theatrical sigh. "Okay," she said as Jenny placed her feet on the floor. She took her mother's hand and led her to the door, calling out, "Brucie!"

"Brucie" arrived in good time, stomping up the stairs. Jenny said to him, "Keep an eye on the angel for a bit?"

Bruce nodded, then allowed himself to be pulled downward as Angelina reached up and grabbed his vest. When he was bent over double, he slung her over his shoulder, much to Angelina's noisy delight, and carried her off.

Jenny watched them go from the door, then slowly closed it and returned to her desk, waving me to a seat on the other side.

"She's beautiful," I said. "How old is she?"

"Four and a half, going on thirty-three and a third. So what's up? Anything good for Tony and Katerina?"

"I'm afraid not."

Jenny's look turned serious. "I was afraid of that. And I still can't believe it. Tony wouldn't kill anyone."

"It's worse than that. I hate to be the one to tell you, but it's probably going to be in the news soon. I was with the police when they went to Tony's office today. Someone put a trap inside his office, and an officer got caught in it."

She shook her head, her blue eyes blazing. "Trap? What the hell are you talking about?"

"Some kind of homemade pipe bomb thing, rigged to nail the first person who came through the office door."

Jenny shook her head again, hard. "This is just so whacked. Wait a minute. Do you think someone put that there to get Tony?"

"It's a possibility," I said carefully, remembering Tony's words: *They're going to kill me.* "You told me the other day that Tony called you up and said he wanted you to agree to sell the theater because the needed money?" I asked her.

"Yeah, he did. At first he tried to make it sound like a smart business move, but when I tried to pin him down as to just how much money he was talking about, he couldn't answer me."

"Did he sound desperate?"

Jenny thought for a moment. "Yeah, in a way. Although at the time I just thought he was lying to me to get me out of here, like Malcolm wanted."

"This may sound like a strange question, but did Tony mention any problems with anyone who was Russian?"

"Russian? Katerina's Russian, if that's what you mean, and no, he didn't say they were having any problems."

"I see. Well, and this part doesn't get any better, I heard a little while ago that Tony now wants to make a statement to the police."

"A statement? What kind of statement?"

"I'm not sure, but at this stage of the game it usually means that he's got something to trade. Something he's been holding back so far."

"Jesus," she breathed. "You weren't kidding when you said it was getting worse."

"Sorry."

"Yeah," she sighed. "Me, too. Especially for Katerina. I should probably give her a call, see if there's anything I can do for her."

"Okay. Well, I guess I'd better be going."

Jenny looked disappointed, I was happy to note. "Oh. Okay. You're sure you don't want to stick around for the next show? Oh, sorry. I suppose you have things you need to be doing for Tony right now."

After all the bad news I was the bearer of, I decided that Jenny didn't need to hear that I was officially off her brother's case. "No, thank you. Some other time, perhaps," I said as I rose from the chair.

Jenny nodded. "All right."

I had almost made it to the door when my phone went off. A glance at the incoming number revealed that Her Highness was calling. "Excuse me, this may be about Tony," I said, and answered it. "Jason here."

Queen Victoria inquired, "Where are you?"

"I'm over at the Castle."

"Is Ms. Chance with you?"

"Yes."

A brief pause. "There are two pieces of news you need to be aware of. One, Paul just informed me that Katerina Sterling called. She has decided to dispense with our services."

"What?"

"We've been fired, kiddo," Mom translated. "But that's not the kicker."

"It's not? I'm afraid to ask."

"You should be. Abigail and I have just come from Anthony Sterling's interview with the police."

"And?"

"He says his sister killed the man behind the theater."

■
CHAPTER FIFTEEN

Jenny mouthed the words "What's wrong?" as I retraced my steps to the chair and all but fell down backward into it. I said into my phone, "You're kidding?"

"Not at all," Mom replied. "Anthony Sterling was quite specific, and that Lori Banks was all too happy to let him talk. Anthony said the only reason he didn't tell the truth before now is that he wanted to cover up for his sister."

I looked over to Jenny, who silently sat back down in her own chair, eyes intent on me the whole way. "Okay," I said calmly. "How about you give it to me from the top?"

"Certainly," Mom said. "But are you sure that's wise? Considering where you are now? Or, to be more specific, whom you're with at the moment?"

"It's okay," I said. "Let's hear it."

"Okay, it goes like this: Anthony Sterling is still in custody. Apparently, Malcolm Sterling didn't manage to get him released yet, although I understand he did visit with Anthony this afternoon."

"Okay."

"So when Abigail and I reached the jail, we had to wait for Detective Banks to show up. God, that woman annoys me. We no sooner have Anthony brought to the interrogation room than he says he's sorry, but now he has to tell the truth. Abigail tried to get him to shut up, but to no avail."

"Go on."

"He stated for the record that he went to the Castle Theater to see his sister, Jenny. When he arrives, he hears a shot, then goes and finds the man on fire in the alleyway."

"So he's claiming to be an eyewitness to the, er, event?"

"Not as such, no. Anthony stated that he saw Jenny leaving the alley. When he went in, he saw the victim and found Jenny's gun on the ground."

"What?"

"That's right, kiddo. He says the murder weapon belongs to your Ms. Chance."

I sat there, my eyes on Jenny as she studied me. "He was sure about that?" I asked Mom.

"Positive. And he said that's why he took the weapon, to try to protect his sister. He also claims that he burned his hands when he attempted to help the man in the alley."

"So what now? What's Banks going to do?"

"Oh, she was busily scribbling notes. At the end of the interview, she said she'd look into it. But she seemed most intent upon asking Anthony about 'the Russians', as she phrased it."

"What did Tony say about that?"

"Ah, now, that was interesting," Mom said. "He claimed not to know what she was referring to, but I thought it was rather revealing, seeing as how that was when his hands began to shake a bit."

"Uh-huh. So I repeat, now what?"

"Now nothing. Like I just told you, when I got back to the office, there was a message from Anthony's wife, saying thank you very much but she no longer requires our services. For what it's worth, she sounded like she was repeating something that someone told her to say. But the end result is we're off the case."

"Damn."

"So," Mom said, "are you going to share any of this information with Ms. Chance?"

"I kind of thought I would."

"I see. Well, son, do as you think best. And stay out of dark alleys, hmm?"

"Uh, right. Sure thing. Bye."

As I folded up my phone, Jenny looked me in the eye and asked, "You're going to tell me that it just got worse, aren't you?"

Childishly, my first reaction was to ask Jenny not to hate me for the news I was about to deliver, but I wound up saying, "Yes."

"What now?"

I took a breath, then said, "Tony's saying now that you did it. That you killed the man in the alley last Sunday."

For a split second, it looked like Jenny Chance was going to laugh, until she read the look in my eyes. "You're serious?"

"Yes."

"Tony said that?"

"Yes. To the police."

Suddenly Jenny's fist pounded the table. "That bastard! That goddamn bastard! I'll . . ." She stopped herself, then seemed to deflate in her chair before saying quietly, "I was almost going to say I was going to kill him. Again."

"Again?"

"Yeah," she sighed. "When Tony started pressuring me about selling the theater, I kind of told him to stay the hell out of here or I'd kill him. Figure of speech, you know?" I didn't respond, and Jenny said, "So what exactly did Tony say?"

"That he was covering up for you. That the man was killed with your gun."

Jenny's eyes narrowed. "My gun?"

"Yeah. Tony says the murder weapon belongs to you. You don't happen to own an old .45, do you?"

"A .45," Jenny repeated numbly. She shook her head. "No. Can't be," she said as she opened her desk drawer and took out a cluster of keys. She stood up and turned to the file cabinets behind her. I stood up, too, and watched as she unlocked and then opened the top drawer. Her eyes widened, her lips parted, and the blood drained from her face. "Oh, no. No," she said as if to herself.

It was in that moment that I knew she was innocent. I wasn't fooling myself, mind you. I was highly aware that I was attracted to Jenny Chance, and I was just smart enough to know how feelings can cloud logic. I was also aware that history is full of beautiful, charming women who were also cold-blooded killers. But I was trained by the best in the detective business how to watch people when I speak with them and to look for the signs that say someone is lying to me, and while a person can fake an expression, I've never met anyone yet who could pull off an involuntary cardiovascular response, like the way Jenny's face paled the split second after she looked inside that cabinet.

"It's gone," Jenny said flatly.

"Jenny?" She turned to me, staring blankly. "Jenny, sit down." Slowly, she did. "It's gone," she said again.

"I take it that you do own a .45 Colt pistol? With ivory grips?"

"Yeah. Not really. It belongs to Father, actually."

"It's your dad's gun?"

Jenny rubbed her eyes and left her hands over her face. "Yeah. That night I ran away from home for the last time, I took it with me. I knew I wasn't coming back, and I'd been running around on the streets long enough to know how bad it could be out there. I took it for protection. Hell, I didn't even know how to shoot or load it or anything back then. I didn't learn how to handle a gun until after I started doing stunt work. I never even fired the thing." She dropped her hands. "That was just part of my inheritance I helped myself to that night."

"Okay. Who knew you had it?"

"No one, really. Not even my soon-to-be-ex husband. Guns kind of freaked him out. I guess Tony knew about it. We found out where Dad kept it hidden in the house when we were kids."

"Okay." I went to the filing cabinet and examined the lock. The cabinet was old, but the lock showed no signs of being forced. "Did you always keep the gun locked up?"

"Hell, yes. I didn't want it in the apartment with my baby. I figured it'd be safer to keep it locked up here."

"Who else has keys to the cabinet?"

Jenny looked at the keys lying on her desk. "Well, me, of course. And Bruce. He's got a full set."

"Did you ever show him the gun?"

"No."

I looked at the keys. They all appeared to be recent copies. "Didn't you tell me that Tony has a set?"

"He's the one I got my keys from, so yeah, he's got to have a set. What are the police going to do?"

I thought of the unpleasant Detective Lori Banks. "Unless I miss my guess, they'll try to check Tony's story. But if the gun was yours, it's probably going to have your fingerprints all over it."

"My fingerprints? Yeah, I guess it would. Would that be enough for them to . . . what's wrong?"

I had remembered what she told me the night I met her, about how the police took a set of her fingerprints when they were dusting the movie projector. "The police have a brand-new set of your prints on file," I said. "From the other night."

"Yeah, so . . . Jesus," she breathed. "I'm in trouble, aren't I? No matter what, this looks really bad, doesn't it?"

"Let's see. You said that you saw Tony Sunday night, driving down the street after you heard the sound of the gunshot and saw the flames coming from the alley?"

"Right."

"And you also said that Bruce had walked you out to your car?"

"Yes. But after he left, I remembered that I had to go back up to my office to get my insurance paperwork. So I drove back and parked on the street."

"Did you see anyone else? Anyone at all?"

"No," she said definitely. "Only Tony when he drove down the street."

"And you're sure Bruce was gone by then?"

"I guess so," she said. "I really didn't pay attention. Once he drops me off at the car, he just walks away."

"But it's possible he could have still been at the theater?"

Her lovely blue eyes narrowed. "I don't like where you're going with this."

"Sorry, but we have to look at everything. You can't be sure Bruce wasn't still at the theater, can you?"

"No."

"Okay. Did you and Bruce ever talk about what happened Sunday night?"

"Sure. I told him the next day. All he said was, 'Bad neighborhood.' "

"Did the police ever question him?"

"Sure. But he said he didn't see anything. What are you getting at?"

"It's just that you don't have an alibi witness. You were by yourself at about the time the homicide occurred."

"Well, considering that I didn't do it, why would I need a witness?"

" 'Cause you've now got someone pointing the finger at you, namely, your own brother. The fact that the murder weapon belonged to you makes it worse."

"Jesus, I can't believe this!" she said.

I thought for a moment. "As I recall, Detective Dolman said there were two witnesses that night. He was originally counting you as one, but unfortunately he never told me who the other witness was. Damn."

"So you think that person could be my alibi witness, as you say?"

"Hopefully." I flexed the fingers of my left hand; the bandages were starting to give me an itch. Another unwelcome thought occurred to me. "Jenny? You told me you knew about explosives and such?"

"Yeah, why?"

"Enough that you could make a bomb from scratch?"

"Sure. Nothing to it when you know how. Oh, crap," she said as she followed my thoughts. "You said that someone set a bomb in Tony's office, didn't you?"

"Yeah."

"So now what can I do?" she asked quietly.

"A good lawyer would be a start."

Her lovely lips took on a bitter twist. "I figured that one out, Sherlock. If I could afford a lawyer, I'd be on the phone right now."

"Oh. Sorry."

"Can you get hold of that other witness?" she asked. "Find out what he or she saw?"

"Probably not," I said hesitantly. "What I haven't mentioned yet is the fact that Katerina took us off the case today."

"She did what? That doesn't make sense!"

"Whether it makes sense or not, if my office no longer has a client, then we no longer legally have access to any of the case information. Unless . . ." I flipped out my phone and dialed Abigail Glass's cell. She picked up right away.

"Hello, sailor," she answered.

"Hey, Abby. How did you know it was me?"

"I didn't. I always answer the phone that way, hoping I might get lucky. What's up, pup?"

"Did you get any copies of reports from the DA's office today?"

"Sure. They couldn't get rid of me fast enough, but didn't your mom tell you? We've been canned."

"Yeah, she did. But I want the ID on the other witness. Did you get that?"

"Should be in the initial police report," Abby said. "Why? What are you up to?"

My neck in trouble, I thought. "Can you get a copy of that over to me?"

"Yes, I could, and no, I won't. Not until you tell me why you want it at this late date."

"Uh, let's just say I've still got an interest in the case."

"You? The only thing you've ever been interested in is . . . oh. Aha! You've got the hots for that idiot Sterling's sister, don't you? Or is it his wife? Maybe both?" she asked expectantly.

"That information will cost you a copy of that report," I said.

"Ah, well. What the hell. But you're gonna have to come across with all the juicy details, you got that?"

"While we're on the subject, how do you feel about taking on a new client? Pro bono?"

"Hey, watch that talk, young man. If I'm going to be giving myself away, there's got to be something in it for me. What have you got?"

"A strong feeling that you could make the police look really, really bad. Does that qualify?"

"Maybe," Abby said cagily. "Although that kind of action doesn't take much effort on my part anymore." While I was bartering with Abby, I heard Jenny's phone ring and watched her answer.

"Okay, Abby, my love; you send me that report, and I'll get together with you tomorrow with more details. Deal?"

"Sure. What the hey. No promises, though. I want to know for sure what you're trying to get me into."

"You got it. Later." I snapped my phone shut, then stopped as I saw the look on Jenny's face.

"That was Bruce," she said, wide-eyed. I knew I wasn't going to like what I heard next. And I didn't.

"The police are here."

CHAPTER SIXTEEN

I closed my eyes for a moment, feeling dizzy from how fast things were moving. That I was running on too little fuel and no coffee didn't help at all. When I opened my eyes, I saw Jenny sigh resignedly and stand up. "Where are you going?" I asked.

"Downstairs. To talk to the police."

"Whoa. Hold it. Bad idea."

"What do you mean?"

"Do they know you're here?"

Jenny's eyes narrowed. "Probably. Bruce just called to say a couple of cops are downstairs."

"But did he say you were here? Now?"

"I don't know."

I was betting that the less than loquacious Bruce hadn't volunteered the information to the police. "Wait a minute," I said as I went to the office door. I opened it just enough to look out with one eye down to the lobby floor and saw Detective Lori Banks, looking somewhat disheveled in jeans and a plaid wool shirt, standing next to the officer I knew as Harold from Tony's office this morning. Bruce, with little Angelina perched on his shoulders, was standing guard by the front door and ignoring the officers. "Okay. Can you get Bruce back on the phone without tipping anyone off that you're here?"

Jenny frowned and picked up the phone. "You better explain just what the hell you think you're doing. Hey, David? Put Bruce on. Don't say it's me."

I closed the door and held out my hand for the phone, which Jenny handed to me, albeit hesitantly. I heard Bruce say, "Jenny?"

"No, it's me, Jason. Quick, now, did you tell the police Jenny was here?"

There was a pause, then a pair of grunts that I took to mean no. "Okay, good. Listen, I don't think it's a good idea for Jenny to talk to the police right now. Did they say anything about having a search warrant or an arrest warrant or anything like that?"

Two more grunts signaled a negative. "Okay, final question. Do you think you'd mind lying to the police and saying Jenny's not here right now?"

My answer to that was a low, rumbling chuckle. "Good," I said. "Okay, stand by, and we'll see if we can get Jenny out of here."

I handed the phone back to Jenny, who said into the receiver, "Look, I don't know what Jason has in mind, but I don't want you or anyone else getting into trouble over me, you got that? Bruce? Bruce?" Jenny looked at me suspiciously. "He hung up."

"All right. Now, is there a back way out of here?"

Jenny placed her hands on her desk and leaned in toward me. "I don't know what you think you're doing, but I'll be damned if I'm going to sneak out of here and go hide from the police. Didn't it occur to you that's going to make me look guilty?"

I leaned in and faced off with her. "Listen, if that was Detective Dolman waiting for you down there, I'd be a lot more inclined to go and talk with him. But for your information, you've got what I'm afraid is a very overenthusiastic cop who just might not care about your innocence at this stage. Now, all I'm saying is that I think we need more time to try to work things out. Once we've figured out exactly where you stand in all this, then we can talk to the authorities. With an attorney."

"Forget it," she said shortly. "I've run away from bad situations twice in my life already. I'm not going to run away again. No way."

"What about Angelina?"

"What? What's she got to do with this?"

"You want her to see her mommy marched out of here in handcuffs? Who's going to look after her? I can tell you right now, in a case like this, they'll take your daughter to the Children's Receiving Home, then a social worker is going to give her to her father or the next closest relative, who happens to be Malcolm Sterling. So, Jenny, which is it gonna be?"

She sat back down, looking miserable.

I sighed and pushed myself away from the desk. "Look, all I'm asking is for you to trust me just for tonight. Let me see what we can figure out, and tomorrow, if you still want to talk to the police, I'll go with you. And by then we can find a safe place for your daughter. Deal?"

She closed her eyes and rubbed her temples. "What choice do I have? All right. But just for tonight." She opened her eyes and looked at me. "How are you going to get my daughter and me out of here?"

Damn good question. I quickly surveyed the white-painted brick walls of her office. "Is there a back way? Secret passage? Anything?"

"Sorry, no."

"What kind of castle is this?" I complained. "Okay, I'm going to go down and see if I can get rid of the cops. Stay put up here."

"What about Angelina? I'm not leaving here without her."

"Noted. This may not work, but be ready to leave in a hurry if it does."

"I hope to hell you know what you're doing," she said as I slipped out of the office door.

So did I. I eased the door shut behind me, flattening myself against the wall. Below in the lobby, I could see Lori Banks and Harold, heads close and talking to each other. So far, so good, as long as they didn't look up. I made my way down the curving stairs, catfooting it on the faded carpeting. I reached the bottom, then angled my way behind Harold, the taller of the two, and tried to affect a casual air. "Hey, guys," I greeted them. "What are you doing here?"

Harold turned around, and Lori Banks frowned in recognition. "What are *you* doing here?" she shot back.

"I was looking for Jenny Chance."

"What for?" Banks demanded. "You and your mom haven't got a client anymore."

I smiled. "I know. I just needed to get a few questions answered to close out the file."

"Like what?"

"Oh, about the billing and stuff."

"Which reminds me," Banks said. "I want a copy of all your case notes."

"Well, sure, Detective. We'll just need a subpoena. You know, for form's sake."

Banks gave me an irritated look and turned toward Bruce. "Hey! I thought you said you were calling her to come down?"

Bruce, I saw, had placed Angelina on the floor and was whispering in her ear. The little blond girl was smiling and nodding, holding her hand to her mouth. When Detective Banks called to him, Bruce gave Angelina a quick kiss on the top of her head, and she immediately giggled and scampered off toward the stairs. Bruce walked slowly over to us. "I said what?" he rumbled.

"You said you were calling Ms. Chance to come down. Where is she?" Banks asked.

Bruce blinked his dark eyes and muttered, "Sorry. She's not here."

Banks shook her head as if to clear it. "What do you mean, she's not here? Where did you call her?"

"Cell phone," Bruce said.

"Did she say she was coming?"

"Nope."

"But you told her we were here?"

"Yep."

"So she's coming?"

"Nope. Not until later tonight."

Banks did not take frustration well. "Why the hell didn't you tell me that?"

Bruce blinked. "You didn't ask."

I was trying very hard not to laugh, watching the way the color was rising in Detective Banks's face. She drew in a deep breath, obviously on the verge of a verbal explosion, when Harold stepped in and said to Bruce, "Would you be kind enough to have Ms. Chance give us a call? Detective Banks will give you her card."

Bruce grunted in assent. Lori stood there, holding her breath, then finally let it out all at once. "Yeah. Here," she said, digging a card out of her badge wallet. "Tell her it's important. And to call real soon. Got it?"

Bruce shrugged, and Banks started for the door. Harold called after her, "Be right there."

Bruce returned to his station by the front door while Banks went on into the now dark street. Harold turned to me. "I wanted to say thank you for the way you jumped right in and helped Walter Dolman today. How's the hand?"

"Fine. Thanks."

"I knew your father, you know."

"Really?"

Harold took off his glasses and looked at me with soulful brown eyes. "Yeah. One of the things I remember best about your dad was how he was the smartest thing around. If you're half as smart as your old man was, you're twice as smart as most people."

"Well, I can think of quite a few who'd disagree with you. My mother included."

Harold laughed softly. "Yeah, I remember her, too. Haven't seen her in years. How's she doing?'

"Fine."

"Good. Tell her Harry Caldwell asked about her."

"I will, sir."

Harold put his glasses back on and half turned to leave, then said suddenly, "The other thing I remember about your dad was that he was always a straight-up guy. Always honest. You know?"

The way Detective Caldwell looked at me translated his words into *I know you're playing a game here. Don't screw with me.*

"Yeah," I answered seriously, telling him *I got the message.*

Harold Caldwell smiled and patted me on the arm. "Okay, son. See you around."

I damn near made a total rookie mistake; I almost went right back up the stairs to Jenny. Trying to keep a self-deprecating frown off my lips, I walked past Bruce and out to the sidewalk. I kept going straight ahead, fighting the urge to look around and see if I could spot where the detectives had gone and wondering if they were going to lurk around in hopes of catching sight of Jenny Chance. I waited until I was alone in the parking garage elevator before I took out my cell phone and dialed Jenny's office.

The phone picked up, but there was no greeting. Smart girl, I thought. "It's me," I said.

"Okay, Sherlock. I see you got rid of the police. Now what?" Jenny asked.

"Stay put. I'm not sure if I got rid of the police or not. They could still be around. I'll call you back in a minute."

"Okay," she said dubiously.

I hung up, got out of the elevator on the fifth floor, and went over to look down on the post–five o'clock traffic, trying to spot any police types of my recent acquaintance. As I scanned the street, I speed-dialed Mom's direct line. "Well, how nice," she answered. "Is this my son calling to take his poor old mother out for dinner?"

"No, this is the idiot you spawned that may be in over his head. With the police, no less."

"Oh. That son. Abigail already called and told me that you wanted what the DA gave her on Sterling. You do recall that we are no longer involved, don't you?'

"Well, *we* may no longer be, but it looks like I am."

She sighed. "Give it up, kiddo."

I did, and gave her a rundown in record time. When I finished, she asked, "You lied to that Lori Banks? And she fell for it?"

"Yeah, although I'm pretty sure that your old friend Harry Caldwell saw right through me. He just didn't call me on it."

"Harold's a good guy," Mom said. "He should have made captain by now, but he's way too honest for that. What exactly are you trying to do?"

"Like I told Jenny, I just want to get all this into perspective before she talks to anyone. And it'd be great if Abby would help her out. So do you mind if we have some company for dinner?"

Mom was silent for a moment, then she laughed. "Surely not. Why, I haven't harbored a fugitive from justice in far too long. Besides, I happen to agree with your assessment."

"You do?"

"Yes. I sincerely doubt that Lori Banks would be a good person for your Ms. Chance to have to deal with. I get the impression that Banks is the kind who wouldn't let the facts interfere with her case."

"Thanks. You're the best mom I ever had."

"You're welcome. But before we go any further, have you considered the alternative?"

"What's that?"

"That Jenny Chance is indeed the killer?"

"I have a foolproof plan for discovering that," I answered.

"What's that?"

"I'll let you figure it out."

Mom laughed. "Flatterer. Okay, get your guests over here, and I'll have Abigail fax the file. See you soon. Unless you get yourself arrested in the meantime, of course."

I clicked off and called Jenny back. "Okay, I think we're ready for the next move."

"What's that?"

"I'm taking you to consult the smartest, slickest, most cunning and downright conniving person I know."

"Who?"

"My mother."

■

CHAPTER SEVENTEEN

As masterfully planned escapes went, this one left a lot to be desired.

"Great," Jenny said flatly. "Do you want to give me directions so I can meet you there?"

"What? No. It's best that you don't take your car. I was thinking that you can take the back alley over to Jib Street. I'll come and pick you up."

There was silence on the line, then, "Are you stupid?"

"What do you mean?"

"You expect me to take my daughter into that alley. After dark. I repeat, are you stupid? Or do you think I am?"

"Uh, I think the answers are no and no?"

"And tell me, do you have a car seat?"

"Car seat?"

"Yes. Car seat. As in I'm not driving anywhere without my daughter being in a proper child's car seat. Did you think of that?"

I hadn't. But before I could say another word, Jenny announced, "Look, I'm going to walk right out of here with my daughter. We're going to cross the street, at the crosswalk, mind you, and then I'm going to go to my car. If you insist on driving, meet me there and we'll put Angelina's car seat in your vehicle—if I think it's safe for her to be in your car. I have no idea what you drive."

"What if the cops are still here?"

"Do you see them?"

"No, but that doesn't mean—"

"If they're still here, then I'll just have to talk to them, won't I? But you can forget me running around dark alleys with my daughter."

Hell hath absolutely nothing on a mother protecting her child.

"Okay," I capitulated. "Where's your car?"

"Across the street. I have a monthly space, number 247 on the second floor."

"All right. I'll meet you there."

She hung up, and I stayed at my vantage point, ignoring the chill wind and scanning the streets for signs of potential trouble. Eventually Jenny and Angelina, who was dressed in a bright red coat, came to the Castle's front doors. I watched as Jenny and Bruce exchanged some words—his body language conveyed the fact that he didn't like what he was hearing—and then Jenny, holding Angelina by the hand, walked to the crosswalk. They made it across Ketch Street without being stopped by the law, I was happy to see.

I got my car and drove to the second floor, where I found Jenny and Angelina waiting for me, and slid into a berth next to a white Toyota van. As I got out, I heard Jenny say to her daughter, "See? It's our friend Jason again."

"Evening, ladies," I greeted. "Made it with no mishaps, I see."

Jenny picked up Angelina, who cooed, "Ooo. I like his car, Mommy."

"Yes, it's a pretty green one," she said to Angelina. To me, she said, "Looks like you keep this old thing in good shape." I watched as Jenny maneuvered a child's car seat out of her van and into my Mustang's abbreviated backseat. Angelina came over to my side and looked up at me. "This your car?"

"Uh-huh.

"I like it."

"Thanks."

"Where we going?"

"Well, we're actually going to meet my mommy."

Angelina looked like she thought that was funny. "Your mommy?" she said, as if she couldn't believe I actually had one.

Jenny backed out of my car (I admit, I was watching) and said, "Okay. Give me the keys."

"Why?"

"Because I'm driving. For all I know, you could be an absolute doofus behind the wheel."

"But it's my car."

"And she's my daughter."

Trumped again. I smiled in concession and surrendered my keys. There was another delay as Angelina got into my car and did some exploring, testing the switches and dials she could reach. Finally her mother told her that was enough and settled her in her seat. I slid into the passenger seat while Jenny took the driver's. After I paid to get my car out of hock, I directed her to Galleon Street. Angelina amused herself by kicking the back of my seat in rhythm.

As she drove, Jenny said, "You really think your mother can help with all this?"

I nodded. "Absolutely. She used to be a River City detective herself. That was before, as she puts it, she started working for a living by solving other people's problems."

Jenny just looked thoughtful as she drove the rest of the way, handling my car with smooth, practiced ease. When we reached the 1300 block of Galleon, I told her to pull up in front of the office. "We're here, big kid," she said to her daughter, shutting off the engine. She held the keys up to the interior light, before handing them to me. Examining the small brass token on my keyring, she looked at me with a raised eyebrow. "Captain Midnight Medal of Membership? Who's Captain Midnight? Is that supposed to be you?"

"No. My dad."

She handed over the keys. "You're going to have to tell me that story."

I waited as Jenny assisted her daughter out of the car. "Whew," she said, taking in the old brick Victorian. "Is this where your mother lives?"

"And works," I said. "It's also the office. Come on, I'll show you."

Jenny crouched down by Angelina. "Okay, munchkin, I need you to do your big-girl manners, okay? Mommy needs to talk business." Angelina nodded, and Jenny stood up and took her hand. I led them up the steps and into the reception area. Paul had long gone for the day by this hour, so I knocked on the carved wooden door to the office. "Come in," Her Majesty bid from within.

I unlocked the door and stood aside to let Jenny, now holding Angelina, enter the room. Mom had positioned herself in the center of the office doing her best lady-of-the-manor-receiving-company routine, complete with a homey fire going in the fireplace. "It's good to see you again, Ms. Chance," Mother said warmly. "And who do we have here?"

As bright as Mom's smile was upon seeing Angelina, it was nothing compared to the way the little girl suddenly started jumping in Jenny's arms, pointing and saying, "Doggie! They got a doggie!" when she caught sight of Beowulf at Mom's side. "Wanna see the doggie!" Angelina insisted.

Jenny shot me a look. "Is it all right?" she asked.

"Of course it is, dear," Mom said. "Beowulf is a very good doggie."

Jenny let the squirming Angelina down, and she hurried over to Beowulf, who turned his head up to Mom as if to say, "Save me!" Mom merely smiled as Angelina started petting and stroking the beast.

Jenny whispered to me, "Are you sure it's all right?"

"Well, I suppose," I said uncertainly. "She hasn't bitten anyone in days. Oh! You mean the dog? Well, sure. He's fine."

"What his name?" Angelina asked, not taking her eyes off the pooch.

"His name is Beowulf, dear," Mom said.

"Beywoofdear?" Angelina said with a little frown.

"No, just Beywoof," Mom replied, smiling. While Angelina petted and fussed over Beywoof, Jenny said, "I'm sorry to be dropped on you like this, Mrs. Wilder. And please call me Jenny. But your son kind of insisted. I really don't want to be a problem."

Mom, who was watching Angelina with undisguised pleasure, said to Jenny, "Not at all. Jason told me a little about the situation, and I agree that it would be best if we analyzed some of the facts before you have to deal with the, um, authorities, shall we say."

Jenny smiled with gratitude. "If you're sure it's not a problem."

"Not for me," Mom said. "I enjoy twitting the police from time to time. Rather a hobby of mine. Now, I've been looking over the police reports. Please, have a seat."

Jenny glanced at Angelina before she sat down. The little girl was deep into a soft, one-sided conversation with Beowulf. Mom reached over to her desk, picked up a fat stack of paper, and sat in the other guest chair, leaving me to sling a hip on her desk. She threw a look at Angelina and said quietly. "We'll have to talk around some issues, so if I'm not clear, please let me know."

"Thanks," Jenny said. "I appreciate that."

"First," Mom said, "is the matter of the other witness. The report identifies him as one Daniel Shaw, age forty-six, unemployed and residing at the Benson Hotel."

Jenny frowned. "The Benson? That's the place behind the Castle. It's been closed for months."

Mom nodded. "Precisely."

"In other words, he's homeless," I said.

"Evidently, the detective who spoke with Mr. Shaw didn't bother to check his stated address," Mom went on. "He was probably using the closed-down hotel for shelter last Sunday night. And he got a bird's-eye view of the incident. Well, a part of it anyway. Here," she said, handing me the report.

It was a typical police report—boring and repetitious, full of opening phrases like "This officer then." Daniel Shaw's statement was rendered "I woke up when I heard the noise and went to the window. I looked down from the window and then I saw the fire. I could not see what was on fire. The smoke was coming up and it stank real bad. There was burning stuff flying all around the place. I then saw a guy come out of the other place. I could not see how tall he was because he wore a hat. He had what looked like a big white pipe in his hands. I heard him scream, and it sounded like it was maybe a woman I heard. The person started to reach into the fire and then he started slapping things around. Smoke was coming up real bad and then I could not see anything. I saw this guy bend down and he picked something up off the ground. I yelled at the guy and he looked up at me. Then he ran away. I did not see which way he went. Then I heard the sirens and I came down. An officer told me that it was a body. I am willing to go to court."

As I finished, I thought to myself that I'd read worse reports, contradictions and all. I handed the report to Jenny. "Did you see this guy while you were talking to the police that night?"

Jenny shook her head as she read. When she finished, she said, "That's weird. If this guy is right, then someone came out of the Castle that night."

"Carrying a big white pipe, according to the report," I noted.

"What's more interesting is the physical evidence the police collected," Mom said. "Along with empty cans of very flammable turpentine, the forensic team discovered what appears to be a homemade electrical device. In other words, whoever was there that night may have had arson in mind."

Jenny's eyes flew open, then narrowed intently, but before she could speak, Angelina called out, "Mom!"

"What, baby?"

Angelina stood next to the dog and gravely announced, "Doggie's only got one eye!"

Mom answered, "Yes, dear. He hurt the other one."

Angelina frowned. "How did he hurt it?"

"By being very brave," Mom said seriously.

Angelina threw both arms around Beowulf. "Poor doggie."

Beowulf was clearly enjoying all the attention. "Must run in the family," I said.

Jenny blinked. "What do you mean?"

"Your dad really liked Beowulf, too."

Jenny looked surprised. "Malcolm? That's weird. Tony and I weren't allowed to have pets while we were growing up."

We were again interrupted by Angelina announcing, "I'm hungry, Mommy."

"Where have I misplaced my manners?" Mom said, rising. "You and your daughter are to be my guests this evening. I'm afraid we'll have to make do with what's in the pantry."

"About time, too," I said. "I'm starved."

"You'll have to forage elsewhere," Mom said to me. "I've called James and Timothy to come here. You, dear boy, are going to find Mr. Daniel Shaw tonight."

"Say what?"

"I really don't want to impose," Jenny joined in.

"Nonsense," Mother replied. "It's Girls' Night In and Boy's Night Out. The sooner we can get a more detailed statement out of Mr. Shaw, hopefully one that nails down some facts that will clear you, the better. Now, ladies? If you'll follow me?"

Mom, Jenny, and Angelina, with Beowulf in tow, went through the concealed panel into the kitchen. My cell phone went off. Jim Bui greeted me, "So, what kind of trouble have you gotten us into this time?"

"Oh, just a little hunt through an abandoned building for a homeless guy. You know, the usual."

"Really? Good thing I had dinner first. Sounds like it might be an all-nighter."

Since the ladies were no longer present, I commented on just how happy I was for him and what I thought he could do with his dinner.

CHAPTER EIGHTEEN

We circled the block between Jib and Ketch streets three times, both to take a look at who might be lurking about and to give me time to finish my drive-through dinner. Jim Bui, Tim O'Toole, and I had driven over in the plain white van that we used for street-level surveillance. The thing was a rolling arsenal of electronics that probably cost more than the vehicle itself. The van was also equipped with a selection of removable magnetic signs that could be plastered on the sides. For tonight's excursion, the van was dressed as a vehicle from Anubis Plumbing Services. While Jimmy drove, Timmy stayed in the back, belted into one of the bolted-down chairs as he trained the hidden turret-mounted camera on the alleys we passed, scanning them with a light-enhancing scope. "Looks clear," Timmy announced. "So what's this guy we're looking for look like?"

"Caucasian, five ten, one seventy, hazel eyes and reddish hair, forty-six years old," I repeated from the police report.

"Hmm," I heard Bui muse beside me. "That could almost be Timmy, if he were much taller, quite a lot younger, and a whole lot less fat."

"Fat! I'll have you know that my body fat is—"

"Nothing compared to your brain fat," Jimmy finished for him. "Well, I suppose we could drive around the block a few more times."

"Not with you at the wheel," Timmy cut in. "We're risking life and limb here. If junior is finished with his heart-attack-on-a-bun, let's pull over and take a look-see. If we can find this guy quick enough, I might have time to go out on the town and find the next Mrs. Timothy O'Toole tonight."

"Women of the world, unite and run," Jimmy muttered as he pulled over. We parked across Jib in front of the Benson Hotel. It was just past seven o'clock, and the traffic seemed equally divided between the cars heading west toward Old River City with its bars and nightclubs and the vehicles going east to where the better restaurants were. We got out, hurried across the street through a break in the traffic, and stood in front of the Benson. The eight-story gray hotel was an all but deceased landmark of days long gone, leaving behind a stylish stone skeleton wrapped in a barbed wire fence. A large blue and white sign stated that it was now in the hands of the Haven Property Development Corporation. Notices warning people to keep out were plastered on the plywood affixed where the windows used to be.

"So much for the front door," Jimmy mused.

"Well, there's got to be a way in, suitable for a middle-aged man," I said. "We just have to find it."

We headed for the alley off Jib, the one where the night before I chased a couple of potential burglars down to a waiting SUV. Not that my gang looked any less suspicious. Tim O'Toole was decked out in a black sweater and windbreaker, a woolen watch cap pulled over his gray head. He was carrying a big Maglite flashlight, suitable for use as a club. Jim Bui looked even more ominous in his long black raincoat, and I briefly wondered what kind of personal armory he was keeping under wraps. I'd stuffed my own pockets with a compact collection of gear: camera, binoculars, flashlight, multitool, and my Ruger revolver. The gun was small enough to fit into my right front pocket, although it made an awkward lump in my pants. I was now fairly ready for any contingency short of falling into water over my head, and since I was in the pleasant company of the two most dangerous men I knew, dark alleys and abandoned hotels didn't worry me at all.

We silently crept down and away from the amber streetlights, the sounds of the traffic eerily fading behind us. Timmy shot a quick beam of light every few steps, illuminating the obstacles and trash. About halfway in, we found a spot on the fence that had been broken away from a metal support rod. Lifting the fence revealed a man-sized flap that we ducked under. We followed the wall back to the front, where we found that the plywood covering on the first window was loose, allowing the panel to be swung to the side. Timmy leaned in and played his light around. "Okay," he whispered.

"Need a boost, shorty?" Uncle Jimmy inquired softly.

Timmy snorted and levered himself up onto the ledge and through with no apparent effort. He's always prided himself on his physical fitness regimen. As Jimmy puts it, "He's strong as a mule. And just as smart."

I was next, and I confess I made a bit of noise when my left hand reminded me that it was still on the injured list. Once in, I reached out and gave Jimmy a hand, pulling him up and inside. I eased the plywood panel back into place, and the three of us stood still in the darkness, intent on listening.

All that came to my ears was the muted sounds of the traffic outside. My nose, however, was assailed with a plethora of scents, none of which were inviting. After a minute or two, we all lit up our flashlights and surveyed the area. It would take a lot more imagination than I possessed to picture this gutted, trash-littered cavern as the foyer of a luxurious hotel. We silently climbed stairs, which groaned in protest under our weight, to the second floor. On either side of the landing, a wide hallway stretched between the rooms. Our intrusion hadn't gone unnoticed, judging by the skittering sounds that the rodent population made at our approach. I flipped a mental coin and led my troops to the hallway on the right, heading in the direction of the back of the Castle Theater. All the doors had been removed from the place, and

I stopped briefly to shine my light around inside a huge open area that must have been the grand ballroom, with an arched ceiling that was adorned with a faded fresco of cherubs lounging among the clouds. But it was the dust on the now naked hardwood floors that caught my attention, with its trail of foot traffic, that we followed, evidence of recent occupation.

As we approached the end of the hall, I held up my hand, signaling for a stop. When no other noise reached us, I took a gamble. "Hello?" I called. "Anyone home?"

"Who's dere?" a slurred, masculine voice demanded. I quickly stepped over to the last room on my left, where I thought the voice came from. I shot my light in, and found myself confronted with a shambling mound of cloth in the center of the room. "Go way," came a muffled shout.

Jimmy and Timmy played their lights around the room, which was decorated, if you could call it that, with a host of shiny pictures, evidently removed from magazines, plastered all along the walls. They were all of women, and they were all pictures from the neck down. The heads had been carefully removed. On the right-hand wall, where a window overlooking the back of the Castle Theater would be, was another plywood covering.

Timmy went over to the heap of cloth covering the room's occupant and gently prod it with a booted toe. "Hey, buddy, you've got company."

"I said go 'way!" came the response.

I crouched down and addressed the bundle. "Mr. Shaw? My name's Jason Wilder. It's important that we speak with you, sir."

There was a flurry of activity that sent a wave of sour scents my way, then a face that was mostly a shaggy, reddish brown beard appeared. "How'd you know it'd be me?" he slurred.

"We had a good description of you, sir." I managed not to laugh.

Daniel Shaw's face, what I could see of it, was a thin, pallid thing, foreshortened by a lack of teeth and ringed with greasy,

145

rust-colored hair. His watery hazel eyes blinked through the lights we held. "Ah, go 'way," he grumbled.

"We're here to talk about what you saw last Sunday night. Down in the alley," I said.

"I didn't see nuthin'."

"Well, you told the police you saw something," I prompted. "You know, the fire?"

Shaw's eyes grew wide and seemed to lose focus. "Fire? Oh, yesss," he hissed.

I tried to capture his attention again. "Mr. Shaw? Did you see a woman that night? A woman with dark hair?"

He nodded, blankly. "Yesss. They're everywhere. Always lookin' at me."

Jimmy and Timmy did their best to cover up their chuckles while I tried to keep exasperation out of my voice. "Yes, sir. I'm sure they do. But did you see a dark-haired woman last Sunday night when the fire happened in the alley?"

Daniel Shaw's head bobbed. "Sure. If you say so."

Timmy cut in with, "Mr. Shaw, who's the President of the United States?"

Without missing a beat, Shaw replied, "Ronal' Reagan."

"Guy's a head case," Timmy whispered.

I stood up then, but the distance I gained from my aromatic new friend didn't comfort me much. No doubt about it, Daniel Shaw was a head case. I could see now why the officer who spoke with him last Sunday night didn't bother to take a more detailed report. As a witness, this guy was a total loss and wasn't going to be any help to us—or, more important, to Jenny.

Jim Bui had pushed the plywood aside and was looking out through the crack. "Jason," he said quietly, "I think I got something."

I glided over to the wall near Jim and stole a peek out the window. Down in the alley there was a flickering light. It came from the back of the Castle. "What do you think that is?" Jimmy whispered.

"It's the back door," I said softly. "I think someone's propped it open. I think those burglars could be back." I could feel my heart start to hammer. "Tim," I hissed. "Let's go. Jim, you cover us from up here."

Quick as a blink, Jimmy had his Glock automatic out and was snapping his palm-size flashlight to it. Timmy knelt down by Shaw and said, "Quiet! The Reagans are coming!" Shaw made a muffled howling sound as his head disappeared under his covers. Timmy stood up, grinning, and followed me out of the room at a run. When we made it to the lobby, we doused our lights and lifted the plywood flap over the window we had used as an entrance. The streetlights revealed a familiar dark SUV parked in front of the alley to the right of us. "Looks like my friends are back," I whispered. "I think someone's trying to break into the Castle Theater."

"Hot damn!" Timmy hissed. "How do you want to handle it?"

"Give Jimmy a call and let him know we're going around back to the alley. Then let's circle around the other way over to the Twelfth Street side."

Timmy nodded and got on his cell phone. "Wake up, sunshine. Junior's spotted some company, and they may be sneaking around in the alley. We're going to come up right beneath you. Try not to shoot us by accident." There was a pause, then he clicked his phone off. "He says if he shoots us, it'll be no accident. Let's go."

We eased the plywood covering aside and slid out to the ground, keeping an eye on the SUV. I crept up to the fence line and was able to get a look at the back license plate. Using my Space Pen, I jotted the number down on my bandaged wrist. Timmy and I continued over to the Twelfth Street side of the hotel. We found a spot in the fence where we could lift up the wire high enough to crawl under, and from there run quietly back to the alley entrance between the theater and the hotel. I had a picture of the terrain in my head from when I'd visited the area the night before.

Leaning around the corner, I saw the faint, flickering glimmer of light again and heard low strains of music. The music became more distinct as I crept in. It was music with a lot of synthesized keyboard. It reminded me of the 1980s. As Timmy and I approached the back double doors, I saw I'd been right about the source of the light: Someone had propped the door open about an inch. I reached over and gave Timmy's shoulder a squeeze, then slowly pulled the door open enough to slip through.

Ahead of me was the back of the movie screen, bordered in bright, pulsing light from the projector. The music was much louder back here, a driving beat overlaid with a chorus yelling "Destruction!" over and over. I hoped that wasn't an omen. The wings of the stage were shrouded in inky black. I pointed to Timmy to take the right side, and I went off to the left, trying to move by feel—until I got a face full of bright flashlight myself.

As I threw my left arm up to cover my eyes, I was suddenly body slammed and knocked to the ground. I instinctively tucked my chin in and rolled with the blow, winding up in a backward shoulder roll that sent my flashlight flying off God knew where. I grabbed at whatever it was that hit me and came up with a lot of nothing, flopping painfully on the hardwood stage in the process and ramming the gun in my pocket into my upper thigh. I heard something banging into the metal doors at the same time Timmy yelled, "Watch it!" over the music, followed by the sound and feel of something slamming onto the stage floor. I rolled over and got to my feet just in time to hear the back doors swinging closed. I couldn't see Timmy; he must have been beyond the flickering gash of light that came from the side of the screen. I sent my left hand into my pants pocket, painfully peeling my bandages loose, and came up with my key ring with its little emergency light. Its blue-white beam showed me Uncle Timmy crouched over a struggling form. "Timmy?" I called out.

"Over here, junior. I got one," he yelled back. I hurried to get a look at his prize.

Only to have the grimacing face of Bruce come glaring back at me.

CHAPTER NINETEEN

Timmy had Bruce's left arm cranked behind his back in a painful-looking wristlock and one knee planted on his spine. "It's okay, Timmy," I said. "This is Bruce Roberts. He works here."

Timmy released his hold and stood up. We both took a couple of cautious steps away as Bruce slowly rose to his full, towering height. "Bruce, it's me, Jason," I said, hoping he was listening.

"What are you doing back here?" Bruce rumbled.

I had to talk loudly to be heard over the music. "I spotted a car parked on Jib," I said. "The same car a couple of guys who tried to break in here the other night ran off to. What are you doing here?"

Bruce ignored my question. "Where's Jenny?"

"Having dinner with some friends of mine. That's all you or anyone else needs to know right now."

Timmy had clicked on his flashlight, pointing it at the floor. Lit from underneath like that, Bruce looked more like Frankenstein's Monster than anything else. He was rubbing his wrist, the one Uncle Timmy had recently abused. "One of the boys said he saw someone from the audience sneak backstage from the theater. I went to go look."

Maybe the crew I surprised trying to crowbar their way into the back doors got smarter and had one of the team pay admission and then sneak the other guy in. Unless, of course, Bruce was lying and he was the one who let them in back here.

"What do you think they were looking for?" Timmy wondered aloud.

For some reason, my brain chose that moment to connect what Mom had said about the cops having evidence of a possible arson attempt here last Sunday night with the nasty, fire-breathing booby trap in Tony's office. "Oh, hell," I heard myself say. "I think they wanted to plant some kind of bomb."

"Christ!" Timmy said, sending the beam of his flashlight arcing out around us. "You sure?"

"Sure enough. Bruce, you've got to get these people out of the theater! Now!"

In the darkness, Bruce said, "The movie's almost over. Unless you want to cause a panic?"

I could hear the music rising to a crescendo, with a beautiful female voice singing something about how love can't hide. But bombs could, I thought. I yanked out my cell phone and called Jim Bui. "Uncle Jim? Did you see the guys who ran out the back?"

"Yes. I was just about to call you. I got a quick light on them. Two to be exact. Both Caucasian."

"Did they have anything in their hands?"

"Not sure. You want me to come over?"

"Not yet. Sit tight," I said, and clicked off the phone. "Okay, come on, let's look around real fast. Bruce? Where would you hide something around here?"

He grunted and walked toward the back wall. Suddenly there was a harsh bright light coming from above. I blinked to get my bearings and saw Bruce swiveling his head from side to side. "Don't see anything," he said.

I spotted my little flashlight on the floor by the back wall, scooped it up, and scanned the area. I could hear Bruce and Timmy stomping around somewhere behind me. "What are we looking for?" Timmy called out.

"Maybe something that looks like a big pipe," I answered. Having covered all the floor space of the stage on my side, I saw

I had two other options. There was a ladder bolted into the wall that led up to a scaffolding above, and a set of stairs going down. I took the stairs, using my flashlight and spotting a collection of footprints left in a layer of whitish dust. At the bottom of the stairs was a green wooden door, secured with a heavy padlock. I retraced my steps and took to the ladder.

My climb took me to the catwalks and the pipe grid holding the stage lights. I was looking for signs of anything out of the ordinary when I felt the catwalk sway a bit and saw that Bruce had joined me on the other side. "Anything look out of place?" I called.

In the light coming from below us, I saw him shake his head as he slowly walked around, checking every light he came to. I waited for him to finish his inspection before saying, "Is there anyplace else we haven't looked back here?"

"No."

"You sure?"

Bruce looked at me balefully. "I know every inch of this place. There's nothing here."

My breath seemed to come out of me all at once, the relief making me feel like a deflated balloon. "Okay. Good. Maybe we were in time and scared them off."

"Or maybe you're wrong?" Bruce asked quietly.

"Or maybe I'm wrong," I admitted. "I just didn't want to take the chance." I placed my hands on the metal safety bar of the catwalk and leaned over, getting a look down. It was a hell of a drop, I saw, and realized that I was up here with a rather large guy who probably didn't like me very much. I looked over at Bruce and wasn't reassured to see the nasty grin on his ugly features. "Long way down," he commented.

"Yeah."

"I want to talk to Jenny."

"Okay. Let's get down and give her a call."

Bruce made an after-you gesture, and I retraced my steps to the metal ladder. I went back down in a bit of a hurry, as Bruce seemed intent on crowding me as he followed. I jumped the last few feet to the stage floor to get out of his way.

The music had stopped. From the sides of the screen I could see that the house lights had come on, and I heard the murmur of the departing audience. I stole over to the side of the screen and saw maybe a hundred people slowly marching up the aisles. I got a chilling feeling as I pictured the same people clawing and trampling each other to get away if I had yelled "Bomb!"

Timmy had left the stage and was looking under the front row of seats just past the empty orchestra pit.

"Anything?" I called to him.

"Nada."

I took the stairs down from the stage, peeked under the first chair I came to, then more or less collapsed into it. I pulled out my phone and called mom. "Is it too late for me to go back to law school?" I asked when she answered.

"Why? Have you lost your mind, or just your morals?"

"Let's just say I haven't been exactly successful this evening." I gave her a quick rundown of the night's events. When I concluded, she said, "So, Daniel Shaw is of no help?"

"He has a problem with, eh, women. That, and he's delusional. How are our guests?"

"Jenny's up in your old room trying to get Angelina to sleep. Beowulf seems to have collapsed from all the attention, and I've been working."

"Oh? On what?"

"The next potential lead. Come on back home, kiddo. The night's not over yet."

"Great." I noticed Bruce watching me from a distance with intense scrutiny. "Have Jenny call Bruce up when she gets a chance. But remind her not to let on where she's staying," I added softly. I closed my phone, heaved myself off the chair, and went over to Bruce. "Jenny's going to call you later, okay?"

His grunt gave me the impression he didn't like my announcement. I got out my wallet and gave him my business card.

"Here. If anything else squirrelly happens tonight, call right away." He took the card in one fast swipe.

"Where are you going?" he asked as I turned to leave.

"With any luck, I'm going to figure out what the hell has been going on. In the meantime, parting is such sweet sorrow, - etcetera."

As I walked away from Bruce with Timmy falling into step behind me, I heard a low grumble behind me: "That I shall say goodnight till it be morrow."

"What was that he said?" Timmy asked as we walked back up to the stage.

I shook my head. "Shakespeare."

"Well, ol' Godzilla there is full of surprises, isn't he?" Timmy commented. I pushed open the back door to the alleyway, taking a cautious look around with my flashlight, feeling I was growing all too familiar with this dark and foul-smelling place. As Timmy went to the corner and shined his own light around, I phoned Jimmy. "We're heading back to the barn. Unless you want to stay here with your new friend."

"Thanks, but no," Jimmy said. "If it's all the same, Timmy's company is slightly preferable. We calling it a night?"

"I don't think so. Her Majesty just informed me that she's got another chore for me, but she didn't mention anyone else."

"Gotcha. Meet you out front," he said, and clicked off.

The boys and I drove our company van back to the office, where Timmy and Jimmy let me off at the front before going to return the van to its place in the garage. I found Mom in her throne room, reading glasses in place, busily working her desktop computer. " 'Bout time, kiddo. I was about to give up on you. You missed the party."

"I can see I missed something. What were you guys doing all evening?"

"Girl talk, mostly." Mom stopped typing and regarded me over her glasses. "When are you going to gift me with grandchildren of my own?"

"Hey, it's not like I haven't tried, but I can't recall the last time you actually approved of my choice of potential partners."

"Is it my fault you tend toward bubble-headed bleached blonds?"

"Not to change the subject or anything, but I take it we're still working on the Sterling matter?"

"Certainly. After all, we have a client again."

"Good. But I'm afraid Jenny Chance may not be able to pay the going rate."

"Who said our client was Jenny? For the record, we are now employed by Miss Angelina Chance. She not only declared that she wanted us to help her mommy, but she gave us a retainer."

"A what?"

"One original portrait of Beywoof. Hey, I've worked cases for less, you know."

I couldn't help but smile. "You softie."

"Now, here's where we earn our keep," Mom announced. "I've compiled a list of tasks we need to accomplish. One, we have to speak with Anthony Sterling again and find out why he's implicated his sister. That, however, has to wait for morning before we can visit him in jail."

"Okay, then what?"

"Then we need to get a good look at the physical evidence. Namely, the handgun used in the homicide and the pipe bomb booby trap. Again, we'll have to wait for tomorrow before we'll be allowed access to the police evidence warehouse."

"Okay. And I'm missing out on my beauty sleep now why?"

"Because we still haven't interviewed all the people potentially involved. You have noticed, have you not, that there seems to be more than a little interest shown by the authorities in our Russian community?"

"If by authorities you mean Detective Lori Banks, then yes. She seems to have Russians on the brain."

"Perhaps for good reason. Your friend Robin over at the coroner's office told you that the victim may be Russian, did she not?

155

That brings us to Katerina. I called her tonight and inquired why she decided to dispense with our services. She was nervous and uninformative, which leads me to believe that the decision to fire us was not hers."

"Okay. So?"

"So tonight, we're going calling on Uncle Georgi. Didn't it strike you as odd that he waited for Katerina outside the jail? In the pouring rain?"

"Maybe he's claustrophobic?"

"Uh-huh. Dikephobic is far more likely."

"Come again?"

"Fear of justice," Mom said, then regarded me bleakly. "And here I spent all that money on your so-called education. Did you notice how he was seemed friendly, but he was reticent to give us his last name? A little too suspicious, if you ask me."

"If we don't know his last name, then how do we find him tonight?"

Mom cupped her chin in her hand. "You know, detection is kind of a hobby of mine."

"So I've noticed. Especially the way you've always done background checks on my girlfriends. How did you find dear old Uncle Georgi?"

Mom tapped her computer screen. "I went to the Recorder's Office records on-line. Katerina Sterling's maiden name on her marriage certificate is Pakhomov. Granted, her uncle might have a different last name, but I tried the property database using Georgi Pakhomov just to see what came up. Lo and behold, this particular Georgi Pakhomov has acquired several pieces of property in a short amount of time. In particular, he's the owner of the Café Mediterranean bar and restaurant."

"So?"

"So I thought we'd go over there tonight and take a look. Evening is a restaurant's busiest time; it's quite possible we'll find him there. It would give us a chance to have a little chat with him."

"A little chat, huh?"

"Yes," Mother agreed. "Mind you, we'll have to be subtle and diplomatic at this stage." I watched her take her pistol from her desk and pop the magazine out to check that it was loaded. She rammed the magazine home and flipped the safety. "Let's go be diplomatic, shall we?'

CHAPTER TWENTY

The Café Mediterranean was a single-story white stucco structure on the outskirts of the northern residential district of Rio Del Oro. Mom navigated her Jaguar around the crowded parking lot to get a feel for the clientele. "Bingo!" I called as I spotted a dark-colored SUV of my recent acquaintance. "That's the car I've seen lurking around the Castle."

"You sure?" Mom asked.

I pulled up my sleeve and consulted my hastily scribbled license number. "Positive match."

"Good," Her Majesty nodded. "Next time use your notebook. I thought I taught you better than that."

I laughed and retrieved said notebook from my briefcase in the backseat, then pulled out a copy of the photograph I took of my alleyway neighbors as they tried to force the Castle's back doors open. "Okay," I said. "What do you want to bet that we find these guys in the photo inside?"

"I'd bet that photo will match roughly half the people here. But's let's go and see for ourselves, shall we?"

Mom parked the Jag, and as I got out of the car I carefully folded the picture and slipped it inside my jacket pocket. It was coming up on 10:30. We approached the front entrance, passing a cluster of young men around the front door, smoking and talking quietly among themselves. I tried to spot one who matched the faces in my photo, but as Mom had predicted, I came up with too many potential candidates.

Inside, the place was noisy and dark, with low lights and candles in red globes burning on numerous tables. The noise came from the dance floor, where disco music was blaring. I tried to place the song, but gave up when I heard the chorus "Ra-Ra-Rasputeen, he seduced the Russian queen," or something to that effect. As my eyes adjusted to the gloom, I noticed that the customers seemed to be on the young side and exclusively Caucasian. Almost all the men wore black leather car coats. Mom made her way over to the bar, where she flagged down a darkly bearded bartender. I watched a brief conversation that ended in Mom handing the bartender a business card. The man nodded, then slipped out from behind the bar and disappeared into the crowd. He reappeared shortly and waved us toward the back.

Mom and I eased our way through the clouds of smoke and cologne and were led to a short hall that opened up into the restaurant room. At the moment, it could have been a classic gentleman's club; the "diners" were exclusively male and were grouped at white-clothed tables where lots of alcohol was in evidence. The whole scene was shrouded in cigarette smoke. Uncle Georgi himself came up to greet us. He was looking a lot more casual now, dressed in dark slacks and an open white dress shirt with the sleeves rolled up, and acting the part of jolly, overweight favorite uncle. "Mrs. Wilder!" he boomed. "Come in! Come in! It is good to see you again. And you, too, of course, young man. Come, have a seat. May I offer you a drink?"

"Why, thank you, Mr. Pakhomov," Mother said graciously. "We'll have what you're having."

Georgi Pakhomov waved us to a table, scattering three men who had been sitting there eying us with open suspicion. Mom unbuttoned her expensive overcoat but left it on as she took her chair. I sat down next to her, and Georgi snapped his fingers at a waiter and called out something in Russian. Almost instantly, a shot glass of clear liquid appeared before each of us. "So, tell me please," Georgi inquired as he sat down opposite, "what it is that I can do for you? Little Katerina told me that you had to leave her today but sent a man in your place. The police found nothing at her house, of course."

Mom took a sip of her drink, and I followed suit. And had to swallow twice. It was vodka, of rocket-fuel grade. Mom said, "I was curious, Mr. Pakhomov, as to why your niece Katerina decided to dispense with our services?"

Georgi's deep brown eyes widened in surprise. "She did? I did not know this. When did this happen?"

"Late this afternoon," Mom replied. "Shortly after Anthony decided to speak to the police."

Georgi made an expansive gesture. "Tony talked to the police? This I also did not know. What did he say?"

Mom smiled in apology. "I'm sorry, but I really can't repeat what Anthony said. Especially as we no longer work for your niece."

Georgi's frown went deeper. "I have no idea why Katerina would do that. Unless she thought she did not have the money to afford to hire you? If that is true, then she should have come to me. I will speak to her about that. Now, is poor Tony still in jail?"

"As far as I know, Anthony is still in custody," Mom answered. "I was under the impression that his father was going to post his bail and have him released, but I don't know if he's managed to do that yet."

I was listening to Mom and Georgi as I surveyed the room. No doubt about it, we were the center of attention, and the looks we were getting were not favorable.

"Well," Georgi said, "this is strange news. I will speak to my niece tonight. But is this what you came here to tell me?"

Mom tossed off her drink as though it were weak tea. "Actually, I had a question for you, if you don't mind."

"Certainly," Georgi said generously. "What can I tell you?"

"You can tell me why your men have been trying to break into the Castle Theater."

Georgi's smiling face fell into a blank slab, as if a mask had been slapped into place. "What do you mean?"

I found his reaction interesting, but I would have enjoyed watching Mom question him more if I hadn't been distracted by the feeling of quiet menace emanating from the sullen-faced men all around us.

"I mean precisely what I said," Mom replied pleasantly. That was my cue to take the photograph out of my pocket and hand it to Georgi. All the other men in the room seemed to tense up as my hand went into my jacket.

Georgi, his face very still, studied the photo, his eyes darting off to the side once, then back. "So why is it you bring this to me?"

"Because of the facts at hand," Mom explained patiently. "Anthony Sterling, a relative of yours by marriage, was in that alleyway at the Castle Theater the night a man was murdered. We believe, from his dental work, that the murdered man was Russian. And now we have men who have made at least two attempts to break into the Castle Theater near the spot where the man was killed. Those facts, like a certain vehicle parked outside your restaurant, come right to your doorway, Mr. Pakhomov."

Georgi settled back in his chair and tented his thick fingers, studying us. Finally, he said "It would mean a lot to me to know the name of the man who killed . . . the other man that night. A great deal indeed."

"I'd be happy to tell you, if I knew," Mom said evenly, "but I need more information if I'm going to figure that one out."

"Information such as?"

"Such as what the victim was doing behind the Castle Theater in the first place."

Another pause. "Mrs. Wilder, there is business, and then there is family business. If this was just business, then we could talk, yes? But with family business . . ." He let his words trail off with a shrug, then said, "It would perhaps be best if you did not pursue this matter anymore. You did say my niece does not want you on the case, yes?"

Mom nodded. "Yes. But be that as it may, my agency may

remain involved. And if we do, then I believe it would be beneficial to both of us to come to an understanding."

The tension was growing thick enough to cut with a knife, if you happened to have a very sharp one handy, and I had the uncomfortable feeling that sharp knives were not in short supply in my immediate vicinity. Georgi leaned forward, his eyes glittering redly from the reflected candlelight. "So let us speak plainly, yes?" he said.

"Fine," Mom agreed. "You and your men stay clear of the Castle Theater. In return, if I or my son can uncover the identity of the person who murdered your friend last Sunday, I will inform you."

Georgi's mouth turned downward. "I will consider what you have said. Now, you will hear me: I do not like people who try to interfere with my family or my business. And I cannot be responsible for anyone who does."

"Has someone interfered with either one lately?" Mom inquired.

Georgi nodded. "Oh, yes. Most assuredly."

"Would you care to tell me how?" Mom asked.

"I would not," he said shortly. "Let us agree to stay out of each other's way, shall we? But if I may be allowed a question?"

When Her Majesty nodded, Georgi said, "Mrs. Wilder, let me ask you. Theoretical, okay? If a man was going to do something not so legal, but that thing never happened, could he still be convicted of a crime?"

"Well, there's always the crime of conspiracy," Mom said. "That can still apply even if the actual crime never occurs."

"And would you be compelled, so to speak, to report such a thing to the law?"

"Possibly not. As long as I wasn't aiding and abetting anyone by my silence."

Georgi rubbed his stubbled chin. "I see. What if I were to tell you that Tony needed money for a debt. Very badly. And perhaps he was going to do a desperate thing. A thing that never happened."

162

"You mean, like burning down the theater for insurance money?"

Georgi's smile came back, but it wasn't a nice thing to see. "Theoretical, right?"

"To whom did Anthony owe money?"

Georgi shrugged.

"All right," Mom said, "So, theoretically, may I ask again why your men keep trying to break in to the theater?"

Georgi spread his hands. "I have perhaps said too much already."

"All right, Mr. Pakhomov. But be advised: Nothing, I repeat nothing, had better happen to the Castle. Do I make myself clear?"

Georgi nodded once. "And, Mrs. Wilder? As I have already said, I would very much like to know the name of the killer."

"I'll keep that in mind," Mom said as she arose. I got up, too, tossing off the rest of my drink in the process. Then I spent a moment desperately trying not to cough out loud. Mom suddenly turned back to Georgi and said, "One more thing. You wouldn't have a reason to place a booby trap in Anthony Sterling's business office, would you?"

Georgi's mask slipped back into place. "No," he said shortly.

"And I should believe you why?"

"For two reasons," Georgi said stiffly. "One, Tony is family. I, too, read about what happened at Tony's office. It makes sense to me that whoever killed . . . the young man at the theater may be after Tony, too. That, I think, is the person someone should be looking for."

"I see," Mother said. "And your second reason is?"

Georgi Pakhomov smiled again. "Because if I were out to get somebody, I would not use something like a cowardly trap. It is too . . . impersonal."

Mom nodded to Georgi, and he returned the gesture, the two of them like a pair of duelists who've come to a draw. For now. It didn't escape my attention that the whole damn room seemed to stand up as we did, only to be stopped in their tracks by a slight wave of Georgi's hand.

Her Majesty and I made an orderly retreat back though the bar. The music had shifted to another disco song, but in this one the squeaky-voiced singer was declaring that "she's a Barbie girl, in a Barbie world." None too soon, we were outside in the cold, clear night.

"Family business, indeed," Mom muttered as we walked to her car.

"Well, that was slightly productive," I commented. "Seeing that we lived to tell the tale and all. So what do you make of what we got out of Uncle Georgi tonight?"

"Well, if we can believe him; and that's a big, fat if, it looks like Anthony Sterling was in the process of torching the theater for insurance money. Probably with a little help from one of dear old Uncle Georgi's associates. Only something went entirely wrong."

"Yeah. Someone stopped them big time." The word "big" brought to mind the towering form of Bruce, and I wondered how far he'd go to protect the Castle Theater—a place that Jenny Chance loved.

The traffic was fairly thin at this hour, and Her Majesty made good time getting us home. As she pulled the Jag into the garage, she said, "You look all washed out, love. Why don't you stay the night? You've still got a set of clothes here, right?"

"It's been a day and then some," I agreed. "Wait. We've got company. Where am I going to sleep?"

"In the den, of course. I gave your room to Jenny and Angelina."

Mentally, I flipped a coin: my comfy bed at a distance, or the foldout couch right here. "I'll make sure you get breakfast," Mom said temptingly.

"Sold. Eating has become a real novelty lately."

I followed Mom in as far as the back room, where I stopped to boot up my computer and check my e-mail. Roland Gibson had forwarded the old news stories concerning Jenny's parents. The last article, the one that mentioned that arrest warrants for grand theft and embezzlement had been issued for Angelique Sterling and Malcolm's former business partner, Anthony Worthington, had picturers of the fleeing couple. Anthony Worthington was described as six-foot-two with blond hair and blue eyes; Jenny's mom was a petite five-five with dark hair and eyes. The black-and-white photo reproductions showed two people who could have been cast in a Hollywood movie. I was about to print a copy, for my file notes, then realized that I wasn't sure if I wanted to; this definitely wasn't the kind of thing that I wanted to talk to Jenny about. I got up and headed upstairs through the kitchen.

The living quarters were dark, and I moved quietly, not wanting to disturb anyone. From the top of the stairs, there's a single hallway that leads to the front. Mom's suite occupies the forward section. My old room is to the right, with the den and guest bath on the left. I slipped into the den, but before I could close my door I heard Jenny say softly, "Jason?"

I turned to see her standing just inside the door of my old room. "Yeah, it's me. How's the short blonde?"

"Fine. I was able to get her to sleep hours ago. I just can't seem to get there myself. Your mom stopped by to check on us on her way in. I take it it's not going well?"

A classic understatement, I thought. "Well, there are still some things we can do," I said. "You should try to get some sleep."

"That's easier said than done. Are you going to bed now?"

Not if I can spend some time with you. "Well, probably not right away."

"Care for some company?"

"Sure. Come on over."

Jenny opened the door wider, and I could make out that she was dressed in her dark pants and white shirt, tail out. Leaving the door open, she padded over barefoot to the den, and I turned the lights on, but with the dimmer switch keeping them low. Jenny made a slow tour of the room, examining all the photographs on the wall. "Is this one your father?" she asked, pointing to one that showed a rough-looking group posing with a collection of guns. "Yep, that's him," I answered. "Captain Midnight himself."

"Oh, my God," Jenny breathed as she took another look. "Is that one your mother? The one holding the shotgun?"

I came up behind her and had to resist the temptation to breathe in her scent. "Yeah. That's a picture of the original Crime Abatement Team. CAT Squad, they used to call it."

"So what's all this about Captain Midnight?"

"If you're looking for a bedtime story, that's probably not the one to tell."

"Hey, no fair. I spilled my guts about my family to you."

I sighed. "Okay. Have a seat."

Jenny descended to the couch, folding her legs up under her and watching me with expectation.

CHAPTER TWENTY-ONE

Once upon a time, there was a girl born into wealth and privilege. Only she decided to break with her family tradition and actually do something with her life."

"This is your mother, right?" Jenny asked.

"Yep. Mom's family name is Larsen, one of River City's first families. She always said that her side of the family got kicked out of Europe, settled in California and probably made their fortune ridding the early gold miners of their excess wealth. Anyway, instead of growing up to be a trophy wife, she shocked her family and joined the River City Police Department, getting herself damn near disowned in the process."

In the near darkness, I saw the gleam of Jenny's smile. "I knew I liked your mom right off."

I sat down on the couch, turning to face her. "While she's working her way up to detective class, she meets Dad, otherwise known as Wild Bill Wilder. Now, on my father's side, we Wilders have always been policemen, probably due to some genetic inability to do honest work."

"So why didn't you become a policeman like your father?" Jenny asked.

"According to Mom, there never was a policeman like my father, and never will be again. But your question gets a little ahead of the story. Mom and Dad met during what has been referred to as the drug wars. The River City PD was directed to put together a crime abatement team to combat the evil drug pushers and stuff like that. Dad was the head of the team that in-cluded Mom."

Jenny uncoiled from the couch and went over to the picture. "Okay, I recognize your father from the picture in the office. Who are these other guys?"

"The Asian guy is Jimmy Bui. The short guy who looks like a red-haired gorilla is Timothy O'Toole. Only they've always been Uncle Jimmy and Uncle Timmy to me. They work for Mom now."

Jenny returned to her spot on the couch. "Where does the Captain Midnight thing come in?"

"Everyone on the CAT Squad had their own call sign, sort of like a nickname. Uncle Timmy was 'Samurai', Jimmy was 'Cowboy', and mom was the 'Iron Maiden.' "

"I can see that for your mom," Jenny murmured.

"As for dad, he was the team leader: 'Captain Midnight.' "

I dug my key ring out of my pocket, being more careful with my bandaged hand this time, and handed it to Jenny. "That little brass disc there was a present from Mom. It's an original Captain Midnight Medal of Membership, from the old radio show."

Jenny held the disc in her hand. "When I saw this on your keys earlier, I thought it was some kind of holy medal like I used to see girls at parochial school get from their parents." She placed my keys in my hand, then gently turned my hand over and ran her finger lightly over the silver ring I wore. "So what's this? A secret decoder ring?"

I held my hand up, letting the wan light play over the face of the ring with its engraved clock-at-midnight symbol. "No. But that used to belong to my father, too." Actually, the ring did have a special function. But I never spoke about it.

"So what happened to him?" she asked.

"My dad? Well, he and Mom got married. I came along. And then he was murdered."

I heard Jenny's sharp intake of breath. "How awful!" she whispered.

"It was a long time ago. I was just a kid. He was set up, an out-and-out assassination. And to make a point, he was killed at exactly midnight. No one was ever able to figure out who his killer was, but during the investigation it turned out that certain members of the police department were getting big payoffs in drug money, so a lot of people either got arrested or were quietly allowed to resign. After that, Mom quit the force. I have it on good authority that she wrote out a lengthy letter of resignation, pinned her badge to it, then wrapped the whole thing up in a brick and threw it through the police chief's office window. Now she gets to play the game by her own rules."

"The Midnight Investigation Agency," Jenny said quietly.

"Yeah. So everyone would remember. Even the company's initials make a point: Captain Midnight isn't dead, he's just MIA. Missing in action."

In the dim light, I could see Jenny's face become thoughtful. "We're kind of alike, you know," she said. "I grew up without my mother, and you without your father."

"Well, I did have a couple of male role models as I grew up," I said. "Uncle Jimmy and Uncle Timmy were always there for me. Not to mention the time and trouble they took teaching me the manly arts, as Uncle Timmy refers to them."

"Oh?"

"Oh, yeah. I'm a regular danger to myself and others. Between the two of them, I've probably had more combat training than any ten policemen."

"I wouldn't mind having Angelina learn some of that when she's old enough," she said thoughtfully. "So you just kind of grew up into the family business?"

"Well, I didn't start out in that direction. There was some talk about me going to law school, but that bored me silly. In the end, being a PI just came easy for me. I probably learned more about the detective business around the dinner table than anywhere else. I guess I sort of absorbed it by osmosis. Not that Mom was crazy about the idea, mind you, but she always said I could be anything I wanted to be, with the exception of unemployed."

Jenny was silent for a bit, then she said, "So, Sherlock, what do you make of your most recent case?"

I tried not to sigh too loudly. "It's a little confusing," I admitted, "and it still looks bad for your brother. From what we can see, at the very least he was intent on burning the Castle down for insurance money."

Jenny shook her head. "You know, that's still almost as crazy as the idea that Tony killed someone. Tony would never do something that . . . flat-out wild. It's just not him."

"Did he have any money problems? Something that would make him desperate enough to try something like arson?"

"No. All I know is that one minute he's saying we have to sell the Castle, and then he goes and changes the insurance policy without telling me. Did you find out why people have been trying to break into my theater?"

"No," I said. "I thought at first that someone might have been trying to finish the job of burning it down, but now I'm not so sure. It may be that certain other people are trying to find out what happened to the man who got torched in the alley there. And they may be the same people who tried to kill Tony, too, by setting that trap in his office."

"That's . . . that's really scary," she said softly.

"Not to mention the fact that Tony is now trying to put the blame on you."

Jenny pulled her knees up and hugged them to her. "I can't believe he did that."

"Even if he really thinks you did it?"

Jenny looked at me, then said slowly, "Even then. I was the closest thing he had to a mother, for God's sake."

"What about that gun of yours? Are you sure Bruce didn't know about it?"

"What are you getting at?"

"From what you tell me, Bruce is always hanging around. You ever get the feeling that he might be in love with you?"

Jenny looked surprised. "Me? How would I know? He's never said anything, or done anything out of line. I know he adores Angelina, and she loves him, too. He'd never do anything to harm her, that's for sure."

"Okay," I said carefully. "But what do you think he'd do if he thought that he needed to protect you from something? Or better yet, protect Angelina?"

"I think I see where you're heading. I don't like it, but I see your point. You think Bruce may have done something, thinking he was protecting us?"

"I don't know. I'm just guessing," I admitted.

I was torn. The day's trials and tribulations had caught up with me, making me tired and confused, but I didn't want to let Jenny go just then, either. Finally I decided I was being selfish. "You'd better go and try to get some rest," I said.

"Yeah," she agreed. "Tomorrow's going to be a busy day. And night."

"What do you mean?"

"I've got to be at the Castle tomorrow night for the masquerade party. I have to be there to run the thing."

"Are you crazy?" I blurted out. "What part of 'the police may try to arrest you at any moment' didn't you understand?"

"Look," she said, with more than a little heat, "I've got to be there. If I'm not, the whole thing could turn out to be a disaster. It's my theater and my responsibility," she finished firmly.

"I don't believe this," I said. "What about your daughter? What's going to happen to her if you get arrested?"

"Your mother and I discussed that possibility tonight. She's having a lawyer come over tomorrow morning so I can sign a power of attorney and emergency custody order. Just in case I . . . have to go away for a while."

"Custody order? Who's going to be the guardian?"

"You are," Jenny said.

I heard a small strangling sound come out of my throat in lieu of the words I didn't have.

"Actually, your mother said she'd be the temporary guardian," Jenny said evenly. "I just wanted to see your reaction."

I shook my head. Even at a time like this, the girl could make jokes. "Okay, I guess," I said, "but it's still crazy for you to show yourself in public. Especially at a place where the police are bound to be looking for you. Hell, even your own mother was smart enough to know when to go and hide from the cops."

Jenny looked like I'd just slapped her. I regretted the words as they left my tongue.

Jenny's large, lovely eyes narrowed as she said, "So. You know about that, huh?"

I shrugged and sighed. "Yeah."

Jenny looked away from me. "It's all right. It's okay that you know. Maybe now you'll understand."

"What do you mean?"

Still not looking at me, she said, "Growing up, all I ever wanted to know was why my mother left Tony and me. Leaving my father, that I could understand, thoughtless bastard that he's always been. But I could never come up with an excuse for her to abandon her own children. So when it came to be my turn to run away from Malcolm, I went to Hollywood. One of the few things I knew about my mom was that she had been an actress. I guess I had this stupid thought that if I was going to find her anywhere, it would be there. I didn't, of course. It wasn't until a few years ago that I found out about how she ran off with Malcolm's old partner, Tony Worthington. My brother's named after him, you know."

"I kind of figured that one out," I said.

She looked at me then, with a fierce determination burning in her deep blue eyes. "So I've decided that I'm not going to be like my mother anymore. I could never, ever abandon my daughter, and I'm through with running. Now and forever."

I heard myself sigh. "Look, I've had a certain amount of experience with stubborn women. I was spawned by one. And I can tell when I've met one it's useless to argue with. So how about I save us all a lot of trouble and just lock you up in the basement until all this is over?"

"You could try," Jenny said simply, "but the last guy who tried to boss me around wound up singing soprano."

"I'm not that musically inclined," I said. "Okay, if you're bound and determined to go, then all I can do is try to get all this figured out by tomorrow night. You don't believe in making things easy for a guy, do you?"

"Hey, if the son of Captain Midnight can't help a girl out, who can?" she asked with a wry smile on her full lips. It faded as she said seriously, "Look, I know you're just trying to do what's best. For me, and for my daughter. And don't ever think that I don't appreciate all this. All my life I've had to fend for myself, and it's difficult for me to accept that someone wants to help me for a change. But it's still my life, after all is said and done, and I've got to do things the way I think best."

Jenny got up slowly and came to me, bending over and giving me a soft kiss on the cheek. "Goodnight, Captain," she said before quietly walking out. I heard the door to my old bedroom close softly behind.

I sat there for a while, not quite feeling up to the task of getting undressed for bed. Finally I stirred myself to action. When I took my keys out of my pocket, I held the small brass medallion up to the light, looking at the symbol of the clock with its hands on the hour of midnight—a constant reminder that a clock was always ticking somewhere.

I was running out of time.

CHAPTER TWENTY-TWO

Jenny Chance woke me up with the three little words that every man loves to hear: "Breakfast is ready."

I opened my eyes and looked around, discovering myself alone on the foldout couch in the den. Jenny knocked on the door and said, "Hey, we girls have been slaving away in the kitchen. Are you getting up? Or do I have to send in the Marines?"

"I'm up," I called back. "I, uh, just need a moment. I'll be right down."

"Better hurry. I think your mother said something about giving your breakfast to the dog."

She would, too, I thought. "On my way," I said. I waited a bit to let the coast clear, then got up and peeked out my door. I made a dash across the hall for my old room; the bed had been made and all signs of occupancy erased. I put on a set of workout sweats from the closet and padded down to the kitchen.

The welcome aroma of pancakes hit me before I made it to the stairs, and as I turned the corner of the landing I was greeted by the sight of Mom, Jenny, and Angelina all pitching in to set the table. Mom spotted me first. "Well, I guess we don't need to get the garden hose out after all. Come get a plate, kiddo, before it gets cold."

Jenny and Angelina were dressed in their matching theater outfits, but they both looked fresh for the day. Mom, of course, looked like she was ready for high tea, dressed in gray with her best pearls. Her Majesty gave me the up-and-down once-over.

"Geez, kid. What's with your hair? You didn't stick something in a light socket again, did you?"

"Sorry. I thought speed was preferable to proper grooming."

Mom turned to Jenny. "I tried to bring him up better. Oh, how I tried."

"Well," Jenny said with a smile, "I think you did a fine job."

Mom and I traded looks. "Thank you, dear," Mom said. "I attribute it all to regular beatings. Now, shall we?"

Angelina came up to me and said, "You sit with me," taking my hand and leading me to the table, where there was a vase of Mom's freshly cut roses.

"Okay, angel, let's see some big-girl manners," Jenny said to her daughter as she helped her with her plate.

"That goes for you, too," Mom said to me from across the table.

I poured syrup on the blueberry pancakes. "Has our guest informed you of her plan to show up at the Castle tonight? I was hoping you'd be so kind as to explain the proper procedure for hiding out from the authorities."

Mom took a sip of her coffee. "Jenny and I have discussed that already. And while I can't approve of her proposed actions, I cannot fault the reasoning behind them."

I managed not to spit out my own sip of coffee. "What?"

"It's Jenny's decision, son. I can't say I wouldn't do the same if I were in her shoes."

My eyes bounced back and forth between Jenny and Mom, seeing a certain resemblance in their eyes.

Angelina looked up at her mother. "We go to work today?"

"No, baby," Jenny replied, "but Mommy has to go to work later tonight."

And hopefully not to jail. I raised my cup back to my lips and said quietly into it, "Damn female conspiracy."

"What did you say, dear?" Mom inquired sweetly.

"I said, 'Darn, no camomile tea.' "

Angelina announced seriously, "That's not what he said, Mom."

Now I was getting it from the single-digit age bracket. I sighed loudly. "All right, I offer unconditional surrender. So that gives us what? Less than one day to wrap this case up and hand all the guilty parties over to the authorities? I guess I'd better get started."

Mom glanced at her watch. "Indeed. I've already called the police property warehouse. James will meet you there at nine to look over the physical evidence. Then you'll have to arrange to meet all the parties involved for interviews. I suggest you start with Anthony Sterling. It's possible he's still in custody."

I was finishing my pancakes and silently juggling my thoughts. I definitely wanted to talk to Tony, that was for sure, but I also wanted to have a private and hopefully revealing chat with Bruce. I suddenly noticed Angelina was smiling at me while whispering into her mother's ear. "Something I should know?" I asked.

Angelina squealed and giggled, while Jenny gave me her sunburst of a smile. "It seems that some people think you're a nice boy. But I can't tell you who thinks that, because it's a secret," she said as Angelina playfully tried to put her hands over her mother's mouth.

We were interrupted by Paul Merlyn's voice through the intercom system. "A Mr. Malcolm Sterling is here. Without appointment," Paul added dryly.

Jenny's eyes widened. Mom's face took on its predatory cast. "Well, well, well," Mom purred. "How interesting." She picked up the phone and dialed Paul's extension. "Good morning, Paul. Has Mr. Sterling told you why he's here? . . . I see. Well, tell him that he's come at an inopportune moment, but we shall accommodate him presently. In other words, tell him to sit down and stay put. Nicely, of course." Mom hung up and said, "All Malcolm told Paul was that he was here on an urgent matter."

Jenny pulled Angelina over to her lap. "Urgent? Like what?"

"We'll find out," Mom assured her. To me, she said, "Looks like your first job of the day, kiddo."

I looked down at my sweats. "Uh, you mean now?"

"Certainly. Malcolm Sterling responds much better to his fellow men, or haven't you noticed? So you're elected. We'll watch from the back room."

"Great."

Angelina kept looking from her mother to mine. Mom said to her, "Angelina, dear? Would you like to keep Beowulf company upstairs for a while? The grown-ups have some work to do."

"Beywoof?" Angelina asked happily. "Mom, can I?"

"You bet, baby," Jenny said. "Let's go get him."

"Give us five minutes to get set," Mom said to me.

The ladies joined hands, Angelina in the middle, and went out the back. I finished my coffee and tried to get my thoughts in order. Not only was I going to have to interview Malcolm Sterling in a state of undress, but Mom was going to be listening and watching, courtesy of the pinhole cameras and microphones in her office that she could monitor from the back room.

When I figured I had stalled long enough, I went into Mom's office and sat on the throne. I opened the drawer that held the phone and called Paul. "Tell Mr. Sterling that Mr. Wilder will see him now."

"Of course, Mr. Wilder," Paul said with a sarcastic undertone. The door from the reception area opened and admitted Malcolm Sterling, who stopped in his tracks as he caught sight of me behind the desk. "Good morning, sir," I greeted him casually.

Malcolm's eyes showed surprise, but he quickly recovered. "I, uh, am sorry if I've come at a bad time. I didn't know what else to do."

"Quite all right. Please, have a seat. Sorry I'm not dressed, but you said you have an urgent matter?"

Malcolm limped to the nearest chair and lowed himself down with his cane. "It's my son," he said. "I think he may have been kidnapped."

I blinked. "Tony? Kidnapped? Wait a minute. The last I knew, he was still in jail."

"I know," Malcolm said earnestly. "I was going to try to bail him out yesterday, but later I thought . . . well, I thought that he might be safer in there. After what happened at his office. But when I went to see him this morning, the officers at the jail said he was bailed out last night."

"When? And by who?"

"I don't know!" Malcolm said, his face twisting. "All they could tell me was that he was released. At about ten o'clock last night. Mr. Wilder, if my son got out of jail, he would have called me, at least. I know."

"Did you check with Katerina?"

He nodded. "Yes. I called Tony's house as soon as I found out. She says she hasn't seen him. But I think she was lying."

I leaned back in Mom's leather chair. Ten o'clock was roughly the same time Mom and I were talking with Katerina's uncle Georgi. "Why do you think Katerina lied to you?"

Malcolm gripped his cane until his knuckles went white. He locked his brown eyes on mine and said, "Because I think that somehow she's mixed up in this. Her or that family of hers. And now the police have told me that they're looking for Jenny, too."

I tried to look convincingly surprised. "They are? Who told you that?"

"Some woman policeman," Malcolm said dismissively. "She said that they just want to talk to Jenny about what happened last Sunday at the theater. But I think there's a lot more to it than that."

"Mr. Sterling, when did you last speak with Tony?"

"Yesterday."

"And what did you talk about?"

"I told him that he needed to be a man, stand up for himself and tell the truth. And I made him promise me that he would. But he didn't really tell me anything."

And right after that, I thought, he goes and tells the police that it was Jenny who must have murdered the man in the alley. "Mr. Sterling? You do know that Katerina told us yesterday that she doesn't want us working on your son's case anymore, don't you?"

Malcolm looked shocked. "That proves it! Don't you see?"

"See what?"

Malcolm shook his head impatiently, then explained carefully, as if to a child, "Don't you see? If that woman my son married was on the up-and-up, she wouldn't have gotten rid of you. She only did that because she has something to hide. Something she thought you might find out."

"Possibly," I admitted. "But even if that's the case, we still can't work on behalf of your son at this point." I wasn't about to admit that we were already working for his daughter.

"Mr. Wilder, please. You found my son once. Do you think you could do it again? For me?"

"Well, uh, certainly we could try," I said slowly. "But as we told his wife when she hired us, Tony is an adult. If he wants to go and hide, then that's really his business as long as he isn't breaking any laws. Come to think of it, if someone is out to get him, then no one could blame him for hiding."

"But he should have come to me!" Malcolm insisted, then lowered his head until it almost rested on his cane. "And if you're right . . . oh, God . . . it may be too late."

I remembered Tony's words from the first night I met him: *They're going to kill me.* "Mr. Sterling," I said gently, "if you want, we'll try to find him again, sir."

He raised his head, hope in his eyes. "Cost is no object," Malcolm said firmly. "And I really do believe my son is in danger. Someone has tried to kill him, for God's sake! So you'll take the case?"

"Well, sure."

"And you can start right away?"

I kept myself from looking down at my attire. "As soon as possible."

Malcolm leaned back in his chair with relief. "Good. You'll call me and let me know how you're doing?"

"Certainly, sir. Now, if you'll just stop by our receptionist's desk, you can fill out a standard contract. I'll get on it this morning."

Malcolm pushed himself to his feet. He turned toward the door, then stopped and looked back. "You don't happen to know where Jenny is, do you?"

"No, sir," I lied. "Why?"

"Because I couldn't help but notice how close Jenny and that woman my son married were acting over at the jail yesterday. It makes me wonder if there's not something going on between the two of them," he said darkly. "You might want to look into that as well." He nodded to me, limped to the door, and let himself out.

As the door shut behind him, I let out a breath I didn't know I was holding in. I hit the intercom button for Paul's desk. "Paul? Have Mr. Sterling fill out a contract. Standard rate. And make sure he has my cell number." I clicked off the intercom and went to the back room, where I found Mom and Jenny over by the large-screen TV. "Brilliant performance, kiddo," Mom said as I entered.

"Really?"

"No, not really. But at least we have more puzzle pieces to play with."

I looked to Jenny. The color was up in her face, and her full lips were compressed into a stern line. "That bastard," she hissed. Then she took a breath and sighed. "I'm sorry. But to sit here while he practically says I'm a murderer, or worse. And the way he talked about Katerina!"

"Um, actually, he may have something there," I said. "You know her uncle Georgi? Mom and I definitely get a Russian godfather feeling about him."

Jenny blinked. "Georgi? Really? But what's he got to do with anything?"

"A good question. One that we won't answer sitting around in our underwear," Mom said, looking pointedly at me. "And I

180

couldn't help but notice that Malcolm Sterling didn't engage our services to find you, my dear," Mom said to Jenny.

"Why should he?" Jenny said. "He never went looking for me when I ran away from home."

I escaped the awkward moment by announcing, "I'm off for the shower. Sounds like I have a day ahead of me."

"I'll go get Angelina," Jenny said.

As Jenny and I walked together through the kitchen toward the stairs, she said, "God, he's really looking old now."

"Malcolm?"

"Yeah. He's hardly ever used that old cane. I always thought that he never wanted anyone to see any kind of weakness in him."

"What's wrong with his legs?"

Jenny shrugged. "He's been that way all my life. I once caught a glimpse of him when I was a kid. Made the mistake of running into his room before he got his pants on. Old Malcolm's legs are pretty ugly; he's got a ton of scar tissue. Not only did I get spanked for coming in unannounced, but I had nightmares afterward."

As we reached the top of the stairs, Jenny called out, "Angel? Come out, come out wherever you are."

"In here, Mom," we heard from the bathroom, where we found Angelina and Beowulf. Angelina was giving the dog a good brushing—with my hairbrush. "Okay," I said. "Everybody out. I need to get presentable."

Angelina carefully put my brush back on the counter and said, "Come on," to Beowulf, who obediently got up and followed her out. Jenny fell in behind her, saying to me over her shoulder, "She's got the boys following her already."

Once alone, I ran through my shower-and-shave routine quickly. I was about to remove the bandage from my left hand but suddenly thought of a potential use for it and kept it on. When I came out of the bathroom, I was surprised to find Mom waiting for me in my old room.

"I can dress myself, you know," I said.

"Ah. But can you take care of yourself?" she asked seriously. When I didn't answer, she continued, "What did you think of Malcolm Sterling's statements this morning?"

"Bad news. Especially as this might make Tony difficult to talk to again if he's run off and hidden somewhere."

"More important, what did you think of his theory concerning Katerina and Jenny?"

"What are you getting at?"

"We have to be prepared for the possibility that Jenny may, indeed, be responsible for a homicide. And maybe more."

"You still think she's a suspect?"

Mom looked at me levelly. "Of course. Despite the fact that I personally like her, there's some compelling evidence that points to her."

"Then why did you allow me to bring her over here in the first place?"

"My concern now is for Angelina. Abigail Glass is going to come over today with the papers to appoint me guardian ad litem in case of emergency." Mom folded her arms and displayed a look with no room for mercy. "Even if that emergency turns out to be the fact that I have to turn her mother over to the police."

■

CHAPTER TWENTY-THREE

Mom left me to get dressed in the dark blue suit and dark turtleneck I kept there while having even darker thoughts. As much as I didn't like it, I couldn't escape the fact that my mother, the smartest person on the planet, could well be right about Jenny Chance. Dressed, and with my handgun and briefcase, I went back downstairs.

I stopped at my desk in the back room and checked my phone messages. Then I wished I hadn't. My one recorded ca' came from Detective Lori Banks, and it went, "Wilder? Y call me as soon as you get this. We have to talk," followe her cell phone number. I made a note of the number ar cided I'd get myself away from the office before I cal' back. I noticed that I had forgotten to shut my compu' the night before, and as I tapped the keys the screen the copy of the newspaper report Roland Gibson ! I took another look at the photographs of Jenny' Anthony Worthington as Mom and Jenny hersel' back room.

"Good," Mom said. "I see you haven't left have Jenny give Katerina a call and see if we want you to listen in."

I waited as Jenny went over to Jim B' call. Mom and I picked up other exter heard Katerina's, "Hello?"

"Kat? It's Jenny."

"Jenny! Are you all right? I've been worried about you and Angelina."

"We're fine, Kat. Listen, I heard that Tony got out of jail. Do you know where I can get hold of him?"

Silence. Then, "Oh, Jenny. I am so sorry. I cannot tell you."

"Kat, it's really important-"

"I know," Katerina said quickly, "but I cannot tell you. I am so sorry."

"Please, Katerina? If not for my sake, for my daughter's? The police are after me, and Tony is the only one who can help."

Another pause. "Jenny, listen. Don't tell anyone. Not a word, do you promise?"

"I do, Kat. I do."

Katerina's voice dropped almost to a whisper. "Tony called last night. He told me not to worry and that everything is going to be all right. But he needed me to go and make a bail for him, to get him out of jail. He told me how to get the money from the savings. But then he said that I will not see him after he gets out and that he has to go away for a while. But when he comes back, everything will be fine. Better than fine, he said. But for now I must not speak to anyone or tell anyone I have heard from him."

Mom was writing something down. She tore off a sheet of paper and handed it to Jenny.

Jenny glanced at the paper and said, "Did Tony tell you to get rid of the detectives you hired?"

"Yes," Katerina said. "He said I must not speak to anyone. Including you and my uncle Georgi. But I do not know why he would say such a thing."

"Okay, Kat. Thanks," Jenny said. "Look, since I think I may be in trouble, would you do the same for me? Not tell anyone we spoke?"

"Of course," Katerina responded. "And remember, Tony said everything was going to be all right. I'm sure he meant that for you and Angelina, too."

"Why? What do you think he meant?"

"He said to me that he found something. Something wonderful."

What the hell? I heard Jenny say, "Thank you, Katerina. I'll call again when I can."

"Are you all right, Jenny? Is Angelina all right?"

"We're fine. I'll call when I can. Good-bye."

We all hung up our phones. Mother spoke first. "Something wonderful?"

Jenny shook her head. "Beats me." She put her elbows on the desk and buried her face in her hands. "Oh, God. What is that man up to now?"

Mom leaned over and placed her hand on Jenny's arm. "We'll just have to do our best to find out, won't we? Jason? I believe you have some work to do."

As I stood up and grabbed my briefcase, something flickered in the corner of my eye. I turned to see my computer screen, with its pictures of Angelique Sterling and Anthony Worthington, staring back at me. Something about those pictures bothered me, but whatever it was, the thought had fled as soon as it arrived. "Okay, I'm off to meet Jimmy at the police evidence warehouse," I said. "I'll keep in touch."

Mom said, "We'll hold down the fort here and bar the gates. Hopefully, the police won't show up and try anything stupid, but that may be asking too much of them, I know."

I smiled, saluted Her Majesty, and winked at Jenny. I went out with my head high, trying to exude the confidence that I certainly didn't feel. Once I made it outside, I was surrounded by fog, the kind River City is famous for this time of year—a perfect reflection of what was inside my own head at the moment.

I carefully piloted my Mustang over to the lower industrial side of town, grateful that I was heading opposite the incoming workday city traffic. By the time I arrived at the plain concrete warehouse that is the home of the police evidence repository, I noted that it was almost 9:30 in the morning and I was late meeting Jim Bui. I wrapped myself in my black raincoat, picked up my briefcase, and marched into the front reception area. Jimmy was lounging against the wall. "Sorry I'm late, Uncle Jim."

"No problem," he responded. "They've kept me stooging around here anyway. I asked for the evidence over half an hour ago. Any other leads show up lately?"

"Tony Sterling got bailed out last night, but no one's seen him since. He called his wife to say he'd be out of touch for a while, but not to worry. Which, of course, makes me worry."

Jimmy smiled thinly. "I hate to think of what would happen to me if I tried that with my wife."

I smiled in return. In a break with police tradition, Jim Bui had been married to the same woman his entire adult life. Knowing his wife, Mary, as I did, no man could have made a better choice.

The door next to the bulletproof glass in the far wall opened, and a lean, mean-looking older man in a police uniform called, "Someone here about evidence in case number 0310485?"

"Right here," Jimmy replied.

The officer gave us a pair of unwelcoming looks. "Okay. It's ready. Sign in." I followed Jimmy through the door, where we had to wait as the officer reviewed our identification and had us sign the logbook. We were then led to a small room with a single table where two brown paper bags stood next to a clipboard. The table also held a pair of boxes for dispensing both latex and cotton gloves for examining evidence. "Okay," the officer said. "Sign, date, and put the time down, then have at it."

While Jimmy signed us in again, I popped the stapled bags open. The first one contained a plastic bag that held a braid of copper wire, bare at both ends with a lump of electrical tape in the middle. Jimmy, finished with the paperwork, came over and nodded. "Hmm. If I had to guess, I'd say you hook up one end of the wire to a wall socket or something. The other end would go into something flammable."

"Like turpentine?"

He nodded again. "Sure. That would do it. That bit in the

middle probably creates enough impedance to let you get a safe distance away before the whole thing goes poof. Then I'd assume that the wires and tape melt to obliterate the device. Simple and elegant."

I opened my case and got out my camera and a ruler. I set the ruler next to the packages and snapped a few pictures. "Where are the turpentine cans?" I asked the officer lounging against the wall.

He shrugged. "Maybe getting printed. I dunno."

I replaced the wires in the paper bag and opened the next one. Peering in, I saw the .45 Colt pistol lying inside. Jimmy and I slipped our hands into cotton gloves—I had to wrestle mine over the bandages on my left hand—and Jimmy lifted the gun out.

As he held it to the light, I could see that someone had spent some time trying to make the basically ugly handgun into a showpiece. The blueing on the metal parts was deep and rich, and the grips appeared to be genuine ivory with a small golden eagle etched on either side. The gun showed a couple of nicks and scratches here and there, but overall it looked close to pristine. A plastic cable tie ran through the barrel and out the ejection port to make sure no one could load and fire the thing. Jimmy frowned as he pulled the slide back as far as the cable tie would allow and peeked in the chamber.

"What? What do you see?"

"Funny," he murmured. "But I can't get a better look."

"Oh. No problem," I said. I got my key ring out and opened up the little utility tool. Just as our officer friend said, "What the hell are you doing?" I cut through the plastic tie, freeing the gun's action.

"Hey! You can't do that!"

I batted my eyes at the officer. "Really? Oh. Gee whiz, sorry and stuff. But seeing how it's already done." I shrugged helplessly.

The officer levered himself away from the wall and hurried over, but not before Jim Bui had the gun fieldstripped. He laid the barrel, slide, magazine, and frame out on the table like puzzle pieces.

"Now you put that back the way you found it!" the officer demanded.

Jimmy smiled. "Certainly," he said, nodding to me to take some picturers. I did, and that's when I noticed that, in contrast with the rest of the weapon's pieces, the exposed barrel was a lighter color. I finished with my photography, and Jimmy put the pistol back together. I took some shots of the gun in its assembled form as well.

Jimmy and I packed up, thanked the officer for his time, getting ignored in return, and walked out into the fog-shrouded morning. A few feet away from the door, Jimmy asked, "Did you see it?"

"The barrel? Yeah. It didn't seem to match the rest of the gun."

"That's because it didn't. Someone, somewhere along the way, swapped barrels. Not unusual in itself, really, but that's usually done when you've worn your gun out. That weapon has hardly been used."

"Were you able to dig up any information using the serial number I gave you?"

Jimmy shook his head. "Yes. I was able to trace the numbers you gave me through the Colt company. That led me to a local gun shop. They weren't happy about having to go back through their records to the 1960s, but they did. That gun was sold to one Angelique Sterling."

"Ah. That's the name of Malcolm Sterling's wife."

"From the look of the weapon, it was probably a present for her husband," Jimmy said.

We'd stopped by my car. I said to Jim, "Okay. Well, I'm off to do some sleuthing."

"And I've got interviews on some other cases lined up," Jimmy said. "But if you need anything else, just call."

Jimmy went to his car as I got into the Green Hornet. Remembering my telephone message from Detective Banks, I reluctantly got out my phone and dialed her number. When she answered, I greeted her cheerily. "Good morning, Detective. This is Jason Wilder. Sorry it took me a while to get back to you."

"Cut the crap, Wilder," Banks said shortly. "I just need you to tell me one thing."

"Well, certainly, Detective. What's that?"

"Tell me why I'm not arresting you right now."

CHAPTER TWENTY-FOUR

Arrest me? What for?" I demanded.

"Let's start with felony breaking and entering and move on to assault and battery, to put it in civilian terms," Lori Banks said.

My jaw dropped. "Okay," I said reasonably. "Who says I committed a 459 followed by a 240 and 242?" I deliberately employed the California Penal Code designations for burglary and assault and battery just to show I could use cop-speak as well as she could.

"We talked with Bruce Roberts," Banks said. "He tells us you and some other guy broke into the Castle Theater, then assaulted him. You want to tell me why you did that?"

Damn. "What else did Bruce say?" I asked.

"Hey, I'm asking the questions here," she snapped.

"And I'm not answering them until I get a clearer picture."

"Look, you want to avoid a whole lot of trouble? You tell me everything you know. Especially about that Jenny Chance woman."

Ah, the picture got a bit clearer. Detective Banks was trying the old squeeze play, telling me I was in big trouble, then using that as leverage to try to get me to talk to her. Well, screw that.

"Forget it," I said. "You're barking up the wrong tree. But if you want to start acting nice, I do have an angle you could be working on. A foreign angle, in a manner of speaking."

"Forget it, Wilder. I don't make deals."

"Oh, really? What was that you just tried to do with me?

Telling me you want to arrest me and then asking me for information. Shame on you, Detective."

For a moment, I thought I'd pushed too many of her buttons. There was an ominous silence on the phone, then she said, "All right, you want to play games? Fine. I want you to come downtown. Let's see how you like it in an interrogation room."

I changed tactics. "Sorry, Detective."

"What?"

"Sorry," I repeated. "I shouldn't have talked to you that way. And I apologize."

There was another silence, and I could almost hear Banks's brain grinding to a halt. Before she could recover, I said, "And I do have some information on that Russian angle. You might want to take a look at one Georgi Pakhomov. He's Tony Sterling's wife's uncle. Does that make him an uncle-in-law? Anyway, he's a really interesting character. You might want to get to know him."

"Where does he fit in?" she asked.

"I'm not sure, but if I had to make a guess, he's connected to the victim from last Sunday somehow. You might want to look into that."

"But what do you know about Jenny Chance?" she insisted.

I'd pushed my luck with the law enough for one day. I started blowing into the tiny speaker on my phone, saying between quick breaths, "Sorry . . . you're breaking up . . . can't hear you," and terminated the call.

I exhaled for real after that, feeling like I'd just run a marathon. Playing games with a detective with no apparent sense of humor was dangerous. I pulled out my car keys. The brass disc with its clock-face symbol was a reminder that I seemed to be running out of time. Grimacing, I fired up the engine and decided on my next stop of the day.

I aimed the Mustang in the direction of River City General Hospital and drove through the lightening midmorning fog. My watch told me that it was now approaching 10:30, and the flow of traffic had slowed to a crawl. Just because I was in a hurry, I thought.

I finally arrived at the hospital, then spent quite a bit more time trying to wheedle the location of Detective Walter Dolman's room out of the first-floor reception staff. They were understandably reticent about giving out the location of a police officer wounded in the line of duty, but I managed to convince them to call his room and say I wanted to see him. Rather to everyone's surprise, Detective Dolman agreed.

I made my way to his private seventh-floor room and was admitted by a uniformed officer who looked to be on the verge of retirement. I found Walter Dolman sitting up in the hospital bed, ominous wires trailing off to a machine close by. "Hey, Detective Dolman! You're looking well, sir," I greeted him.

He looked up from his newspaper and said over his reading glasses, "Uh-huh. And you're a damn liar. What are you doing here?"

Truthfully, his normally dark features looked a bit grayish, but his deep brown eyes were wide awake. "Why, Detective Dolman! I'm shocked. And here all I wanted to do was see how one of River City's finest was faring after his heroic ordeal."

"That's why you come in here waving your poor little bandaged paw around? Or are you trying to remind me that I owe you something?"

I helped myself to one of the guest chairs. "What? This?" I asked, holding up my injured hand. "Why, it's nothing, sir. I was just happy that I could be of some small assistance while you were all on fire and such. Think nothing of it."

Dolman grinned ruefully and took off his glasses. "Cut the crap, son. It's bad for my blood pressure."

I sat there doing my best to look wide-eyed and innocent while holding my left hand up in a casual fashion. Dolman sighed and said, "Okay. Let's get this over with. What are you after?"

"How about some conversation between friends? Like, oh, let's say, everything you've got on the Sterling matter."

Dolman grinned again. "Conversation, huh? Okay. You go first."

I did, telling him everything I knew about the case—except that Mom and I were harboring Jenny and her daughter, of course. When my story ground to a halt, Dolman said, "Damn. Tony Sterling goes and gets himself out on bail, and now he's skipped out? Or do you think his dad is right and somebody grabbed him?"

"I don't know," I admitted. "First it looks like he's involved in an attempted arson at the Castle Theater. Then he's a homicide suspect. Then he tries to point the finger at his sister Jenny while at the same time someone puts a deadly booby trap in his office. After that, he gets out of jail and disappears, telling his wife it's all going to be okay and that he's found 'something wonderful.' So you tell me; I get dizzy just trying to keep it all together."

"But the sister has disappeared, too," Dolman said carefully.

"Yeah. So tell me, how bad does it look for her? What have you guys got?"

"Well, we got the gun. The sister's prints show up on the magazine, and there's a partial print of hers on the slide. The only other prints on the gun belong to Tony."

"That figures, since he had it when I caught up with him."

"And Banks told me recently that he spilled his guts and said that the only reason he took the gun was to cover up for his sister. He now says she did the deed."

"Did Tony say he saw Jenny shoot the guy?"

"No," Dolman said. "Just that he found the guy on fire, recognized the gun, then saw his sister right there. He never said he saw her pull the trigger, and by now it's way too late to do a gunshot residue test on Jenny Chance, providing we catch up with her. Her disappearing like that looks real bad, though."

"Yeah," I agreed. "I guess it does at that. What about that shotgun booby trap thing we found in Tony's office?"

Dolman rubbed his chest as he spoke. "That was a piece of work. Everything was homemade. The barrel was a standard plumber's pipe, and the projectiles were a cluster of fishing weights. It was packed with a mixture of black powder and the stuff they put into emergency road flares. That's why it burned so badly."

"Damn," I said reverently.

"You're telling me?" Dolman asked dryly.

"Sorry."

"Yeah. Me, too. Sorry I didn't let you go in the door first."

When I didn't respond, Dolman said, "Aw, hell. I didn't mean that."

"I know." We lapsed into an uncomfortable silence, then Dolman asked, "You think there's something to Banks's Russian angle after all?"

"Something? Yes. What? I'm not sure. And speaking of the good Detective Banks, could you get her off my back? One wounded soldier to another?"

Dolman did laugh then. "You're on your own for that one, son. When 'Pit Bull' Banks gets her teeth into something, she doesn't let go. But I will ask her to give you a little more rope so you can go ahead and hang yourself. As a matter of fact, she said something about dropping by and seeing me this morning."

I shot to my feet. "Okay, it's been great, but I have to be going now. Take care, Detective."

"You, too, son. You, too."

In my haste to flee before the threatened arrival of Lori Banks and my desire to get away from the cloying hospital smell, I almost missed an opportunity. I stopped just shy of the door, turned, and wagged my fingers, the bandaged ones, at Dolman. "Ah, Detective, I forgot to ask about one tiny little thing. What did you guys turn up from the search warrant at Tony's office?"

Dolma smiled, somewhat bitterly, and said, "Now, you know I can't talk about that."

"Nonsense. I know good and well that search warrants are a matter of public record, so unless you got a judge to slap a seal on it, you're just saving me the trouble of looking it up at the courthouse after it gets filed. Think of this as giving your rescuer a sneak preview."

Dolman looked at me suspiciously. "You sure you're not a lawyer?"

"No, sir. I work for a living."

I got a dry laugh out of that one. "Okay," Dolman agreed. "The geek squad ran through Tony Sterling's computer hard drive. Seems like he went and made himself a deal that turned out pretty bad."

"What kind of deal?"

"You familiar with what's called a Nairobi scam?"

"Well, sure. That's getting to be an old one. Wait a minute. You don't mean?"

Dolman nodded. "Yep. Only this one had a little twist to it. Looks like Mr. Tony Sterling made a deal with someone who called himself a representative of Prince Kashulah of the Republic of Benin. There's a string of e-mails where Tony and this guy discuss the possibility of Tony investing $850,000 in cash."

"Cash? You're kidding? What happened then?"

"What do you think? Apparently this mystery man agreed to meet Sterling and relieve him of all that excess money. I understand there's a flurry of e-mails from Tony after the so-called representative disappeared. Along with all that cash money."

I shook my head. "But where did Tony Sterling get his hands on that kind of money? In cash, no less?"

Dolman shrugged, then winced. Apparently his wounds still gave him some trouble. "Beats me. But it is interesting, isn't it?"

"Yeah. Really interesting. Okay, Detective. Thanks for the chat. Hope you feel better."

"I intend to," he said. "Starting right after you leave."

I smiled and beat a hasty retreat in the hopes of avoiding Banks. When I got to the first floor, I hunted up a washroom, where I used my trusty little utility tool to cut away my bandages now that I didn't need them for a passport to Dolman's goodwill.

I washed my lightly grilled hand throughly and painfully, then gingerly dried it.

By the time I made it back to my car, the fog had lifted into a low ceiling over the city, obscuring the tops of the buildings. Feeling I had secured a tentative reprieve from the police, I decided that it was now time for an intimate conversation with Bruce Roberts.

As I drove to the theater, I thought about how little I, or anyone else for that matter, knew about Bruce. I figured that if I didn't catch up with him at the Castle, I'd try a little computer research, but with a common name like the one he claimed to possess, it would take a while to narrow a search.

I found a parking space on the seventh floor in the above-ground lot across from the theater and took a stroll to the Ketch Street side for a look. The Castle stood silent guard on the corner amid the swirl of vehicular and pedestrian traffic, and from my vantage I thought of how much it reminded me of a real castle. One that was under a siege.

I took the elevator down to street level and made my way to the drawbridge gates. Through the glass, I saw that the lobby was dark, but there were posters in evidence proclaiming that the Grand Masquerade Ball was to commence at eight o'clock tonight. I also saw that someone had festooned the lobby with strands of something that resembled white spiderwebbs, accentuating the haunted look.

I took the sidewalk around to Twelfth Street and flowed with my fellow pedestrians until I reached the back alley, where I ducked in. In the overcast light of day, this concrete valley appeared less inviting than ever. I looked up to the boarded-over windows of the Benson Hotel but didn't spot any signs of life; I wondered if Daniel Shaw was out and about somewhere or was still up there hiding out from the Reagans.

I went down the alley to the first graffiti-camouflaged metal door to the backstage area. Glancing left and right for possible observers, I took out my lock picks and went to work. It took a few minutes for me to manipulate the rusty old lock, but I was finally rewarded by its giving way slightly. I had to use the screwdriver portion of my utility tool to force the cylinder to turn the rest of the way.

I eased the door open and slipped in, trying to close it quietly behind me. The lights were dim, backstage. "Hello?" I called. "Anyone home?"

My response came in the form of heavy, stomping feet and the sudden impression that I'd been hit from the right by a truck. Before I could move, a pair of viselike arms clamped around my chest, pinning my own arms to my side as I was hoisted off the ground. Without thinking, I immediately threw all my weight arcing backward, then forced myself forward and down. The body leverage trick worked; my assailant was thrown over my left shoulder and came crashing down on the hard wooden stage, leaving me hunched over on all fours. I saw Bruce, flat on his back, shake himself and start to roll over and clamber to his feet.

I called out, "Bruce! It's me! Jason!"

The monster turned his head toward me and smiled. "I know," he said almost gently as he gathered himself for another charge.

CHAPTER TWENTY-FIVE

When you've had to do something thousands of times, you can get pretty fast at it. I had my revolver out and pointing at Bruce in a split second. The trouble was, he kept coming. He launched himself at me in a flying tackle; I sidestepped it with a smooth pivot, then assisted him on his flight path by whacking him on the back of his left shoulder with the flat of the gun. The shuffle pivot I used to get out of his way was another move I'd rehearsed ad infinitum, but the use of a gun as a club was not standard procedure, and I was glad Timmy and Jimmy weren't here to see that one. Bruce's dive flopped him noisily on the floor and sent him sliding almost to the edge of the curtain.

As he was pushing himself to his hands and feet, I shouted, "Damn it! Cut it out! I just want to talk!"

I watched as he grabbed the curtain to pull himself up and turned to face me again. "Now stop, damn it! I've got a gun here!"

I was treated to another one of Bruce's ugly smiles as he rumbled, "I've been shot before."

I raised the gun until it was lined up with his eyes. "Not by me, you haven't."

Bruce's face fell into a frown, an expression I definitely preferred. Pressing my temporary advantage, I said, "Look, I just came here to talk to you, and I don't think you getting your brains splattered all over her stage is going to make Jenny very happy. So what do you say?"

It seemed like an eternity as I stood there breathing hard with the shakes starting to hit me before Bruce shrugged, as if this were all no big deal. "Okay. So talk," he said.

"Great. Can we go and sit somewhere?" I asked, happy to note my voice didn't shake like my legs. Bruce shrugged again and pulled the curtain aside with an after-you motion of his free hand. I gave him a wide berth as I walked out the opening and made my way down the steps to the first-row seats. I chose the fourth chair over to collapse in, reholstering my gun in the process.

In the dimmed lights of the theater, I saw that Bruce had changed back into his black leather jacket and biker boots. "Where's Jenny?" he asked. "I haven't heard from her."

"She's fine," I answered, "but she and Angelina are in a safe place where no one can get to them."

"Says you," Bruce complained.

I sighed and took out my cell phone, punching in Mom's direct line. We exchanged hellos, and she asked, "How's it going?"

Looking at Bruce, I said, "It'll be a good day if I can keep from killing someone. Is Jenny close by?"

"Yes. Just a moment."

Jenny came on the line. "Jason? What's going on?"

"Would you be so kind as to tell Bruce to quit trying to kill me barehanded? It makes it difficult to have a conversation. I've got him right here." I handed my phone to Bruce, who took it and said, "Jenny? I've been worried . . . uh-huh . . . uh huh . . . Yeah, but he started it . . . Okay . . . How's Angelina? . . . Oh . . . Tell her I miss her, too . . . Tonight? . . . Good . . . Here," he said as he handed the phone back to me.

Bruce's expression had seemed to melt during the brief phone conversation, and I no longer felt in imminent danger of being stomped by him. I said into the phone, "Jenny?"

"Jason, what are you up to? Have you and poor Bruce really been fighting? Shame on you."

"Me? He was . . . oh, forget it. I just wanted to talk with him, that's all."

"Well, you two boys," Jenny said with emphasis on the last word, "kiss and make up, or go and buy each other a beer, or whatever. Just so long as you stop picking on him."

While Jenny was reading me the riot act, Bruce stood there looking smug. "Yes, ma'am," I said. "By the way, while I've got you on the phone, do you know where Tony would get his hands on close to a million dollars in cash?"

"Did you say million?"

"Yeah, as in roughly $850,000. According to the police, Tony recently lost that much to a con artist's scheme."

"No, I sure don't. Malcolm would know if anyone would."

"Why do you say that?"

"Because Father is a total control freak. Frankly, I was amazed when I learned that Tony took over the business. I never thought that Father would ever let him do anything by himself."

"Hmm. Okay. Do you think you might give Katerina another call to see if she could shed some light here?"

"Sure. Oh, your mother wants to talk to you again."

Her Majesty said, "What's all this about you fighting?"

"Relax. The war is over and a truce was declared. No casualties."

"Well, if there were any casualties, they had better be all on the other side. Or should I have James and Timothy schedule you for some more training? You've been looking a bit soft recently."

I kept myself from moaning at the thought. "Not to rapidly change the subject, but is there anything new on your side?"

"No, dear. I've been busy shopping."

"Shopping? Must be nice to be the boss of your own detective agency."

"Sometimes," Mom said breezily, "unless you count having to deal with problem employees. Speaking of which, what are you doing now?"

"Working," I said flatly.

"I see. Well, there's a first time for everything, I suppose. So I take it you won't be joining us for lunch? I think little Angelina was looking forward to seeing you again. You seem to be her new favorite fella. After Beowulf, of course."

I said good-bye, and closed my phone, and turned my attention back to Bruce. My heart rate had calmed down to its accustomed pace, but I was slightly vexed to see that Bruce showed no signs of recent exertion whatsoever.

"So," I began, "why are you here, anyway? Jenny said she doesn't even pay you."

I got another shrug. "I like it here."

"Uh-huh. Did you know Jenny kept a gun here?"

"No."

"I see. If you did happen to, say, catch someone breaking in here, what would you do?"

His lip twisted in a smile. "I think you know the answer to that."

"You wouldn't bother to get a weapon first?"

"What would I need a weapon for?"

It was my turn to shrug. Big and tough as he was, he did seem to have a point. "So the night the man was murdered in the alley, you didn't see or hear anything?"

"No."

"What did you do that night after you walked Jenny to her car?"

"I went home."

"And that is?"

"Where I live."

"Okay, I get the impression you're a bit on the shy side, but we'll let that pass for a moment. Why did you tell the police that I broke in here last night and assaulted you?"

"I didn't," Bruce answered. "I said that you broke in here and that little runt you brought with you assaulted me." Bruce lifted a massive, scarred hand and rubbed his wrist. "Did a good job, too."

"And you told the cops this why?"

"It was true. I don't owe you anything. Besides, it got them off the track from talking to me about Jenny. I didn't tell them she was with you."

"Okay. Good. Anything else weird happen here recently?"

"No. I stayed here all last night. Nothing happened."

I decided to stop questioning Bruce. He wasn't going to give up anything anyway. I got to my feet. "Okay. You've got my card with my cell phone number on it. Call if anything else happens around here. You going to be here tonight for the masquerade?"

"Sure. Jenny said she's coming tonight, too."

"Yeah. Against better judgment. I hope the cops don't decide to come calling at the same time."

Bruce gave me a smile that seemed to say that it would be a huge mistake for anyone to try to mess with Jenny Chance as long as he was around. Surprisingly, that made me feel better about her being here tonight. I started to make my way to the aisle, then stopped and said to Bruce, "What did you mean when you said you've been shot before? What happened?"

"I was shot," he said simply.

"And?"

"And then somebody died."

"Okay," I said. "By the way, I'm sorry I hit you. How's the shoulder?"

Bruce rolled his shoulder around as he said, " 'Tis not so deep as a well, nor so wide as a church door."

I shook my head. *"Hamlet?"*

His sneer told me I was wrong before he said, *"Romeo and Juliet."*

I turned and trudged up the aisle before Bruce could see my own smile. Monsters spouting Shakespeare was a new one to me. On my way to the exit I passed a fading mural that depicted a knight in battle with an enormous, fire-breathing dragon. I nodded a salute to the knight, feeling that we were kindred spirits.

I got to my car and spun it down to street level, where I paid my bail and slipped into traffic, inching my way to Tony Sterling's office. I really didn't have any idea what I might be able to find there; I didn't even know if I'd be able to get in. But at the moment, I had no other options—and nowhere else to go.

CHAPTER TWENTY-SIX

The hallway that led to Tony's office was barred with a flimsy strip of yellow CAUTION tape. A large portable fan was busy clearing the air at the doorway.

I slipped under the tape and walked down the hall to the office as if I knew what I was doing. Reaching the door, I looked around the corner and said, "Hello?" I repeated myself a bit louder—another fan was noisily doing its job from inside. There was plenty of light coming from the floor-to-ceiling window, even diffused as it was by the low-hanging clouds and mist outside. The carpets had been scrubbed, and there was a strong chemical smell on the machine-made breeze. I could see the black scorch marks on the rug where Detective Dolman's flaming bulletproof vest wound up, and I wondered why anyone had bothered with the cleaning. My hand began to hurt again, as if it had some kind of independent memory of the event.

In the outer office, everything had been removed from the surface of the secretary's desk. The drawers were open, and I spent a little time poking around in the bric-a-brac they contained, but I found nothing informative. It would have been too much to hope that the police search warrant team would have left anything as useful as an address book or a Rolodex behind. The computer had been disconnected, and all its parts were now on the coffee table near the couch.

The door to Tony's office was wide open, with the second fan placed just inside in an attempt to blow away the water that had soaked the place when the sprinklers had gone off. As I stepped over it, I couldn't help but remember, in vivid, red-toned flashback, the nightmarish event of the day before.

I could now see the marks on Tony's wide desk where the booby trap had been clamped, directly in line with the door. The office had been ransacked with typical police efficiency and disregard for personal property; all the drawers in the desk were open and in disarray, and the filing cabinets had their locks drilled out. I spent some time over by the files, randomly leafing though them, but it would take hours of concentrated effort to make sense of any of the documents, and I definitely had a limited amount of time here.

The closets were unlocked as well, and I had a moment of surprise when I saw what I thought was Daniel Shaw's "big white pipe" leaning inside. I was disappointed to find that the tall cylinder was nothing but a rolled-up sheaf of papers. I pulled them out and unrolled them on the desktop, not understanding what I was seeing at first. They were apparently blueprints, but they didn't make any sense to me until I spotted the address on the lower right side. It was the location of the Castle Theater.

I turned the papers sideways, and then I could make out the lines and grids. I could see where the stage was, and the audience seating area. I was about to roll the plans up again when I saw a faint circular indentation, roughly in the middle of where the stage would be. I was tempted to bring the blueprints with me but reluctantly decided, since theft is frowned upon, to get my little camera out of my briefcase instead. I had to do a bit of juggling as I laid the plans out on the floor, holding the ends down with a stapler on one side and a tape dispenser on the other, but I managed to shoot pictures of all the plans eventually.

I then spent a little time going through the drawers in Tony's desk and the credenza but found them to be both uninformative and downright boring, holding absolutely nothing of interest. The telephone was vexing; it was a nice modern one with no external answering machine for uninvited guests to play with. That left Tony's personal desktop computer. It had been soaked, but if the police forensics team had managed to make a copy of the hard drive, it should be still functional. I got out my cell phone, noting it was near 1:30 as I made my call.

Felix McQuade answered, "Now what?"

"I'm in the middle of a surreptitious ingress and could use a little help," I said.

"A syrup-covered what?"

"A breaking and entering," I clarified.

"Oh. I liked the way it sounded the other way you said it. Didn't sound like something that would screw up my probation and stuff."

"How quickly can you get to Twenty-first and Lighthouse?"

"I dunno. How bad do you need me?"

"Just get over here. It's the gold-colored glass building that looks like an anorexic pyramid. Come up to the fourteenth floor and go down the hall marked with the yellow tape until you reach the office where a fan is holding the door open. You can't miss it. Oh, and bring your bag of tricks."

"I didn't think you wanted me for my awesome looks," Felix said, and hung up.

I called Paul at the office and got Malcolm Sterling's cell phone number. Malcolm answered right away.

"Mr. Sterling? It's Jason Wilder."

"Did you find my son?" he asked expectantly.

"No, sir. Not yet. I'm over at his office right now, and I was wondering if you could give me his secretary's phone number."

"Heidi? Well, certainly. But I spoke with her myself today, and she hasn't seen him since last Friday. What are you doing at the office?"

"I was taking a look around to see if I could find any clues to Tony's whereabouts, although I don't think the police left much behind."

"I know," Malcolm said heavily. "I saw the place myself last night. My God, if Tony had come in there while that device was set . . ." His voice trailed off.

"Yes, sir. I was here when it went off. I know."

"You were? You were there with the police?"

"Yes, sir." I didn't bother to mention that I was damn near the victim of the blast that hit Dolman instead.

"What I can't understand is how anyone got in there in the first place," Malcolm continued. "According to Heidi, Tony's door had been locked all this week."

"Had she been here the whole time?"

"Yes. Well, during the day of course. I suppose someone could have come in while she was at lunch or on a break."

"I see. Well, it might be helpful if I could meet with her. She might know something that will help me find Tony."

"Of course. Let me give you her number."

I set my notebook on the desk, then made the mistake of sitting down in Tony's chair. The cloth upholstery apparently held the water from the sprinklers like a sponge, and I was instantly soaked through my pants. "I'm sorry," Malcolm said in response to my involuntary expression, "what did you say?"

"I said, 'luck.' As in we could use some right now," I said hastily.

Malcolm's pause led me to believe that I didn't cover up my expletive as well as I hoped, but he ignored my outburst and gave me Heidi's number. "Okay, thanks," I said. "I'll let you know if I turn up anything here. Oh, by the way, I wanted to have one of our experts come over and see if we can get into Tony's computer."

"Really? Can you do that?"

"Well, if the machine hasn't been ruined by the water from the sprinklers, then we should at least be able to find what the police came up with. I think it's worth a try."

"Very well. Call me if you find out anything."

"Yes, sir. I will." I hung up and pried my wet pants away from my gluteus, smiling ruefully at myself. The thought occurred to me that my sodden state reflected the nature of the detective business: You never know what you're going to wind up stepping in, or in this case sitting on. I decided to avail myself of one of the floor fans. With the current of air aimed at my backside, I dialed Heidi Mulligan's number. A rather breathless female voice answered, and I introduced myself. "I was hoping we could meet today," I wound up.

"Oh, of course," she said. "Oh, this is just so awful. Poor Mr. Sterling is going through hell right now."

"Yes, ma'am," I agreed, not certain which Mr. Sterling she was referring to. "Is there a good time and place we could meet?"

"Well, you could come over to my place, if you don't mind."

"Certainly. Is this afternoon all right?"

"Of course. I'll be happy to do anything that'll help, but like I told the police, I'm afraid I don't know very much."

"Well, in cases like this, sometimes the littlest things make a big difference. Let me have your address and I'll be over this afternoon."

Heidi Mulligan supplied the information, and I hung up. Then I spent over an hour waiting for Felix McQuade, tardy technical wizard. At least my miracle-fabric pants had a chance to dry out by then.

Felix paraded into the office and announced, "*Hola, compadre.* I have arrived."

He was dressed in his standard goth black, from trench coat with turned-up collar to wide-brimmed hat. "I'm surprised you made it past the security in the lobby," I said.

"*No problemo,*" he said as he unlimbered his black leather

backpack. "I'm like the Ghost Who Walks and stuff. I'm unseen and unheard. So what's the gig?"

I pointed to Tony's computer. "Just drain it dry and take whatever it has back to Her Majesty. Hopefully there'll be some useful information in it."

Felix bent over and examined the machine over his blue-tinted glasses. "I can tell you one thing right now," he said. "This sucker's got one too many wires coming out of it."

"Say what?"

Felix picked up a cable and showed me. "See this one? Connected to the splitter? Notice how it goes over to the wall and under the carpet."

We followed the strand to the floor where it disappeared between the carpet and the wall. By pushing down on the wet carpeting, I could follow by feel as the cable traveled around the wall and back of the credenza under the window. The wire made a reappearance as it went up and terminated in the back of a clock radio that faced the room. "Now, that's weird," Felix mused.

Not to me, not really. In the private investigation business, I've been hired to work on inside embezzlement jobs from time to time. In many of the cases, we would place surveillance cameras to monitor locations where suspected criminal activity occurred. I got out my key-ring utility tool, flipped the clock radio over and unscrewed the plates on the underside. In a couple of minutes I had the covering off, exposing a small pinhole video camera nestled along with the more mundane components.

"Whoa, dude," Felix said, "looks like someone wired this place up for sound and stuff. So who was the star of the show?"

The camera was aimed at whoever sat in Tony Sterling's chair, and I wondered who it was that set the camera up. Devices like this weren't hard to get hold of; they could be bought at almost any electronic equipment or security products store. Tony himself could have placed it there, if he thought that someone might have been sneaking in here and accessing his computer.

As a chill of excitement ran through me, I realized that it also could have photographed whoever had placed the deadly booby trap on the desk, catching the attempted murderer in the act.

CHAPTER TWENTY-SEVEN

I left Felix with the disc out of my camera and instructions to make blown-up copies of the blueprints I photographed, then got my car and headed out to Heidi Mulligan's house. On the way I remembered I wanted to call Katerina about the missing money. I found a place to pull over and dug her number out of my folder. After the second ring, a familiar faintly accented voice answered. "Hello?"

I was glad that I'd pulled the car over, as my surprise almost made me jump. "Georgi?"

"Ah, it is young Mr. Wilder, yes? You have some news for me?"

"Actually, sir, I have a number of reasons for calling. Approximately 850,000 reasons."

"Indeed?" he asked. "I find that a very interesting number of reasons. Very interesting indeed."

Aha. "I thought they might be. So tell me, would it be fair to say that those reasons I gave were your reasons?"

"You could say that, yes," Georgi said carefully.

"And would it also be fair to say that Anthony Sterling was somehow involved with those reasons?"

"You could say that, too. Now you must tell me, have you found anything . . . like those reasons?"

I decided that now would be a bad time to tell Georgi Pakhomov that, as far as I could see, his $850,000 worth of reasons appeared to be long gone. "Let's just say I may be getting close to an answer," I said.

"Well, let me tell you this," Georgi said. "If, say, all those reasons could be found, then a great deal of trouble could be avoided for a number of people. Do you understand what I say?"

"I believe I do, sir."

"Good. Just so long as we understand each other." He hung up without a further word.

I damn near threw my phone in disgust. From what I could now see, that idiot Tony Sterling went and lost a huge chunk of money that belonged to the local Russian mob guys. No wonder he'd been so desperate for cash lately, desperate enough to try some silly arson scheme probably to try to make up for a money-laundering scheme he screwed up. Only he ran into someone who seemed to want to protect the Castle at any cost. The fact that he was hiding out didn't surprise me, especially since someone had set a deadly trap in his office, but I again had to wonder about that "something wonderful" he told his Katerina he had found that was going to make everything all right again.

I'd followed my train of thought right past my turnoff to Heidi Mulligan's house and had to backtrack a bit. She had a place in the 4000 block of Eastwind Street, which contained some of River City's oldest and nicest residences. Heidi's place was a small, single-story redbrick home in the middle of the block with a sedate Chevrolet sedan parked in the driveway. She answered the door right away.

"Ms. Mulligan? I'm Jason Wilder," I said as I offered her my business card.

"Come on in," she said, stepping aside for me. Heidi Mulligan was a plump, pleasant-looking middle-aged woman with a crown of curly light brown hair and hazel eyes that were minimized behind her gold-toned glasses. She was wearing a flowered peasant dress that came almost to the floor. As I entered I heard a sharp, repetitive high-pitched barking coming from within the house. "Oh, I hope you don't mind dogs, Mr. Wilder," she said apologetically. "My little Andrew gets upset when I leave him in his room."

"No, I like dogs, as a matter of fact," I said. "And please call me Jason."

Heidi nodded, almost making it a curtsy. "Good. I'll go and let Andrew out, then, if you don't mind. Otherwise he'll just bark up a storm while we're trying to talk."

The front room was cozy, with a small fireplace and hardwood floors covered with rugs here and there, and crammed with enough Christian icons to fill a modest monastery. I soon heard the scampering of nail-studded paws as a fluffy white floor-level rocket shot into the room. I stuck my hand down as the dust mop of a dog sniffed and vibrated in apparent frenzy. "Now, Andrew, you be nice to our guest," Heidi urged the dog. To me, she said, "Please have a seat."

I did, and opened the notebook I brought with me. "Ms. Mulligan," I began, "I know you've spoken with the police, but could you tell me what you told them?"

"Of course," she said as she alighted on a well-stuffed, doily-covered couch. "It's like I told Mr. Sterling, Tony's father. Poor Tony's been in a state for weeks now. He's been very nervous, and staying late at the office after I went home. I called his father about it a couple of weeks ago."

"What did Malcolm say?"

"He told me that Tony was a grown boy and that he knew that he could come to him if he needed anything. Well, that really didn't reassure me, especially when those foreigners started coming around."

"Foreigners?" I prompted.

Heidi nodded decisively. "Yes. They started coming on Monday, the same day Tony first didn't show up for work. They were very rude, insisting that I tell them where Tony was. Well I finally told them that I was going to call security if they didn't leave, and they left. But that night, on my way to my car, I'm sure I saw one of them waiting around in the street outside."

"When was the last time you heard from Tony?"

"Last Friday," she said. "He was still at the office when I left.

I told him good night and said I would see him Monday, and he said he'd be there. But he didn't come in after all. I called his wife, and she told me that Tony was missing and that she was going to the police. Well, I immediately called Mr. Sterling, Tony's father, of course, and told him."

"What did he say?"

"That he would get to the bottom of it. That made me feel better. Mr. Sterling has always been a man who took care of business."

"Unlike his son?" I ventured.

"Well, I wouldn't want to be the one to say, but yes. I'm afraid Tony just didn't have his father's head for business. I worked for Mr. Sterling for years, and I can tell when business starts to drop off."

"Did Tony mention anything about needing money?"

"Well, he wasn't doing the business his father did, that's for sure," Heidi said, "but he didn't confide in me, either. And in the past few weeks, I had noticed how sickly he was starting to look; losing weight and such. I did mention that he should see a doctor, but he told me that he was just overworked. Although what he was working on was beyond me."

"Why do you say that?"

"Well, if he was working, then I should have been sending out letters and arranging meetings, shouldn't I? Whatever he was doing, he wasn't having me help out. I swear, some days I would just sit there with nothing to do but field phone calls and tell people Tony wasn't available. Andrew! Mind your manners!"

The dog had apparently decided that he didn't like me and was demonstrating his feelings by latching onto my pant leg with his needlelike teeth and shaking his head violently side to side. I reached down to try to disengage him, only to have him rear back and bark shrilly. "Andrew!" Heidi called again. "You be nice!" Heidi picked up the squirming bundle of fur. "Now, where were we?" she asked.

I kept an eye on Andrew, just in case he wiggled free. Obviously I didn't have Malcolm Sterling's way with animals. "When was the last time you were in Tony's office?"

"That was Friday as well," she said.

"The police said that you told them you don't have a key for the inner office door?"

"No. When I heard of that bomb in there, oh, my God, I just . . . well, I had no idea."

"Yes, ma'am," I said gently. "So, when the police came that Wednesday morning, did Malcolm Sterling call you before they arrived?"

"Yes. He told me that the police were on their way, and that I should let them in and then go home. But when they arrived, there was an officer who asked me a lot of questions."

"Questions like?"

"Oh, like you're asking. You know, when was the last time I saw Tony, and things like that. I was allowed to leave after that. Thank God, now that I look back."

"Was there anyone else you can think of who was trying to contact Tony Sterling?"

Heidi looked thoughtful for a moment, ignoring her struggling canine bundle. "Well, there was that Mr. Cooper. He's been calling quite a lot recently."

"Mr. Cooper? Who is he?"

"His name is Michael Cooper, and he's with the Haven Corporation."

It took me a moment to place where I'd heard that company's name before. "The firm that's involved with the Benson Hotel?" I asked.

"I don't know," Heidi said. "But Mr. Cooper was always insistent that I tell young Mr. Sterling that he was missing the deal of a lifetime, as he put it."

I stood up. "Okay, thank you, Ms. Mulligan. If I have any further questions, may I call you?"

"Of course," she said, standing as well and releasing Andrew in the process. He promptly attempted to reattach himself to my leg, but I managed to make my retreat.

Driving away back downtown, I felt hungry, tired, and overloaded. I'd missed lunch, again, and now I had one more person to try to contact. A call to the Haven Property Development Corporation informed me that their offices were located on Voyage Street, near Old River City. I'd have to get a move on to beat the five o'clock Friday exodus.

The building that housed the Haven Corporation was a straight-up rectangle of concrete lined with regular rows of windows. I parked in an adjacent lot and made my way up to the twenty-first floor, where I found a reception area that afforded a view of the gathering darkness and fog outside. I gave my card to a young and pretty receptionist; she seemed annoyed at my appearance so late in her workday, but she called for Mr. Cooper anyway and curtly informed me that he would see me shortly.

Michael Cooper appeared in the promised under five minutes, and he appeared "shortly"—he was about five-foot-six, not counting the expensive shoes. He was about my age, dressed in a modestly cut business suit that fit him like a shark's skin and went well with his sleek, dark hair and toothy, predatory smile. "Mr. Wilder? I'm Mike Cooper," he said, offering a firm handshake. "What can I do for you?"

"I'm trying to find Tony Sterling," I began, only to have Cooper cut me off.

"You and me both, pal. That guy's going to cost me a lot of money."

"Uh, could you explain that?" I asked.

Cooper looked at me sharply. "You're not a tax guy or anything, are you?"

I offered my identification. "No, I'm in private investigations. Like I said, I'm trying to find Tony Sterling, and I heard you were looking for him, too."

"You got that right. I've been trying to offer him the sweetest deal in the world, but the guy says he can't do it."

"Does this have to do with the Castle Theater?"

"Oh, yeah," he said. "I've got people lined up willing to put good money into demolishing that whole block to make way for some new developments. We've got the other property owners nailed down, but we need Sterling to come in on the other end. Unless he's trying to be smart and drive up the price, he's said he can't sell."

"Why not?"

Cooper made a helpless gesture with his hands. "Hell if I know. At first, Tony's all hot for the deal, then he says that he can't get his old man to relinquish the property. Something about a legal entanglement or something. But that's ridiculous."

"Why's that?"

"I checked into it. The property the theater's on is actually in old man Sterling's wife's name. But the way I hear it, she's long gone ages ago. According to my legal staff, old man Sterling could make a move without her, as long as he tried to notify by publication, or something like that. As far as I've been told, he could move to have her declared legally dead by now. Only he won't do it."

"Do you know why not?"

"Beats me. Tony said something to me about sentimental value, or something like that. Well, I'm as sentimental as the next guy, but when you're talking millions here, well, you know what I mean? Hell, the place has been closed up forever. God knows what it costs just to keep that relic up, what with paying property tax and all."

"So when was the last time you heard from Tony?"

" 'Bout a week or so ago. After his secretary kept telling me Tony was out, I tried calling the old man direct. But all I got was the friggin' runaround."

I nodded and said, "Well, if you hear from Tony, call me, won't you?"

"Hey, same for you. And tell him he's an idiot for screwing up this deal, okay?"

I smiled, and thought I had a lot more reasons than that for calling Tony an idiot. I thanked Mr. Cooper for his time and made my way back down to my car. When I hit the streets, I saw that the amber-underlit clouds of fog seemed to be descending again. I'd felt I'd done as much as I could for one day, but as that thought crossed my mind, my mother's voice came back from inside my head: *The day ain't over yet, kiddo.*

CHAPTER TWENTY-EIGHT

I parked my car out in front of the office, let myself in through the reception area, and more or less collapsed on one of Mom's guest chairs. "How was your day, dear?" Her Majesty greeted me from behind her desk.

"Well, let's see. I spoke to a bunch of people who wound up giving me more questions than answers, and I'm tired, hungry, and not only got my pants wet but was viciously assaulted by a small dog. All in all, it was pretty much just another day in the glamorous world of the professional private investigator."

"That's nice," Mom said absently, studying her computer screen.

"What's been happening around here?"

Mom took off her reading glasses and said, "I've been delving into Anthony Sterling's computer files. It's a fascinating study on how a fool and his money are soon parted. It seems that young Mr. Sterling made arrangements via e-mail with a rather mysterious 'Mr. Akbar.' The plan was for Anthony to bring all that cash to the airport hotel. A key was delivered to Anthony, and he was instructed to leave the money in the hotel room, where he would find bearer bonds worth ten million dollars waiting for him. Anthony was instructed to take the bonds and wait ten days before depositing them, after which he would be allowed to withdraw two million dollars for himself. Anthony apparently waited the agreed-upon time and then discovered that the bonds were worthless. All in all, a classic. Anthony never even met with the scam artist who relieved him of all that cash."

"I can take that scenario one step further," I said. "Dear old Uncle Georgi pretty much admitted to me that the cash Tony had belonged to him. In other words, it looks like Tony went and lost of bunch of Russian mob money. I guess the question is why he'd do something so desperate? By all accounts, he wasn't doing well in his business. Maybe he felt he needed to make a big score to impress his old man? Or maybe Katerina put him up to it? Men have done stupid things over women before."

"Do tell," Mom said dryly.

"That's not all. I also spoke with a professional shark in the property investment business named Michael Cooper. According to him, there's been an offer on the table for the property that the Castle sits on, and it's worth some millions of dollars. Only Tony couldn't touch it because it's in his mother's name, the woman who took off for parts unknown some years ago with Malcolm Sterling's former partner after draining the business accounts."

"Interesting," Mother mused.

"Yeah. By the way, were you and Felix ever able to figure out why the hidden camera was wired to Tony's computer?"

"No, but we did find some snitchware programs loaded on it. Apparently Anthony, or whoever set up the program, could remotely record anyone using the computer, including all the e-mails and Web sites visited. The software was pretty standard stuff, however. Easily available, just like the hidden camera. We've got much better stuff in the basement."

While she was speaking, Mom got up and walked around to the front of her desk and leaned against it. She was decked out all in black, wearing a turtleneck sweater and pants with a wide black leather belt that was loaded with gear, from her Smith & Wesson pistol to a collapsible baton and a tactical flashlight.

"What's with the Batgirl outfit?" I asked her.

"I thought I'd accompany Jenny to the theater tonight," she answered offhandedly.

"And you're going dressed as a ninja gunfighter?"

"No, silly. Here, I'll show you." She stepped over to the maple-wood coat stand and picked up a reddish-brown cloak. Her jeweled signature brooch was affixed to the collar. She slipped her arms in and put up the hood. "Ta-da!"

"You're Darth Vader's mother?"

"No, dummy. I'm Little Red Riding Hood."

"Ah, I see. Only in this case, if you run into any Big Bad Wolves, you just shove your nine-millimeter pistol up their snout. Well, that's a twist on an old fairy tale. So you couldn't talk Jenny out of going to the masquerade tonight?"

Mom took off her cloak and hung it back on the rack. "She's a stubborn woman," she said with an odd tone of approval in her voice.

"Speaking of whom, where is Jenny?"

"She's upstairs with Angelina and Beowulf. I swear, that little girl has bewitched my dog. He follows her around everywhere."

"Which brings up a point. If you and Jenny are going to the theater, then who's going to watch Angelina?"

"Are you volunteering?" Mom asked quickly.

"Me? Hell, no. Children scare the hell out of me."

"Really? She seems to like you. Kept asking when you'd be coming back and such. It might be good for you to spend a little time with her; broaden your horizons a bit. She's very smart and well mannered. Unlike a certain little boy I used to know." Mom must have taken pity on my deer-in-the-headlights look; she said, "Just kidding, kiddo. Paul's volunteered to stay with Angelina tonight. So, what else do you have for me?"

I ran down the events of the day, from discovering that the barrel of the murder weapon had been switched sometime prior to the homicide to my phone conversations with Malcolm Sterling and Georgi Pakhomov to my meetings with Heidi Mulligan and Andrew the Attack Poodle to my interview with Michael Cooper. When I finished, Mom said, "I see what you mean by having more questions than answers. It occurs to me that an interview with Anthony Sterling might clear a few things up."

"Yeah. Too bad he's hiding out. Did Jenny talk to Katerina again?"

"No. We tried to call several times, but she never picked up the phone. I wonder now if Katrina isn't allied with her uncle Georgi Pakhomov."

"Damn. Hey, is there anything to eat around here? I'm starved."

Mom tossed her head toward the kitchen. "You know the drill. It's self-serve tonight."

I saluted and pried myself off the chair. "If you want me, I'll be grazing."

"Good idea. We're supposed to leave here and get to the theater early."

I stopped midstep. "Uh, was that a royal we?"

"Not this time. I thought it might be best if you came along, too."

"Oh. Okay."

"Your costume's upstairs," Mom said.

"My what, now?"

"Costume," Mom repeated distinctly. "It is a masquerade, you know. You'd stick out like a sore thumb without one."

"I'm afraid to ask. What am I wearing?"

"You'll see," Mom said with a broad smile. I gave her my best glare in return and gathered up my briefcase and dignity and took myself to the kitchen, where I helped myself to another round of cold cereal and yogurt topped off with coffee. Thus fortified, I made my way upstairs.

Before I reached the top, I heard music coming from the direction of the den. Turning the corner, I saw that the television was right in the middle of the Munchkins' big song-and-dance number. Paul Merlyn, our normally impeccably dressed receptionist, was sitting on the floor along with Angelina and Beowulf. He had his jacket off and his shirtsleeves rolled up. "Jason!" Angelina called, getting up and scrambling toward me. "Guess who I am?"

She was wearing a blue-and-white-checked jumper with a white blouse and white socks. Her golden hair was in a pair of braids each with a bow. The clincher was the pair of sparkly red shoes. "Well, hello, Dorothy," I greeted her.

Her face crinkled in a smile. "How'd you know?"

"It's the shoes, girlfriend," Paul said from the den. "They always know by the shoes."

Beowulf came up and started showing an interest in the pant leg that Andrew had attached himself to. Angelina threw her arm around him. "He's Toto," she announced.

The den looked like the miniature stockroom of a girls' dress shop. "Where's your mom?" I asked.

Her smile flipped into a frown. "Getting ready for the party. I wanna go to the party!"

I sighed and knelt down. "I'm sorry, sugar, but—"

"My name's not Sugar!"

"Oh. Right. I'm sorry, Dorothy. But tonight it's only grown-ups. And we have work to do."

On cue, Paul came up and said, "Besides, we're going to have our own party here. We're going to have a lot more fun than they are."

"That's true," I said. Then I wondered if the fun at this so-called party I was going to would include Angelina's mother winding up in jail charged with murder. "Tell you what," I said. "Tomorrow I'll take you and your mom out somewhere special. What do you say?"

Her eyes lit up. "Just the three of us?"

"Sure. If Mom agrees, of course."

She ran down the hall, calling, "Mom! Mom! Jason is going to take us out tomorrow, just you and me!"

Jenny was sitting in front of the big mirror in Mom's palatial bedroom, smearing some kind of green stuff on her face.

"That sounds like fun," she said. "Now you thank him and run back to your movie, angel. Jason and I want to talk."

When Angelina had skipped back down the hall, she added,

"As her mother, I have one thing to say: Anyone who makes a promise to my daughter had better keep it. Or else."

I solemnly raised my right hand. "Yes'm. Scout's honor and stuff. Hey! What the heck happened to your eyes?" Her normally deep blue eyes were now coal black.

"Contact lenses," she said shortly. She was dressed in a floor-length black dress with full sleeves. Her glossy raven-black hair was tied up tight to her head. She sighed. "Okay, I know you're being nice, but I had to have an argument with your mother earlier today, so I'm a little touchy."

I said with apparent awe, "You had an argument . . . with my mother? I don't notice any missing limbs. What happened?"

"She had a bunch of clothes delivered here. For Angelina."

"Yeah. I noticed the Dorothy outfit. It's cute."

"And I noticed the price tags. My daughter asked me if it was Christmas already. So I told your mother that, as nice as that gesture was, I was going to pay her back for all that. And if she didn't like it, she could damn well get me my bill and I would take my daughter and leave here." She stopped suddenly and looked down. "I've never taken anything from anybody that I didn't earn. And I work myself to pieces, trying to take care of my daughter. But I'll be damned if I'll take charity from anyone."

"Uh, what did Mom say when you told her that?"

"Oh, she apologized, and we came to a compromise."

"Apology? Compromise? My mother? No way. These things just don't happen."

Jenny shrugged. "Well, they did. She agreed to return the clothes, minus the Dorothy costume, and give me a bill for all services rendered and I'll pay her. Whenever I can. Which I will. Someday, anyway."

I almost felt my head swimming. "No, you still don't get it. If my mother, Her Royal Majesty Victoria, both apologized and compromised, then we have two certain signs of the coming Apocalypse."

Jenny rolled her eyes and returned to her makeup. "So what are you supposed to be?" I asked.

"I thought I'd run true to my personality and go as the Wicked Witch of the West. Hopefully, if there are any cops there tonight, I won't be recognized."

"Clever," I said.

"Well, yeah. Did you think I was just going to show up and hope the police wouldn't be there? Give me a little credit, would you?" She turned back to the mirror. "I almost hate to ask, but did you have any luck today?"

"Every question just brought more questions," I said. "But I do have a few for you. Did you ever change the barrel on that gun of yours?"

"Change the barrel? No. Why do you ask?"

"Because someone did. But apparently not before it was used on the poor guy in back of the theater. Second, did you know that your brother married into the local Russian mob? Which, come to think of it, makes you a relative, too."

"What?"

"Yeah. Good old Uncle Georgi is like the local Russian godfather, or something. And if I'm not mistaken, Tony went and lost a huge amount of mob money to a con artist."

"You're kidding?"

"Wish I was. Which brings me to my next point. I found out today that some local developers would just love to have someone sell them the land that your theater happens to sit on. Worth millions, or so I'm told."

Jenny turned and stared at me. "If that were true, old Malcolm would have that place bulldozed in a heartbeat."

"Apparently he can't. From what I heard, the property is in your mother's name."

"Really? I never thought about that."

"There are ways to get around it," I said, "or so I heard. You think Malcolm has a sentimental attachment to the theater?"

"That *would* be one of the signs of the Apocalypse you talked about. No. No way. I think if Malcolm thought he could get a dime out of the place, he would have done so by now."

"Okay. Well, that leaves me with three more questions. One, are you sure Bruce didn't kill that guy, thinking he was doing you a favor?"

Jenny looked angry. "Would you leave poor Bruce alone? I told you before, he wouldn't do such a thing."

"I think maybe it wouldn't be the first time he's killed someone," I said quietly. "And I really wouldn't be surprised to find out the guy's done time in prison."

"So what? He's always been good to me and Angelina. And that's all I care about."

"Okay," I said placatingly. "So humor me with my next question. What do you think the 'something wonderful' that Tony says he found is?"

Jenny resumed covering her features with the green face paint. "I've been racking my brain about that all day. One thing's for sure, whatever it is he found, he didn't find it in the Castle."

"Why do you say that?"

"Because I've been over every inch of that place. If there was anything wonderful or valuable there, I'd have found it myself by now."

"Fair enough," I said.

There was a pause, then Jenny said, "Three."

"What?"

"You said three questions," she reminded me.

"Oh, yeah. So I did."

"So what's your last question?"

I cleared my throat before asking, "Have you done away with anyone in the last week or so?"

CHAPTER TWENTY-NINE

Jenny Chance stared at me in Mom's gilt-edged mirror, then returned to applying her green makeup. "Considering all the trouble you've gone through to keep me out of the hands of the police. I'm a little surprised to hear you ask me that."

"You didn't answer my question," I said.

"No, I didn't. But I'll say it if you want me to. No, I haven't killed anyone."

"Good."

Without looking at me, she said, "I think one of the reasons that your mother is keeping me around is that she's not so sure I didn't do it, either."

The girl was smart, no doubt about it. "Look," I said, "I don't want to say this, but I think it needs to be out in the open. I hope to hell I'm right about you not being the killer. I'll be sorrier than you'll ever know if I'm wrong. But if I am, don't count on any help from me. I'll be the first one calling the cops."

"I see." With a ghost of a smile playing on her lips, she said, "So you're not going to play the sap for me?"

"What?"

"Humphrey Bogart. From *The Maltese Falcon*. What kind of detective are you that you don't know that?"

"The kind that spends more time working than watching movies."

"Now, if you'll excuse me, I want to get this disguise on, then I want to spend some time with my daughter before I go."

"Okay." I turned to leave, but Jenny stopped me by saying, "Jason?"

"Yeah?"

She turned from the mirror and faced me. "Thank you."

"For what?"

"For being honest with me. There haven't been a lot of men in my life that I've had that experience with."

"Oh. Okay."

She tilted her head and looked at me quizzically. "What are you smiling about?"

I couldn't help it, really. There was something about seeing a beautiful woman trying to make herself unattractive that bordered on the bizarre to me. But even tinted green, she was lovely. "I was just thinking," I said, "that I'll always remember you looking just like this."

A smile touched her own lips. "Just for that, I ought to give you a kiss. A big greasepainted one. Just to see if you'd turn into a prince."

I raised my hands in mock horror. "Hey, even us frogs have our standards, you know."

I beat a hasty retreat, not because I wanted to leave her, but because I needed to before I made a bigger fool of myself than I already had. I went down the hall and stole past the door to the den. Angelina was sitting on the floor, absently petting a supine Beowulf while she watched Dorothy, the Scarecrow, and the Tin Woodsman make the acquaintance of the Cowardly Lion. Paul Merlyn was on the couch and seemed as engrossed in the film as Angelina. I crept past without disturbing them.

Once back downstairs, I headed for my desk, where the light on my phone was silently telling me I had messages waiting. There was only one, but I could feel myself make a face as I played back Malcolm Sterling's recorded plea. I sighed as I looked for his phone number in my notes. This was part of the job I hated, speaking with the left-behind loved ones of people you were trying to find. Malcolm Sterling was now a client of ours, though, and I owed it to him to give him a report, not that it would help. He must have been sitting on his phone; I didn't even hear it ring before he answered, "Hello?"

"Mr. Sterling? I'm sorry, sir, but I haven't found Tony yet," I said quickly, to get it over with.

There was a pause. "I see. Did you talk to Heidi? Was she any help?"

"I talked to her, but she hasn't seen or heard from Tony since Friday."

"I see," he said again. "Mr. Wilder, as I said before, I can't help but think that woman Tony married is somehow involved in all this. And maybe Jenny, too."

"That's certainly a possibility, sir," I said neutrally. "Did Tony ever mention to you that he was having money problems?"

"Money problems? No. You think this could be about money?"

"We have to look at all the possibilities," I said. "From what I've been able to gather so far, it seems that Tony was in fact desperate for money."

"No," Malcolm said with emphasis. "If Tony needed money, he would have come to me. And that he never did. It doesn't make sense."

"I see. Well, I came across another money-related matter recently that maybe you could explain to me. I've learned that the land the Castle Theater is on is worth quite a lot. Did Tony ever talk to you about that?"

"The Castle? Well, yes, he did, as a matter of fact. He thought we should sell. But I had to point out to him that there were a number of problems in doing that."

"What kind of problems?" I asked casually.

"Legal ones," Malcolm said. "It would take quite a while to, well, unencumber the property."

"Wouldn't it be worth it? If the property is valuable?"

Malcolm sighed. "Mr. Wilder, there's . . . well . . . let's just say that there's a family matter at the heart of this. And I don't see

229

what this has to do with Tony's disappearance. Who cares how much the property's worth if it's not going to be sold? My God, someone tried to kill Tony at his office! As I told the police, you should be looking at Katerina and her family."

In other words, I thought, Malcolm didn't want to air out the family's dirty laundry in front of the hired help. "Okay, sir. Now, why do you say I should be looking at Katerina? She says she hasn't seen Tony since she got him bailed out of jail."

Malcolm sounded exasperated that I was just too dense to see his point. "Mr. Wilder, I have strong suspicions about that woman my son married. I'm certain she got him to marry her just so she could stay in this country, and from what I could see of her family here, they're, well, shady, to say the very least. I'm very afraid that someone's got my son tied up in something dangerous."

Knowing what I did about dear old Uncle Georgi and his boys, I had no doubts about that myself, but I didn't want to alarm Malcolm unduly. "I'll certainly look into that, sir."

"Mr. Wilder," Malcolm said with urgency. "Please. Find my son. Before something happens to him. Tony's never, well, he's never really been able to take care of himself."

"I'll do my best, sir," I said sincerely.

"Good. Thank you. Will you call me the moment you learn anything?"

"I will, sir. I promise."

"Very well. I suppose I should let you get to your work. Thank you for calling me back."

I said good-bye and hung up, feeling as if I'd just run an emotional marathon. I forced myself off my chair and started pacing the room, turning over all the facts and theories I'd gathered in the five days since I'd first heard of Anthony Sterling. After a while, I started to feel almost dizzy, so I gave up and turned my computer back on to check my e-mail. Maybe I'd get a letter from a nice Nigerian company who wanted to offer me the financial deal of a lifetime.

I saw that Felix had uploaded the photographs I had taken in

Tony's office—the blueprints of the Castle Theater. On my small screen, it was hard to make out much detail, so I sent the image through the projector, which gave me a wall-sized view to examine. I ran through the pictures until I came up with the one that showed the stage marked with a circle. From what I could see, whoever did it had made the mark right about where the rear double doors were. And just outside that spot, in the alley, was where our mysterious victim met his fate.

I was still staring at the spot when my cell phone rang. Roland Gibson greeted me. "So where's my story?"

"Extra, extra, read all about it," I said, "idiot detective is clueless."

"That's not news," Roland shot back. "How in the hell are you gonna stay my hero if you're going to go and leave me in the lurch like this? Isn't there anything interesting going on?"

"Well, let's see. Anthony Sterling accuses his sister of being the real murderer. He then gets out on bail and seems to disappear. The only other potential witness to the homicide on Sunday is a homeless lunatic. Oh, and it looks like Tony was mixed up with a local Russian gang. On top of that, Tony's father hired us to find him, and I'm striking out in that department."

"Really?" Roland said with evident interest. "All right! But could you hurry up and solve this thing? I've got a deadline here, you know."

"Oh, anything for you. You want I should go and find you the Holy Grail after this? In my spare time, of course."

"Well, in the meantime," Roland said, "if you're not going to be out working on my Pulitzer Prize, how about we go and get a drink? I'm certain it's your turn to buy."

"No can do. I'm going to be lurking around the Castle Theater tonight."

"Why? You think something's going down there?"

"God, I hope not. Jenny Chance is insisting that she has to be there to run the masquerade party tonight. Mom and I are going with her."

"Jenny? Tony Sterling's sister? The babe?"

"Uh-huh."

"Uh-oh. You watch out there, my boy."

"What do you mean?"

"Didn't I tell you? I think that girl's got bad blood or something. Why are the beautiful ones always criminally insane? Hey! Do you think she's the real killer? She'd look great on the front page."

"Yes, you told me about her mother's larcenous tendencies. And no, I don't think she did it."

"Neither did Heracles."

"Say what?"

"Heracles," Roland repeated. "He's the one who got whacked by his wife Deianira. She killed Heracles just because he wanted to take on another wife. Women can be so cruel," Roland lamented.

"Yeah. Well, Rollo, I'd love to go and hang with you tonight, but I have to take up the sword of Damocles and cut the Gordian knot to open Pandora's box."

After a pause, Roland said, "You just say stuff like that to make my head hurt. So why can't you find this Tony guy? How'd you find him in the first place?"

"Well, I—" My jaw clamped shut as I realized what an idiot I was. I'd been so busy chasing new leads that I completely forgot to revisit the method I used to find Tony Sterling the first time. I hadn't checked on his credit card purchases since last Monday, and by now there could be new clues to his recent whereabouts.

"Hello?" Roland said.

"Rollo, you're a genius."

"I know that," he said in a matter-of-fact manner. "I tell people that constantly. So what's your point?"

"I gotta go and check on some things."

"Okay," Roland sighed. "Fine. Be that way and just go off and leave me. See if I care. Oh, by the way, I dug up some more little tidbits on the larcenous Angelique Sterling, née Raven."

"Oh? Like what?"

"Like the fact that Angelique Raven was not her real name. I was able to track down some documents from various county clerk's offices. Our Miss Raven had her name legally changed in Hollywood back in the sixties. But then again, being born Roberta Jean Roberts might tempt anyone to get a name change. I mean, come on; Bobbie Roberts? Her parents must have hated her."

A pair of mental puzzle pieces went *click* as I made the connection. "Did you say Roberts?" I asked.

"Yeah. I did. That mean something to you?"

Oh, yeah. And I was certain that it meant even more to Bruce Roberts—the man Jenny claimed showed up out of nowhere; the man who was so fiercely protective of her. "Yeah, Roland, it may mean quite a lot."

"Well, don't go and get all mysterious on me. Or do I have to come over and beat it out of you?"

"Look, I gotta go. I'll call you later." I hung up on Roland's protests and found myself staring at the Castle's blueprints projected on the wall. That same circle was where I'd found Bruce hanging around, not once, but twice.

I grabbed my notebook and looked up the information that Katerina had provided us on her husband. I dug out my notes on Tony's credit card information, then punched my computer until I had his on-line credit account information up. Most of his credit cards were either maxed out or up near their limits, a sure sign of financial trouble, but there was another purchase listed. Early on Monday, Tony had rented a space at a storage facility. I cross-checked the address and wasn't surprised at all to see that the storage unit was on Buccaneer Street, less than two blocks from the fleabag motel where I found Tony in the first place. While I was checking my numbers, I heard my mother say from behind me, "The bus is leaving, kiddo."

I spun in my chair and saw Mom in her dark amber cloak standing next to Jenny, now decked out with a black pointed witch's hat and holding a plaid coat over her arm. "I brought your costume down," she said. "What's wrong?"

233

I caught Mother's quizzical look as well and realized my face must have been showing my new suspicions about Jenny. Did she know it seemed possible she was related to Bruce Roberts, and if so, why keep it a secret?

"Sorry," I said. "You just caught me thinking."

"No wonder I almost didn't recognize you, dear," Mom said kindly. "Now, are you coming with us? We need to be going."

"I've got something I need to look into first," I said, touching the corner of my mouth. This was one of our in-house signs; I was telling Her Majesty, "I can't talk now."

Mom nodded. "Well, come along when you can. And don't forget your costume."

"My what?"

"Your costume," Mother repeated. "Jenny actually picked it out. I was all in favor of renting you a flying-monkey suit, but she talked me out of it."

I shook my head as Jenny displayed a short-caped coat with double-billed hat. "I thought this would be appropriate," she explained.

I took the clothes from her and put on the hat. "Sherlock Holmes? You've got to be kidding me."

Mom smiled. "Well, at least for once you'll look like a detective," she said.

CHAPTER THIRTY

Jenny had wandered over to the wall where my photos of the Castle blueprints were displayed. "What's this?" she asked.

"It's the floor plan of the theater," I said. "I found the blueprints in Tony's office."

Jenny pointed to the circle on the diagram. "Why is this here?"

"I'd love to know that myself. Someone drew it there. Does that area mean anything to you?"

"It's upstage center, I can tell you that," she said. "And it's right near the back doors. But there's nothing special about that place."

Mom joined Jenny, crossing her arms and tilting her head as she studied the plans. "Okay. So what's above there?"

"Just the catwalks," Jenny said.

"I can vouch for that," I offered. "I climbed up there the other night."

"And what's below?" Mom asked.

"The old greenroom and dressing rooms," Jenny answered. "But they haven't been used in years. Downstairs is completely empty."

"Greenroom?" I asked.

"Where the actors hang out before a play," Jenny explained. "There's also some storage areas and a bunch of dressing rooms down there, but they'd been gutted years ago. There aren't even any old mirrors left."

I sorted through my set of projected digital photographs until

I came up with a diagram that showed a series of nine rooms with a set of stairs on either side. "That's them," Jenny confirmed.

"And there's nothing down there?" Mom asked.

"Not now. The place was a trash heap when I first took the theater over. I spent a lot of time clearing it out. It used to be quite a fire hazard."

Mom and I exchanged looks at that remark. "Fire hazard, eh?" Mom mused. "I wonder if that was Anthony's intended destination last Sunday night? Maybe he did indeed have a little arson in mind."

Jenny shrugged. "It'd be a good place to set a fire. Or it would have been until I cleaned it up."

"Well, we could speculate all night," Mom said, "but in the meantime, we should get you to the show, my dear. Jason? You'll come when you can?"

"Your wish is my command, etcetera," I replied.

Mom headed for the back door. Jenny gave me an unfathomable look with her now obsidian-black eyes, then silently followed Mom out. I waited until the door was shut, then looked up the telephone number to the storage place.

I was automatically referred to an after-business-hours number, where I had to wait for a human operator. Finally, a pleasant-voiced woman said, "River City Storage and Moving. Can I help you?"

"Yes, you can," I said cheerfully. "This is Anthony Sterling. I rented a unit from you last Monday, and well, gosh, I'm an idiot. I completely forgot to write down my unit number. I'm so stupid."

"That's all right, sir," the woman said. "That sort of thing happens all the time. Do you have your account number handy?"

"Gosh, no. I'm such an idiot. I don't even have that."

"Well, that's okay. Did you use a credit card to rent the space?"

"Why, yes. Yes, I did."

"Well, then, just give me your card number. Oh, and I'll need your birth date and driver's license number to verify."

"No problem," I said. I read off the required numbers from

the information Katerina Sterling provided when she first hired us. Shortly after that, the woman said, "Ah. There you are. You're in space B-17."

Bingo, I thought. "Oh, thank you! I'm such a moron."

"That's okay, sir. You do have your access code, right?"

"My what? Oh, geez. Did I mention I'm an idiot? I've completely forgotten that. Do you have it handy?"

There was a pause, then the woman, who I think was getting suspicious, said flatly, "It's the same number as your birth date."

"Well, I said I was stupid, didn't I?" I muttered quickly before hanging up. I shot out of my chair and was about to dash for the door, then remembered that I'd left my firearm in my briefcase. I took a minute to strap on the holster, check the revolver, and slide it snugly into place. As I was arming myself, I looked at the projected blueprints, and it occurred to me that they might come in handy later. While I was waiting for the printer to spit out a set of copies, my eyes fell on my Sherlock Holmes costume. I debated leaving the stupid thing here but couldn't come up with a reasonable excuse for leaving it behind. When my prints were ready, I folded them up and stuck them in my jacket pocket, put my coat on, took a last look around to see if I was forgetting anything, then grabbed my case and costume, and took my delayed run out the door.

It was a foggy night, the kind where all the sounds are muted and your eyes play tricks on you as you try to peer through the mist. I got into my car and forced myself to drive carefully toward the old warehouse district. Once I was out of the heart of the city, the traffic thinned and I made better time. The unimaginatively named River City Storage and Moving was a series of gray concrete blocks with yellow-painted metal doors surrounded by a formidable barbed-wire-topped fence. There was a black iron gate across the vehicle entrance with a key pad set into a metal post. I punched in Tony's Sterling's birthday, and the gate obediently rolled aside to let my car pass.

I parked, got out, and wandered the complex until I found

a Plexiglas-covered map on a wall that revealed the location of space B-17—on the second floor of the four-story central building. I found a set of stairs and was soon in a maze of harshly lit hallways, all with matching metal doors only distinguished from each other by the numbers stamped in black paint. B-17 was in the middle of a row, with a padlock on the door. I stood still for a minute, letting my ears tell me that I seemed to be alone here, then got out my lock picks and went to work. In a few minutes I had the hasp popped up, and I was as good as in.

Or as good as dead. I thought with a sudden chill of the explosion that blew Detective Dolman across the room in Tony's office.

I took a quick sidestep away from the front of the heavy door and let my heart rate run amok for a while. When it slowed to merely panic level, I tried to think of the best way to get the damn door open without getting into what might be a line of fire. I came up with the best I could do with the tools at hand. I took off my suit coat and tied a sleeve to the door handle. I then slowly backed up against the wall until I was stretched out as far as I could go. Wrapping my free arm around my head, I slowly pulled the door open—and jumped when it eventually thumped into the wall.

I waited a full five minutes before creeping up to the corner. I darted my head in for a quick look. What I saw almost made me collapse: The room was filled with a great deal of nothing.

I shook my head, almost laughing at all my precautions as I turned the corner for a good look. The place seemed entirely empty. I took out my key ring light and played it around. It was then I noticed something rectangular in the corner. I trained my flashlight on it and saw what looked like a short stack of paper, about the size of the blueprints I had found in Tony's office. I picked up the top one and gasped at what I saw. Even though only a half light spilled in from the hallway, my eyes were filled with a riot of color. I was holding a poster-size picture of Clark Gable and Jean Harlow. There were racehorses in the background and text advertising a movie called *Saratoga*. I laid the sheet down carefully and picked up the next, a painted cowboy named Buck Jones in a big hat appearing in *Black Aces*. Next was a picture in rich tones proclaiming "A Thunderbolt of Thrills and Intrigue" with Edward G. Robinson in *The Amazing Dr. Clitterhouse*. A guy named Humphrey Bogart got third billing. But the one that really caught my eye was a poster featuring a woman named Claudette Colbert. She reminded me of Jenny Chance, except that Jenny had much better lips. The movie was *Cleopatra*, which surprised me since I associated that particular film with Elizabeth Taylor.

There were more, of course, each poster as beautiful as the last.

They were, in short, "something wonderful."

I had no idea what these things were worth, but judging by their apparent age and well-preserved condition, I could easily imagine they'd be valuable to somebody. I carefully replaced the posters I had removed on the stack, and even more carefully rolled them up, and as I picked the posters up, I could see where poor Daniel Shaw had thought he saw someone carrying a big white pipe. I locked up the now empty storage room, took a minute to wipe my prints off the handle and lock with the sleeve of my suit, and hurried to my car. I sped away into the fog, the posters safely in the trunk, and dialed up Her Majesty on my cell phone. The first thing I heard when she picked up sounded like a riot in the background. "Hello," she practically shouted.

"It's me, and I've got something wonderful in the trunk of my car."

"I can barely hear you," Mom said. "There's quite the party going on here. Lots of people in costume, many of whom have come dressed as police officers. What did you find?"

"Uh-oh. Any of our acquaintance?'

"Oh, yes. That Lori Banks is here, although she doesn't seem to be having a good time. She's with Malcolm Sterling, and I think she's using him to spot Jenny. We've managed to avoid them thus far. There are also quite a few dour young men in black leather coats, the kind we saw at Georgi Pakhomov's restaurant."

"Oh, crap. That doesn't sound good. Have the cops spotted Jenny?"

"Not yet, but Banks is definitely prowling around."

"Is that Bruce Roberts there?"

"Yes. Jenny introduced us. Now tell me, what's the something wonderful?"

"I'm driving there as fast as I can," I said, "I'll tell you when I get there."

There was a pause, then Mom said, "You know how much I hate suspense."

"Trust me, you've got to see it to believe it, but we have to get back to the office for that. I'll meet you around the stage, okay?"

"All right, but drive carefully getting here. It's a bad night out. And try to stay away from the police."

I drove on through the mist. Closer to midtown, the fog was hovering just above the streetlights, stirred up by the traffic, no doubt, and giving a claustrophobic feeling to the night. When I arrived at Ketch and Twelfth, I saw that all the street parking was taken up and that there were an inordinate number of late-model four-door sedans, the kind the police seem to think are undercover vehicles, parked close to the Castle. I pulled around to Jib and was able to find a place across the street from the boarded-up Benson Hotel.

I parked the Mustang and started to run to the theater, remembering at the last moment the hat and cloak in the car. The coat fit well enough, coming down to about my knees, but the hat was a puzzle. It had two bills, and I wasn't sure which was forward and which was back. I decided it didn't matter and jammed it on my head as I waited for a break in the traffic to dart across the street.

I took the sidewalk down Twelfth Street on the theater side and slowed to a stop as I reached the alley between the Benson Hotel and the back of the Castle. Flattening myself against the wall, I tried to listen, but it was my nose that told me that there was someone smoking a cigarette back there. I eased an eye around the corner. Sure enough, I saw the cigarette glow as its owner took a puff. I took a few quiet steps across the opening and continued down the sidewalk, where the lights of the Castle marquee beckoned.

Turning the corner was like walking in on a mini Mardi Gras. A crowd of people, almost all in costume, clustered outside the theater. I could hear dance music with a heavy beat, and an eerie blue glow emanated from the Castle's drawbridge opening. I eased through the crowd, moving around a group of nuns and a pair of guys wearing full silver-colored space suits. In the lobby, illuminated with ultraviolet black lights, I could see a herd of partygoers around the concession stands. Looking up at the landing, I also spotted Detective Lori Banks, in full police jumpsuit and gear, standing next to Malcolm Sterling. She was right by Jenny's office door and was using the vantage point to look over who was coming and going through the lobby. By the entrance was Bruce, standing guard in a tuxedo as he checked people coming in for the party, taking their tickets and stamping their hands.

I was in a dilemma: If I tried to go in through the front, I ran the risk of being spotted by Detective Banks, and she was the last person I wanted to see right now. On the other hand, the back doors in the dark alley seemed to be guarded by someone who might be a cop or a Russian gang enforcer. I pulled the bill of my Sherlock hat low over my eyes and attempted a casual stroll up toward Bruce. I waited as he checked in a couple of Vikings and a guy dressed as Marilyn Monroe. When it was my turn, I heard Bruce grunt, "Ticket."

I raised my eyes so he could get a look at my face. "It's me."

Even through the music blaring out from the theater, I swear I could hear him growl. He then grabbed my hand and ground a rubber stamp into the back of my knuckles, hard enough to make me wince. He tossed his head, silently telling me to go on in. I looked down at my hand to see if he had drawn blood and saw under the ultraviolet light that I had a glowing, grinning skull on the back of my hand. I carefully pulled the bill of my hat down farther as I made my way through the crowd toward the theater.

And got my first lucky break. I spotted my buddy Hector Morales, in uniform, standing by the left-hand theater doors. I worked my way through a gaggle of belly dancers and some goth vampires until I was under the balcony and out of sight of Detective Banks. "Yo, Hector!" I called.

He scanned the crowd until he spotted me, his dark eyes widening in recognition. He looked left and right, then motioned me over. "What are you doing here?" I asked. "Not that I'm not glad to see you."

"Making overtime," he said. "Roland called and said you'd be around here tonight, probably getting into trouble as usual. I volunteered to help cover this place until my regular shift starts. We're supposed to be looking for the woman who runs it. What's up with you, bro?"

"Roland called? Don't tell me he's here?"

"Yeah. He's up on the balcony, looking as dorky as you do. You want to tell me what's going on?"

"Well, for starters that woman you're looking for is my new client."

Hector took a step back. "Jesus! Should I even be seen with you?"

"Probably not," I admitted, "considering the fact that I'm trying to avoid Detective Banks right now."

Hector's handsome face took on a mournful cast. "Ah, geez. And I had such a promising career."

"Look, could you go find Roland and tell him to meet me by the stage? Then we'll stay clear of each other, okay?"

Hector's face took on that stubborn look I knew so well. "No way, José. We're like blood, man. Something goes down, you find me, okay?"

I confess I got a bit of a lump in my throat at Hector's declaration of loyalty. "No worries, Hec. I plan to go and get my client out of here and be gone before anything goes wrong."

"You'd better, man," Hector said, looking up to the landing where Detective Banks was perched. "Old Pit Bull Banks is on the warpath tonight, and I wouldn't want to be in her crosshairs."

Neither would I, I thought as I patted Hector on the arm and pushed through the leather-padded doors into the theater, stepping right into what looked like hell's own disco.

CHAPTER THIRTY-ONE

I stopped in my tracks when I got inside and almost tripped over a couple dressed in caveman skins. They were making out in the back row of seats. The imitation torches on the walls were casting red illumination; the overhead chandeliers were down to a dim glow. Where the main curtain would have hung, there was a billowing white sheet; projected on it was a scratchy, sepia-toned movie of a hideous fanged creature as it stalked a wide-eyed woman clutching at herself in horror on her bed. From around and underneath the sheet, heavy fog rolled out. Bright beams of light shot here and there through the glow. Blaring, thumping dance music came from the orchestra pit, around which crowds of people gyrated and danced.

I made my way down the sloping aisle past people coming up with empty plastic glasses, no doubt heading for a refill at the concession stand. About halfway down, I saw a tall, heavy guy with a shaved head and dark goatee who was wearing the now familiar black leather sport coat of one of Uncle Georgi's boys. He stood with arms crossed by the side exit, glaring at the passersby. Whatever truce I thought Mom and I had with the Russian contingent seemed to be off.

Three rows from the front, I spotted someone in a black pointy hat sitting next to a hooded figure. I sat down next to Her Majesty, and we all went into a huddle, speaking up to be heard over the music. "Great party. Can we go now?" I asked.

"We really should, dear," Mom commented to Jenny. "I think we've pressed our luck for one night."

Jenny smiled. "I hate to go. I was having a good time trying to calculate how much money we pulled in tonight. Maybe the kids didn't really need me here after all."

I was distracted for a moment by what appeared to be a pagan dance ritual going on near the pit. I wondered if a human sacrifice was on the agenda. "What's supposed to happen after this?"

"Well, there's the costume contest. I was going to be the judge, but I guess I can delegate that. Then at midnight we're showing *The Rocky Horror Picture Show*. I'll tell you this, with all the cops around, I doubt anyone would try anything funny here."

"With the exception of you getting arrested, it's not the cops I'm worried about. It's the Russian Foreign Legion I'm concerned with," I said.

Mom nodded. "I know. Jenny and I ran into one when we came in tonight. We used the back doors and found him in the alley. He made the mistake of trying to follow us inside."

"What happened?" I asked.

Jenny smiled. "It was beautiful. Your mother just threw him down, then held him there, telling him he was being rude." To Mom, she said, "You're going to have to show me that trick sometime."

"Just a simple technique every woman should know," Mom said with apparent modesty. "He apologized before I had to really hurt him."

"Well, just so you know," I said, "he, or someone else, is still lurking back there in the alleyway. And Detective Banks is hovering over the lobby. So if either one of you has a good escape plan, now would be a good time to tell me."

Mom squeezed my arm. "Isn't that your friend Roland over there?" she asked.

I saw Roland Gibson, decked out in a white tabard with a big red cross on it. He had a plastic knight's helmet a bit too small for him on his head and a fake sword and shield. He was carrying a professional camera with a flash attachment and stood looking around the crowd. I dug out my key ring, cupped the small flashlight with my free hand, and flashed a couple of quick bursts in his direction. Roland caught the signal, gave me a smile in return, and headed toward us, homing in on Jenny. "Well, hello there," he said cheerily. "Jenny Chance, I presume?"

"Jenny, this is Roland Gibson," I told her. "Knight erroneous and reporter for the *River City Clarion*."

Jenny looked to Mother and me uncertainly, but Mom reassured her. "It's quite all right, dear. Roland knows I'll hurt him if he tries to step out of line. Don't you, Roland?"

Roland's smile twisted as if he'd bitten into something bitter. "Yes, Mrs. Wilder," he said, like a third grader who'd been bawled out by the teacher.

"That's a good boy," Mom said approvingly.

"What are you doing here, Rollo?" I asked.

He shrugged. "Hey, you know, just hanging out. Seeing if anything interesting happens."

"Well, let me know if it does. We're getting out of here."

Jenny looked to me, almost pleading with her eyes, then nodded. "Okay," she said. "You're right. I guess this place can run without me the rest of the night."

"Good. Besides, I've got something to show you," I said. "Once we get back to the office."

"What's that?"

I couldn't help but smile. "Something wonderful."

"Oh," Roland said with a knowing nod. "Is that what you're telling all the pretty girls lately?"

"Where are you parked?" Mom asked me.

"One block over on Jib."

She nodded. "Okay. Then the best bet is to try to go the way we came, out through the back alley."

"There's still someone back there," I cautioned.

"Well, then, we'll have to go through them, won't we, dear? Come on, children, let's roll."

I led the way to the aisle, looking around for signs of police and other possible impediments. I stood aside to let Mom and Jenny pass. As Roland came out, he leaned in and said into my ear, "Damn, even painted green, she's a babe."

"You coming with us?' I asked.

"Naw. I'll take some photos for the City Scene nightlife section. Then, who knows?" he shrugged.

I had no illusions: Any pictures Roland took that night would be of women in various exotic costumes. I nodded to him and joined Mom and Jenny by the stairs that led up to the stage. After taking another look around, we ran up the steps through the rolling fog and slipped past the white curtain, which now displayed an image of a golden, feminine-looking robot surrounded by levitating circles of electric light. I had taken no more than two steps into the near darkness when I felt a hard, cold metallic bar jam into the back of my neck. "You will stay very still," a harsh voice commanded.

My hands shot up in apparent surrender as I got into position for a rear two-hand gun take-away, high, only to have Mom yell, "Jason!" sharply, short-circuiting my ingrained training. As I felt the shock of fear run through my body, I saw Jenny and Mom with a darkly dressed man in between them holding a gun to Jenny. He was wearing a full-head rubber mask. A hand clamped onto my left shoulder, and I was pushed ahead to join the women. I turned back to my captor, seeing him outlined in the wildly shifting light coming through the translucent cloth the movie was projected on. I didn't miss the way he gestured with the gun, telling us to move to the right and toward the stairs that led down to the greenroom.

We were herded ahead and down, and as I turned the last corner at the bottom of the stairs I saw that the door had been forced open and the padlock was hanging impotently from the hasp. My eyes were speared by a shaft from a flashlight as I was

pushed aside to make room for Jenny and Mom, the second gun-
man bringing up the rear. Over the music that seemed only
slightly diminished down here, I heard a muted yet familiar voice
say, "So. We are to have company, eh?"

"Hello, Georgi," I replied, right before Her Majesty demanded, "Mr. Pakhomov, will you be so kind as to explain?"

I heard a brief command in Russian, and the lights were
dropped from our eyes. As I blinked, trying to recover from my
temporary blindness, I saw a thick figure step forward, pulling
something from his head. As my eyes adjusted, I could see
Georgi Pakhomov standing before me, holding a flashlight pointing downward in one hand and a limp rubber mask in the other.
He shrugged and said, "So it is now the time to unmask. Just as
well. It was hard to breathe in this thing."

"What the hell are you doing here?" Jenny demanded angrily.
"This is my theater!"

I counted four other figures besides Georgi, all behind flashlights. And I figured on there being just as many guns. We were
all crowded in a small hallway; I could see a series of rooms on
either side. "You should be happy to know," Georgi said, "that
we have paid full price of admission. So I hope you will forgive
me if I helped myself to a little unguided tour, so to say." Georgi
held up the rubber mask and played his light on it; it was a mask
of Ronald Reagan. "Not my favorite of your presidents," he said,
"but I could not quite make myself buy the Clinton one."

"The lady asked you a question," Mom interjected. "What
are you doing here?"

"Just looking for something," Georgi said reasonably.

"Let me guess," I said. "You're looking for 850,000 some-
things, am I right?"

"Give or take," Georgi answered.

"And your niece Katerina told you that Tony found something here that may be worth that much?"

I could see Georgi nod. "Yes. Just so. So I am wondering, if
that is true, then where is it? I have been all through your stage,

and I have found nothing. I would be very sad to find out that maybe I have been lied to. Very sad indeed."

"I could have saved you the trouble of sneaking down here," Jenny said firmly. "This is my place, and I know every inch of it. If there were anything worth that much, I'd have found it myself by now."

Georgi played his light over Jenny as she spoke. Somewhere along the way, she had lost the black pointy hat. "Coming from woman who now reminds me of my wife," Georgi said, "I have to pay attention. So I am thinking that maybe you know something? Yes?"

While Georgi was talking, I scanned the floor, illuminated by several flashlights. All the recent foot traffic hadn't erased a set of prints that were outlined in whitish dust leading from the room to the stairs on the opposite side.

"No, I don't," Jenny answered Georgi firmly.

Georgi studied Jenny, and while he did, I made my own study of the walls nearby. They were all lined with some kind of stucco and the same color as the dust trail on the floor. "Did you look everywhere?" I asked.

Georgi looked irritated at my interruption. "Yes, of course I have. There is nothing here. Nothing."

"You mind if I take a look?"

Georgi weighed the idea, then shrugged. "Certainly. Be my guest. You may take your arms down if you do not do anything foolish. My men have had army training."

I relaxed my arms and walked down the hall, looking at the rooms left and right until I came to the one in the middle. One of Georgi's men stood aside and shined his light in, and I could see where a panel had been pried out of the wall, exposing a section bordered by wooden two-by-fours. The broken stucco was scattered around the floor, and at the base of the wall was an electrical outlet. I cautiously stepped inside and up to the far wall, hunching down and pretending to study the outlet. The space in the wall was easily two inches deep. I said over my shoulder, "I take it this is where Tony was supposed to wire up his little do-it-yourself arson kit?"

Georgi said from behind me, "Um, perhaps. I am certain I would not really know anything about that. Officially."

Covering my actions with my body, I picked up a piece of the stucco and could feel that it was lined with paper on one side as I slipped it into my pocket. I stepped out and slowly walked the rest of the way down the hall, checking the rooms as I went. When I reached the end, something didn't add up right. "Well?" Georgi asked.

I sighed and turned around. Everyone had been following my progress. As much to buy time as anything else, I asked, "What was his name, Georgi?"

"Whose name?"

"The man who was killed here last Sunday. The man you sent with Tony to make sure the arson job got done. The man who's now on a slab in the coroner's office. Who was he?"

A low mutter ran through Georgi's assembled gunmen. After what seemed like a long time, Georgi said, "I have made many promises in my life. When this is over, I have promised that I will see he gets a proper funeral. I have also promised something else." Georgi took a few steps closer to me, then said with quiet intensity, "I have promised to find out who it was that killed him."

Georgi turned and walked over to Jenny and Mom. He raised a light to Jenny's face. Her obsidian eyes stared back defiantly. "Some people have said," Georgi began, "that you may be responsible."

Jenny bit her words out. "I didn't kill anyone."

"How sad it is if you are lying to me," Georgi said. "Especially sad for your little girl."

While Georgi's attention was on Jenny, mine was focused on my mother. In Her Majesty's world, there are some things you never, ever do, and threatening a child tops the list. In the flashlight, I saw the look on Mom's face and caught the way her right hand flexed, and wondered how that idiot Georgi couldn't see he was standing right in front of red-cloaked death. With an attitude.

I felt my own hand ready itself to sweep away my coat and grab my gun as my mind automatically went into targeting mode. I was suddenly in one of those slow motion nightmares, waiting for Mom to make her move and start the mother of all gunfights. All I knew at that moment was that I had to try to stop the bloodbath before it started. "Wait," I said quickly. "I think I've got the—"

My words were cut off be a loud, concussive explosion that seemed to shake the walls, followed by the sound of screams from hundreds of voices.

CHAPTER THIRTY-TWO

Everything seemed to freeze for a moment, then Georgi yelled a sharp command. At once, Georgi and his men abruptly turned and ran for the nearest set of stairs, leaving Jenny, Mom, and me in the darkness.

"What the hell?" Jenny yelled as Mom and I broke out our own flashlights.

"Upstairs, now!" Mom barked. I let the ladies lead the charge up the stairs and then followed them to the end of the stage, where Jenny pulled aside the curtain.

Through the near blinding rays of the projector's lights I could see a cloud of black smoke as it roiled up from somewhere near the center of the floor-level seating area. The people were screaming and running for all points away from the sinister-looking mass as it started to block out the light, all while the music continued to thunder and blare. "Oh, God, no!" I heard Jenny scream.

Mom slapped my shoulder to get my attention. "Cut the music," she commanded. Looking down, I saw where the DJ had set up his console in the middle of the orchestra pit. I jumped down and grabbed a handful of wires, jerking them out of the outlet. The music stopped. From above me, I saw bright lights come on as my mother ran to the side of the stage, dragging the curtains open. Above the noise of the panic-stricken crowd I shouted, "This way!" The next thing I knew, I was between a pair of human rivers as they charged up the stairs and poured onto the stage.

Over their heads, I saw my idiot friend Roland, standing on a theater seat and shooting his camera in all directions as fast as he could. While Jenny and Mom called for the crowd to come their way, I yelled his name. He couldn't hear me, of course. I shot my small flashlight at him, and he finally turned in my direction, catching the beam in his viewfinder. I waved my arms and called, "Get the hell over here, moron!" I was relieved to see him grin and give a thumbs-up as he started to clamber clumsily over the chairs toward me.

It was then that I spotted a disturbance in the mob pushing up the left-hand aisle to the front exit. I lifted myself back up on the stage for a better look and saw Bruce Roberts, tossing people out of his way left and right as he fought through the throng. He finally broke free of the last of the upward-bound crowd and charged ahead. Even through the screams I could hear him bellowing, "Jenny!" over and over.

Jenny threw herself off the stage and ran for him, calling, "Bruce! Get back!"

My mother yelled in my ear, "Go get her!" as she shoved me off the stage. I landed clumsily, picked myself up, and took off after Jenny, keeping one eye on the expanding black cloud. As I ran up the aisle, I caught a glimpse of Detective Banks, with Malcolm hobbling behind, following in Bruce's wake as he ran headlong to Jenny.

The five of us, Jenny, Bruce, Banks, Malcolm, and I, all converged about halfway up the aisle. Bruce was battered and bloody, his tuxedo torn to rags on his body. Without another word, he picked Jenny up and turned—and ran full tilt into Banks, knocking her back into Malcolm and putting them both on the floor. I heard Jenny cry, "Bruce? What are you doing?" as he took off with her through the side exit. I stole a quick look to the center of the theater, only to see that the black cloud seemed to be gaining on us. Banks flailed a bit, looking for something to hold on to as she hollered, "God damn it! Where'd they go?" I reached down and yanked her up, and she immediatly shoved past me and ran through the exit, chasing after Bruce and Jenny, leaving me with Malcolm Sterling, who was flattened out on the faded red carpet. I leaned over and offered both my hands, and as he grabbed hold I saw the death's head of my hand stamp as it glowed and grinned at me. "Mr. Wilder? Is that you?" Malcolm asked.

"No time to talk. Gotta go!" I threw an arm around him.

"My cane!" I snatched it up for him. Together, we entered the dark tunnel that was the side exit and climbed for street level. We came out in the side alley, and I could now hear the sirens of the responding emergency vehicles as they started to converge. I helped Malcolm Sterling as he limped until we got to the mouth of the alley that led to the front of the Castle.

It looked like hell's own hospital waiting room. Garishly costumed people milled about aimlessly or were on the ground surrounded by clusters of their friends as a few uniformed police tried to keep some kind of order amid the chaos. Over by the drawbridge opening was a widened circle of people. Pushing my way through, I saw Hector Morales, his uniform in complete disarray. He stood breathing hard and holding a broken nightstick over the fallen form of Bruce, while Detective Banks had Jenny pushed against the headless carved stone knight that guarded the portal. Banks had Jenny's hands behind her back and was locking them into a pair of handcuffs while telling her that she was under arrest.

"Hey! Hold it!" I yelled.

Banks's head swiveled toward me at the same time Jenny's did, and they took on simultaneous looks of pure hatred. But while Bank's eyes locked on me, Jenny shot her look at Malcolm, who now stood beside me.

"Wilder!" Banks said. "Back off! Unless you wanna go for a ride, too!"

"Not as long as I'm around he won't." That came from my mother, who materialized on the other side of the crowd. Her cloak was gone, and she was breathing hard and looking dangerous as she stood there with her hand on her belt less than an inch from her pistol.

Banks pulled Jenny away from the wall, leaving a green smudge of greasepaint on the stone knight's breastplate, as she announced, "I'm taking my prisoner out of here. Anyone that wants to object can go, too. Got it?"

For a flash of a moment, I had the wild impulse to try to grab Jenny to pull her away from Banks, but Mom's glare and small shake of her head quashed my urge.

As Banks pulled her away, Jenny said to me, "I'm trusting you to take care of my daughter." All the while, she kept a baleful eye on Malcolm Sterling.

I let my breath out and more or less fell against the stone wall, letting it hold me up as I closed my eyes for a moment, until I felt a gentle hand on my arm. "You all right, son?" Mom asked though the noise of the crowd and approaching sirens.

I pushed myself off the wall and opened my eyes. Hector was kneeling down by Bruce, his hands hovering by Bruce's bloody head. Mom and I went over and hunched down on the other side. "Jesus," Hector said, shaking his head in disbelief. "The guy just wouldn't give up. That detective told me to stop him. I thought he was kidnapping that girl or something."

"I'll get the medics," Mom said as she rose and slipped into the crowd. Bruce looked bad, but he was still breathing, labored as it was. "It's not your fault, Hector," I said to my friend.

Hector's deep brown eyes bored into my own. "Just what the hell is going on here, man?"

I silently shook my head, then got up and made way for a pair of paramedics as they pushed through and laid a portable gurney down. I turned and found myself facing Malcolm Sterling, who looked around helplessly as he said, "Mr. Wilder? Do you think any of this has to do with my son?"

"I don't know, sir," I said, stalling for time. "Maybe. I just don't know right now."

"But did you know that Jenny was here? When the police called me tonight and asked me to come see if I could identify her, I didn't think to call you. Are the police right? Did Jenny kill that man?"

"I don't know," I repeated. "Look, I don't think there's anything anyone can do here right now, except make room for the police and paramedics to do their job. I suggest you go home, sir."

Malcolm searched my face for a moment, then nodded. "You're right, of course. I'll go home as soon as I can." He looked around, bewildered, and said softly, "I guess someone has to stay and lock this place up."

Mom appeared beside me and took my arm. "Come on. There's nothing more we can do here."

"Have you seen Roland?" I asked her.

"Yes. He got out the back, then kept on running. By now he's probably halfway to the newspaper with his pictures."

"Good."

Mom and I made our way though all the people, most of whom had seemed to have discarded bits and pieces of their costumes, which now littered the ground. I saw that Hector had taken up a position with other police as they tried to keep some kind of control over the people milling about as emergency crews came and went. As we passed by, I leaned in and whispered to Hector, "Find out what the hell that thing was that went off in the theater, then call me. Okay?" He kept his attention on the people in front of him but nodded that he understood me.

Mom and I crossed Ketch Street, now blocked off in both directions by patrol cars, until we stood by the elevated parking garage. I felt a chill as the foggy night air seemed to seep through my clothes to my sweat-soaked body. I took off my Sherlock coat and wrapped it around Mom. The hat was long gone somewhere.

"Thanks, son," Mom said quietly. I noticed she looked as tired as I felt.

"Now what?" I asked.

She sighed. "Now I try to get Jenny bailed out before I have to tell her daughter that her mommy's in jail. Although God knows what that idiot Banks is going to charge her with. I only hope she doesn't try to write up an enhancement on the arrest sheet asking for Jenny to be held without bail." Her Majesty stood up straighter and squared her shoulders. "Well, once more into the breach, kiddo. The day ain't over yet. Let's go."

"You go on ahead," I said. "I've got something I have to do."

Mom paused and gave me her X-ray glare. "Like what?" she asked suspiciously.

"Like maybe try to put all this together. Now you get going and try to get Jenny sprung. I'll call you if anything develops."

"Since when are you telling me what to do?"

"Since now. Only because there's no time: You need to get Jenny out, and I need to go and test a theory. Trust me, okay?"

"I swear to God, boy," she said seriously, "whatever it is you're planning, it better not result in you getting hurt. I swear I'll fire you."

"No problem. The thought of me having to go get another job and actually have to work for a living will keep me on the up-and-up. I'll call you when I've got something solid."

"You better," warned, as she marched off into the foggy night. I waited until she was out of sight, then pushed myself off the wall I was leaning on and made my way down the street. If I was right, then I could put this whole problem to rest.

I didn't want to even think about the consequences if I was wrong.

■

CHAPTER THIRTY-THREE

I'd been waiting in the dark for hours. Again.

The theater had been as quiet as a tomb after the police chased everyone out. And in that time that seemed to stretch into infinity, my thoughts kept bouncing around among all the facts and theories that I'd been living with for the past week. Just when I could almost feel them start to coalesce into something tangible, I'd think of Jenny, and my focus would evaporate. I was so wrapped up in my own mind that I almost missed the slight sounds that told me I was about to have company here in the Castle Theater's greenroom.

My heart raced, and I tried to keep my breath slow and quiet as I got off the cold concrete floor and eased my gun out of its holster. I heard the door creak open and then was blinded for a moment as harsh overhead lights came on. I waited until the aftershock shadows cleared from my vision before I stepped around the corner and raised my gun. "Good evening, gentlemen," I said.

Malcolm and Tony Sterling, both dressed in work clothes and burdened with tools, snapped their heads toward me in unison. Tony's eyes bugged out, and he yelped an involuntary exclamation of surprise. His father just froze, staring at me with intensity.

I raised my revolver. "I hope you don't mind the gun," I said, "but murderers scare the hell out of me."

Behind his glasses, Malcolm Sterling's dark eyes remained calm. "Mr. Wilder, what is the meaning of this?"

"Fair question," I said, stepping up to within a couple of feet of him. "I could ask you the same thing. Seems you didn't really need me to find Tony after all. But let's talk about a few other things, shall we?" I kept my gun level with his chest. "Let's start with what brought us all here together tonight. But first, how about you drop all those tools and stuff, just so I don't get nervous. Don't worry about making any noise. I'm sure no one can hear us down here."

Malcolm and Tony traded glances, then dropped their burdens, making loud clanging noises as a pair of crowbars and something that looked like a putty knife hit the floor along with a couple of boxes of large plastic garbage bags. Just as I turned my head to speak to Tony, Malcolm slashed out with his cane, snapping it across my forearm and knocking the gun out of my hand.

"Get the gun!" Malcolm yelled as he swung the cane in a vicious backslash that I only managed to avoided by falling into a backward shoulder roll. By the time I scrambled to my feet, Tony had picked up my revolver and shoved it in my direction, holding it in both hands. If he pulled the trigger now I'd be all over. I held up my empty hands and shouted, "Hold it! I just want to talk!"

Pale and pudgy Tony went from foot to foot as his head snapped back and forth between Malcolm and me, clutching my revolver in his bandage-wrapped hands. Malcolm, seeing he had the situation under control, straightened up, grounding his cane. "Talk about what, Mr. Wilder?" he asked almost conversationally.

Keeping my hands up, I slowly raised myself to my feet. There was a sharp pain in my arm where Malcolm whacked it. "Well, for one, I happen to know there's a fortune in old movie posters behind these walls. While I was waiting for you guys I pried open another panel down here and found at least two dozen or so." It was the first thing I did when I snuck past the police and came back down here. Using my key ring utility tool, I carefully poked some holes in a random wall, striking colorful gold.

Malcolm looked at me quizzically. "So, you're here for money, is that it?" he asked mildly.

"Well, money seems to be at the root of everything around here, doesn't it, Tony?" I asked.

Tony, emboldened by the gun he held, twisted his face into what I'm sure he thought was a threatening look. "So what if there's something valuable here? It's no business of yours!"

"Maybe," I admitted. "But let's backtrack a little, shall we? Back to where you lost about $850,000 that belonged to Georgi Pakhomov and his, shall we say, business associates?"

Tony's face lost a shade of color, and I continued, "From what I can gather, I'll bet you were approached by old Uncle Georgi to take an embarrassing amount of cash and launder it into some kind of nice, clean investment. I can see where Georgi would think it was great to have a legitimate investment broker in the family, considering that his business is less than on the square."

"I didn't want to!" Tony burst in plaintively. "But . . . I thought I had to."

"Sure," I said soothingly. "Only you wound up getting taken by a con man you met on the Internet. Supposedly from the Republic of Benin, as I recall."

Tony started shaking again. "How did you know that?" he said hoarsely.

"By reading your private e-mail from your office computer. It tells the whole story about how you were conned out of all that cash Uncle Georgi trusted you with. So when you figured out you'd been conned, you knew you had to come up with real money, real fast. I know you tried to talk Jenny into selling the theater, but that didn't go as planned, did it? So I'm guessing that dear old Uncle Georgi told you about a great way to make a bunch of money off the insurance people. All you had to do was burn this place down. How am I doing so far?"

Tony's head started to drop as the weight of my words had their effect. Malcolm was as still as a statue. "Go on," he said neutrally.

I flexed my fingers, trying to keep the circulation going as I held them up. "Tony first tries to up the ante on the insurance policy. Then, because he doesn't want anyone to get hurt, he sneaks in here late Saturday night and sabotages the movie projector, thinking they'll have to close the place on Sunday. And on that Sunday, everything went to hell, didn't it, Tony?"

I watched him nod, then said, "I assume Georgi sent one of his boys along, just to make sure everything went off all right. You had some nice flammable paint thinner and a little device to set it off. Only when you came down here to hook it all up, you made a discovery. Somebody, no doubt years ago, used old, leftover movie posters in the walls down here, packing them in the spaces between the wooden frame. Probably thought they'd make great, cheap insulation or something. Only now, after all these years, they're really worth something, especially preserved as they are."

"And you want a cut, is that it?" Malcolm asked.

"Not so fast," I said. "Before I can make up my mind, I need to know some things. Like, when did you tell your father about all this, Tony?"

"When I was in jail," he said.

"That was kind of risky, wasn't it? They can record jail visits, you know."

Malcolm cleared his throat. "I convinced that black detective that if I could talk to my son privately, I might be able to get him to tell the truth. About Jenny."

"Ah, I see," I said. "So tell me, Tony, what was it like when you came back up from the greenroom here only to find Uncle Georgi's man dead and on fire?"

I could see Tony shiver. When he didn't speak, I went on, "Well, bad as it was, you still saw that old pistol on the ground. I guess it was kind of hard to miss with those fancy white grips on it. You knew Jenny had taken off with that gun years ago, didn't you?"

"Yeah," he sighed.

"So you picked it up. I assume you were wearing gloves during your little attempted arson, so you didn't put your own finger prints on the gun. Then you ran off to hide. You had an armful of the posters that you dug out of the walls down here, so you took them to a storage facility for safekeeping. Now, you had a real dilemma; you needed to get Uncle Georgi's money back and at the same time avoid whoever it was that was out to get you. And while you were hiding out and trying to figure a way to get all these posters out of here, your wife goes and hires the Midnight Agency to find you. Just out of curiosity, when the cops took you away, you said, 'They're going to kill me.' You meant Uncle Georgi and his boys, didn't you?"

Tony gave a quick nod. "And when I caught up with you and the cops got involved, I guess you thought you'd just keep your mouth shut and protect your little sister, is that it? Or you did until your father here told you it'd be best to give her up. Tell me, do you really think Jenny killed that man?"

Tony shook his head. "I . . . I don't know. She must have. There was no one else. And there was that damn gun," he finished quietly.

"Actually," I said, "I had another suspect in mind for a while. A man named Bruce Roberts. That name mean anything to you, Malcolm?"

Malcolm's jaw was so tight that I could see a nerve playing under the skin, like a worm on a hook. "No," he said flatly.

I shrugged, then said to Tony, "It must have gotten really scary when you heard that someone placed a nasty booby trap in your office. Now, who do you think did that?"

Tony's hand seemed to spasm, his knuckles whitening as he held my gun. "I . . . I thought that Georgi's men . . ."

I shook my head. "Wrong."

"What are you playing at, Wilder?" Malcolm demanded. "If it's money you want, then damn it, I'll see you'll—"

"Cut it out, Malcolm," I snapped. "There's already been one masquerade tonight, which you went and screwed up. I got a call from a friend of mine in the police department a while ago;

seems that it was a mostly harmless smoke bomb that went off in the theater. Just enough to cause a panic and then get this place closed down, so you two could come down here and make off with all your valuable posters. But all the smoke and diversions in the world won't cover up the three murders. The three that I know of."

Tony's jaw dropped open. "Three? What murders?"

"The ones your father committed."

I swear Tony almost dropped the gun then. "What?" he stammered.

I was speaking to Tony, but my eyes never left Malcolm as I said, "One was Sunday night, that young Russian man who was your supposed partner in arson. You thought you were being sneaky. I can see you now, going over the blueprints for the Castle in your office, looking for a good place to set up the fire. But what you didn't know was that your office was bugged. Seems your daddy here couldn't quite trust you on your own, so he made sure he'd always know what you were up to. For your own good, I'm sure he thought. Why he didn't stop you from losing all that Russian gang money, I don't know. Maybe he thought that would be a good way to get you separated from your new Russian in-laws. Either way, he couldn't tip his hand that he was spying on you, but he sure as hell knew what you were up to when you came to torch the Castle that night. And he couldn't let that happen. I guess he couldn't think of a way to stop you beforehand without tipping his hand. I'm also betting that Malcolm has the original set of keys to the theater, so he could come and go as he pleased. He mentioned tonight that 'someone' was going to have to lock the place up, that someone being him. The only set of keys I've seen was Jenny's, and they were obviously recent copies. I'm certain it was during one of Malcolm's little secret excursions through the theater here that he found his old gun, the one Jenny took years ago. So you must have discovered the posters when you dug into the wall to hook the incendiary device up to the electrical wiring. You must have made at least one trip up to the alley with an armload of posters, letting the Russian stay up there as lookout as you went down for more. That's when your father killed him, by stabbing him in the back. Only now he has to get rid of the posters up there, and fast. So he decides to burn them. He pours the turpentine you were going to use for the arson on the body and the posters and lights it up—by shooting the body at close range."

From the corner of my eye, I could see Tony as he slowly seemed to melt. Malcolm, on the other hand, seemed rigid as steel. "Malcolm left the gun there, thinking Jenny would get the blame for the killing. Then he could close the theater back up, which was his real goal all along. As for that lethal trap in your office? Well, Malcolm apparently decided that he needed to protect his boy Tony from those evil Russians. He knew that some of them were looking for you and were hanging around your office. He decided that he'd make up a little surprise for them in case they tried to break in. He rigged the trap, then he jammed the lock on the door by breaking off a piece of a paper clip in it so it wouldn't open with a key. That way, you or your secretary, Heidi, couldn't get shot by accident. Only someone who was breaking in would get killed, and maybe the Russians would get the message to back off of Malcolm's little boy. And you know all about booby traps and stuff, don't you, Malcolm? Enough to be able to rig a booby trap from scratch."

When he didn't answer, I continued, "You kind of tipped your hand when you went gaga over that one-eyed dog at my office. As I recall, you said you used to work with a German shepherd. The military uses them as bomb sniffers, among other things. That, and the wounds on your legs, told me that you were probably in some kind of bomb disposal unit in the Army. Judging by your old injuries, I'd also guess you missed one."

"Yes," he said quietly. "So I did."

"But no one died in my office!" Tony squealed.

"No," I agreed. "The second murder came with the third. A long time ago."

Without taking his eyes off me, Malcolm reached over toward Tony and said, "Give me the gun."

That's when I said, "He killed your mother, Tony."

Tony's hands did go limp then, but he still held on to to the revolver as it dangled by his side.

"He killed your mother," I said again. "And Anthony Worthington, the man she was supposed to have run away with. The man you were named after. The man who was Malcolm's partner and friend. Only Worthington and your mother never ran away together. That they were lovers I have no doubt. The proof is Jenny."

Malcolm's face ran red, then drained to a deadly white. "You really only have to see the pictures of your mother and Anthony Worthington side by side to see where Jenny gets her looks," I said. "And Malcolm couldn't stand it. He must have killed them with the old .45. He couldn't get rid of the murder weapon in case the police had questions, because it was his gun. A gun that your mother must have bought for him as a present. But after the killings, he changed the barrel, just in case, so if the bodies were ever found the ballistics wouldn't match. Only he never intended for them to be found."

I could see that my words were hitting the mark. Malcolm's lips slowly pulled away from his teeth in a silent snarl.

I said to Malcolm, "And they're right down here with us, aren't they? If you check the blueprints for this place, you'll see that there are supposed to be nine rooms down here, but there are only eight now. The room where your father put the bodies of your mother and Worthington was sealed up. That was another mistake your father made. Supposedly, your mother and Worthington ran off with a lot of money. So it doesn't make sense that Malcolm closed down the theater. You'd think he'd need the cash flow. But he couldn't risk anyone discovering where he put the bodies. And he'd make damn sure you didn't find them now, either, Tony. Malcolm was going to stay with you until all the posters were out of the walls, making sure you didn't open up the tomb. Then this place would be closed back up. Forever. And that's why Malcolm could never allow the theater to be torn down. So he could keep his secret murders buried."

Tony was staring at his father. "Dad?" he said in a small, child-like voice. "Why?"

And Malcolm Sterling, with the rage of over twenty-five festering years, roared out, "She was a whore! A goddamn cheap whore! Now give me that gun, you spineless bastard!"

Tony gave him the gun, all right. Although not in the way Malcolm wanted. With a shrill cry like a man falling off the edge of a cliff, Tony pointed the revolver straight at his father as he pulled the trigger. Tony kept on screaming, even though the gun never fired.

And would never fire for him. For that gun was my father's, and he had a special safety built into it: There was a metal bar in the handle that kept the gun locked up until it was pulled free by a magnet—a magnet that was made into my father's ring that I wore. With that device in place, that gun wouldn't fire for any-one but me. I'd deliberately let them get hold of my gun, hoping I could get them to talk.

While Tony was screaming and doing his best to kill his own father, Malcolm just stood there, staring at Tony with dawning comprehension, as if Tony Sterling had just done the impossible. It was then that I made my big mistake. I took a few steps to-ward Malcolm, and he seemed to catch me out of the corner of his eye. His head turned to me slowly, and an evil glee seemed to pull his features as he suddenly whipped his cane up, yanking it apart—revealing a long, slender blade.

I heard myself yell as I attempted to throw my body back-ward, out of the arc of Malcolm's backhanded slash, only to feel something that burned like a molten steel whip into my side. I flopped onto the cold, hard ground just as Jim Bui stepped out of the room he'd been hiding in this whole time, yelling, "Freeze!" Malcolm Sterling, a wild look twisting his face, reared back, holding the blade high as he panted and glared. Tim

O'Toole bounded into the room from the end of the stairs and tackled him, flattening Malcolm to the concrete floor and sending the sword cane skittering across the room.

I clapped a hand to my right side as I watched Tony Sterling collapse to his knees, throttling my gun and staring at nothing. While Uncle Timmy cranked Malcolm's arm around into a pain-inducing twist lock, Uncle Jimmy knelt beside me. "You okay, boy?" he asked.

I pulled my hand away from my side and felt the shock hit me as I saw my palm covered in my own blood. My head felt light as I heard myself say, as if from a distance, "Mom's going to kill me."

CHAPTER THIRTY-FOUR

I hate hospitals.

I woke up in bed, and for a while I wrestled with my disjointed memory, trying to piece together exactly where I was and how I got there. I remembered a ride in an ambulance and waiting on a gurney and being pushed into a room with bright light and people in masks. Then I made the mistake of attempting to sit up, only to have a lancing pain in my side remind me. Oh, yeah. I'd been wounded. With a sword.

"Take it easy, kiddo," came a well-remembered voice to my right. I carefully turned my head and saw my mother, sitting in the backlit darkness close to my side. I tried to speak, but my throat seemed to be full of sand.

Mom came over, and the next thing I knew the back of the bed started to raise. "Just relax, and tell me if this hurts," she said. After my head came up halfway to level, she stopped the machinery and placed a straw near my mouth. "Take it in sips."

I did, and when I'd lubricated my throat enough, I said, "Where's Jenny?"

Mom placed the water glass near my bedside and stood there with her arms crossed. Even in this dim light, I could see the stern expression on her face. "She's fine. Which is more than I can say for you. You took a pretty deep cut just below your ribs. Just what did you think you were doing?"

"Solving the case, I thought."

"You feel up to telling me all about it now, or after I formally fire you?"

I took in a cautious breath, feeling the bandages binding my torso. "Not much to tell," I said. "After I figured out that Malcolm was behind it all, everything came together. So where is . . . everybody?"

Mom placed a hand on my brow, a worried expression on her face. "I want you to get some rest. There'll be plenty of time to talk about everything when they've thrown you out of here."

"Forget it. I won't rest until I know what's been happening in my absence. I hate suspense, you know."

I saw a ghost of a smile play along my mother's lips. "Well, we have that much in common, anyway. All right, kiddo; I'll give you the short form, then you rest up, right?"

I nodded, saving my voice, and Mom said, "James called me right after he dialed 911. I was in the process of reading the riot act to the obnoxious Lori Banks. I must say, the news that you boys managed to corral the real murderer came at a good time. By the way, your recording came out pretty good."

The last thing I remembered after Malcolm Sterling perforated me with his sword cane was taking out the digital voice recorder that I had stashed in my coat pocket. Fortunately, it hadn't taken any damage. "Good," I whispered. "What then?"

"The police took custody of Malcolm and Anthony Sterling and released Jenny and her friend Bruce. The only thing that kept me from running over here to the hospital was the fact that I heard you were going to be all right. Well, that and the fact that I was afraid that idiot Lori Banks was going to screw up Malcolm Sterling's interrogation. After this, I'm thinking she may have a rewarding career in parking enforcement. I made a point of gently explaining to her that a man like Malcolm Sterling responds to older Caucasian males a lot better than to young, inexperienced female twits. My friend Harold Caldwell took over questioning Malcolm. And that's when the story came out."

"Go on," I managed to say.

"Malcolm Sterling was overseas when he got the news from his wife, Angelique, that she wanted a divorce. She explained that she and Anthony Worthington were in love, and had been for some time. Malcolm, at the time, was recovering from wounds in an Army hospital in Hawaii. He called Angelique, and she sealed her own fate."

"What happened?"

"Angelique tells Malcolm that she and Anthony had kept their relationship a secret. She wanted to wait until Malcolm came home before she started divorce proceedings. And that's when Malcolm decides he'll kill them both. He arranges to get a seventy-two-hour pass, then flies home without telling anyone. He surprises his wife and Anthony together, kills them both, and walls their bodies up in the theater. He then moves some of the business's money around, making it look as if Anthony made a lot of withdrawals, flies back, reports to the hospital, and waits. When the River City police notify him that his wife and business partner have disappeared, he returns home as the grieving, cuckolded husband and wounded war veteran, acting as if his legs were more disabled than they really were. The police evidently fell for it. He even was able to use the letter Angelique sent him, telling him all about her affair with Anthony Worthington."

"So I was right about him using that gun? The one Jenny took from him later?"

"Oh, yes. He admitted that he changed the barrel of the pistol, just in case."

"Whoa. So what's been happening at the Castle?"

"Well, while you've been malingering here, there have been crowds of people converging on the theater. Looks like a regular invasion. The coroner's office, along with a team of archaeologists from the university, opened up that sealed-off room downstairs. Sure enough, they found two bodies. Mummified. Male and female. There's no real doubt that they'll be identified as

Angelique Sterling and Anthony Worthington. Your friend Robin Faye tells me that they can extract DNA from the bone marrow to test your theory concerning the parentage of Jenny Chance."

"Science is wonderful," I managed to croak out.

"So give it up, kiddo," Her Majesty commanded, though gently. "If you're up to it, that is. Just how did you figure it out?"

"Well, I am a detective, you know."

"No, seriously," Mom said with a dismissive wave. "How did you do it?"

"Well, I used science myself."

"Science," Mom said flatly. "You?"

"Yeah. It was kind of right in front of me at one time. I saw the pictures of Angelique Sterling and Anthony Worthington together. When you look at them, and then look at Jenny, the similarities seem obvious. Then I remembered my high school biology. Jenny has beautiful blue eyes."

"So I've noticed," Mom said wryly.

"Well, Malcolm has brown eyes, and when you read the description of Angelique Sterling, she's listed as having brown eyes, too. So there you go; two brown-eyed people can't have a blue-eyed child. And from there, I could see how it all could have happened. So I arranged to confront Malcolm Sterling. The fact that I caught him at the Castle with Tony helped a bit."

Mom was silent for a moment, then she said, "Blue eyes. You based your theory on that?"

"Yeah."

"Amazing," Mom said quietly.

"Thanks," I said with attempted modesty.

"Amazing that you seemed to come up with the right answer out of a completely erroneous assumption."

"Say what?"

Mom sighed. "The gene for blue eyes is recessive, O ignorant son of mine, but it is entirely possible for two brown-eyed people to have a blue-eyed child, if they carry the recessive gene.

Tell me, just what was it you were studying while you were supposed to be learning biology?"

I cast my mind back to my high school biology class and suddenly remembered Patty Allen, the girl who sat in front of me. She had a penchant for wearing halter tops that displayed a fascinating array of freckles. "Oh."

"Well, be that as it may, you seemed to have stumbled on the truth of it," Mom generously allowed. "Jenny is not only a free woman, but it looks like she's going to be a rather rich one as well. I took the liberty of getting that roll of posters out of your car. The preliminary estimate of their value is impressive. And if it indeed turns out that Malcolm Sterling is not her father, then she and Anthony are the sole inheritors of the Castle and all its treasures. If that whole downstairs area is packed with posters, then Jenny's money troubles are over. Which reminds me, I need to add your hospital expenses to her bill."

"So where is she now?"

"What do I look like, your social secretary? As a matter of fact, she's been dying to see you. I had to put my foot down to keep her out of here, and she relented only as long as I promised to call her as soon as you were ready for visitors. She's a stubborn woman, that one is. Very stubborn indeed." Again, I caught that almost approving note in my mother's voice.

"Seems all I've been doing lately is keeping people away from you," Her Majesty continued. "You've been very popular lately. Your friend Roland has been pestering me to get in to see you. When I told him that if he didn't knock it off I'd put him in the hospital myself, he said that would be great as long as the two of you could share a room. You should see the story he's written already. Front page stuff. Oh, and we got a very interesting message from Georgi Pakhomov. He thanked us for uncovering the real killer of the man in the alley and apologized for his behavior at the theater. He then assured us that if we ever need a favor, then we've got one coming from him. Might come in handy someday," Mom said pensively.

I reached for the water, only to stop halfway as my arm didn't seem to want to complete its task. Mom obliged, and when I had another sip, I said, "So everything turned out right," I said.

"No," Mother contradicted. "Not when my only son is lying in front of me like a doll with its stuffing torn out. Hurry up and get well. So I can punish you myself for putting me through all this. What on earth were you thinking?"

"Well, I did have Jimmy and Timmy there for backup."

"Uh-huh. And a fine job they did not. Marksman that he is, James claimed that he didn't dare shoot Malcolm Sterling, as you were in the line of fire, then Timothy shows up too late to stop you from getting perforated. Not to mention the fact that he was responsible for all your unarmed defensive tactics training in the first place. Or were you just a lousy student of that as well?"

"I should have seen that one coming," I admitted. "Especially when the only time Malcolm didn't have that damn cane with him was when I saw him in the courthouse hallway. He wouldn't have been able to smuggle it past security. But come to think of it, I was only trained on what to do against knives and clubs. Never swords."

"I accept no excuses," Mom said firmly. "Now, I suggest you start taking better care of yourself, or I'll fire you. Got it?"

"Got it," I sighed.

"Good. I love you, son."

"Ditto and likewise, lady. Now, can I see Jenny?"

Mom favored me with a benevolent smile. "I suppose. Although you have a rather insistent visitor waiting outside your door."

"Who?"

"Jenny's friend Bruce. Want me to throw him out?"

"No," I said thoughtfully. "Send him in. I need to have a private chat with him."

Mom cocked her head. "Seems to me, the last time you two boys got together, you didn't play nice. Well, I'll be right outside if you need me."

Less than a minute after Her Highness exited, I heard Bruce come trudging into my room. Even in the half light, he looked worse than usual; his round face might have been a pumpkin someone used for soccer practice. "Have a seat," I offered.

He shook his head, then said, "Came to say I heard what you did. I owe you."

"Good. Then I'll take what you owe me out in an explanation. Does Jenny know you're her uncle?"

Bruce stood like a statue, then took two steps over and dropped into the guest chair. "No," I faintly heard him say.

"Why the hell not?"

The chair squeaked as he shifted his weight around. He turned his head away from me as he said, "Didn't think she'd want to know."

"Again, why the hell not?"

"My big sister," Bruce began slowly, "Bobbie Jean, always was the best in the family. She went and left home. For Hollywood. She was going to be a star. She even changed her name."

"To Angelique Raven."

"Yeah," Bruce sighed. "That's where we're from. Raven's Corner, Louisiana. Anyway, she still wrote to me. Even after I wound up in prison. She sent me a birthday present once while I was there. A big book. The letter she sent with it said that all the great stories were in this book. I didn't understand the words at first. Had to learn to use a dictionary. But I kept at it. Then I started to see."

"Shakespeare?"

"Yeah. All his plays. I read every one."

"That's more than I've done," I said. "So why keep your relationship a secret from Jenny?"

"Bobbie Jean got married. To Malcolm. She said in a letter that she couldn't talk to him about her family, about me. Said he wouldn't understand. Then one day, her letters stopped coming. It was after that I found out what Bobbie Jean did . . . was supposed to have done . . . running off with a man and taking

money. So I figured that maybe Bobbie's children, Jenny and Tony, would be better off if they never knew about . . . their mother's side of the family."

"Listen, Bruce," I said, "I've heard the way Jenny talks about you, and I've seen the way Angelina is when you're around. Those two could only love you more if they knew that you're related, and they certainly could never love you any less. Now are you going to tell them? Or will I?"

Bruce sat for a while, then slowly stood up and walked to my door—but not before I saw the glitter of a faint trail of tears on his face. I heard him rumble, without looking back, "There's a divinity that shapes our ends, rough-hew them how we will." He quietly opened the door and let himself out, closing it softly behind him.

For a while, I don't know how long, I faded in and out of consciousness—until the time when I woke to find what appeared to be an angel sitting close to my bed. "Uh-oh," I heard myself mumble.

Jenny Chance, beaming a look of gentle joy, took my hand and said, "Hello, hero. What's this uh-oh stuff?"

"Sorry. Thought I must be dead."

She shook her head slowly. "Oh, no, you don't. You're not getting away from me that easily. You made a promise, remember?"

My brain still seemed to be stuffed with cotton. "I made a what, now?"

"Promise," she repeated gently. "You told Angelina you were going to take her somewhere. I told you at the time that anyone who makes a promise to my daughter better be prepared to keep it."

"Oh, yeah." I took a look down at my chest. "Um, it may be a while," I said.

"Doesn't matter," Jenny said serenely. "Angelina and I aren't going anywhere. Because of you, we're here to stay. So hurry up and get yourself out of that bed."

"Yes' m. Wait. What do you mean, because of me?"

Jenny reached over and gently ran her fingers down the side of my face, leaving an electric, tingling sensation in their wake. "Everything I have now is because of you," she said. "You gave my daughter and me a future, and you've saved me from my past."

"Your past?"

I saw in her large, deep blue eyes something that shined through the darkness of my room.

"Yes," she said, "you returned my mother to me."

"Your mother?"

"Don't you see?" she said in a half whisper. "She never really left me."